I0618703

HARD JUSTICE

A COBRA ELITE NOVEL

PAMELA CLARE

WWW.PAMELACLARE.COM

HARD JUSTICE

PAMELA CLARE

USA TODAY BESTSELLING AUTHOR

Hard Justice
A Cobra Elite novel

Published by Pamela Clare, 2019

Cover Design by © Jaycee DeLorenzo/Sweet 'N Spicy Designs
Photo credit: _italo_ on Depositphotos

Copyright © 2019 by Pamela Clare

This is a work of fiction. Names, characters, places, and incidents are products of the author's imagination or are used fictitiously, and any resemblance to actual persons, living or dead, business establishments, events, or locales is entirely coincidental.

All rights reserved.

No part of this book may be reproduced, scanned, or distributed in any printed or electronic format without permission. Please do not participate in or encourage piracy of copyrighted materials by violating the author's rights. No one should be expected to work for free. If you support the arts and enjoy literature, do not participate in illegal file-sharing.

ISBN: 978-1-7335251-7-6

This book is dedicated to my mother, Mary White, whose love and support has helped sustain me through two kids, three grandchildren, and thirty novels. Thanks, Mom. I love that you get caught up in my stories.

ACKNLOWLEDGEMENTS

This book would not have been possible without my wonderful Glaswegian sources. Special thanks to Nicola Brooks and Saunders. They helped give Quinn his distinctly Glaswegian voice, though I did have to modify his speech a bit for American readers. We want them to understand it, aye?

Many thanks to my home team—my sister, Michelle White, my son, Benjamin Alexander, and my friends Jackie Turner and Shell Ryan. Writing a book shares more than a few things with climbing, and you help me when I freak myself out by looking down. Thank you for your years of support.

Thanks, too, to Kaylea Cross and Katie Reus for their encouragement and support.

A heartfelt thank you to the men of Scotland for fueling the fantasies and flaming the lust of women around the world for a fair few centuries now. Aye, wear the damned kilt.

PROLOGUE

Mazar-e-Sharif, Afghanistan
November 29
Two years ago

Elizabeth Shields walked down the jet bridge to the plane that would carry her from Mazar-e-Sharif, Afghanistan, to Istanbul, Turkey, passport in hand, a white burka covering her from head to toe. Except that right now, she wasn't Elizabeth Shields. She was a decoy pretending to be Jenna Hamilton, a Cobra client who'd become a target of Abdul Jawad Kazi, the warlord who governed Balkh Province.

She made her way to her seat, handbag slung over her shoulder, burka catching on the arms of the chairs as she passed. She sat, put on her seatbelt, and sent a text message to the operations room to let Quinn McManus and Alex Cross know that she was safely on board.

Quinn replied immediately.

Safe travels. See you in Istanbul.

The big Scot had a soft heart—and was super sexy. Ripped. Six-foot-four. Square jaw. Beard. Thick red hair. She enjoyed flirting with him, though, of course, nothing could come of it. Since that rat bastard Jason, she didn't do workplace flings, and fraternization was against company rules.

She sat back, tension starting to leave her.

This had been a crazy mission. For starters, Derek Tower, one of the co-owners of Cobra International Security, had fallen head-over-heels in love with Jenna, their client. Derek and Jenna tried to deny it, but Jenna, a midwife, wasn't good at hiding her emotions—at least not from someone with Elizabeth's experience.

Elizabeth had worked for the CIA as a counterterrorism analyst, linguist, and interrogator, and had no problem reading every emotion that ran through Jenna's mind. Tower was more closed, but he'd been off kilter this entire mission. The fact that they'd been sharing a room that held only one bed was also a pretty clear sign that they'd become lovers.

Derek Tower had a soft side. Who knew?

On top of that, someone had detonated a car bomb just outside Cobra's compound, damaging their front gate and shaking the building.

They'd put this operation together to get Jenna safely beyond Kazi's grasp. Elizabeth had never been a decoy before, but she wasn't nervous. Three armored vehicles with Cobra agents sat outside the terminal, ready to act in case she needed them. It was exciting, really—a chance to get out of the office and do field work.

Turkish flight attendants helped people with luggage, passengers speaking mostly Dari with some tribal dialects thrown in for good measure. Slowly, everyone took their seats, and the aisles cleared.

The doors were closed, and the jet bridge started to retract.

Then it stopped and reversed, moving back toward the door.

Elizabeth's pulse skipped. Through her window, she saw turbaned fighters with automatic weapons heading for the airplane.

Kazi's men.

She tapped out a quick message.

```
I think they've come for Jenna. Kazi's men
boarding.
```

They might be here for someone else.

A flight attendant gave a shriek as the door to the cabin was forced open and armed men rushed on board.

"Jenna Hamilton," said one, his accent heavy.

Heart thrumming, Elizabeth raised a hand. She needed to distract them only long enough for Derek and the others to take off on Cobra's private jet.

The fighter made his way toward her, three others behind him.

"Passport."

He took the passport, examined it, then compared it to an image on his smartphone.

Damn it!

Kazi must have given them a photo of Jenna.

Elizabeth's false passport had been created with her photo, not Jenna's.

Her fear for Jenna's safety escalated. This could bring their entire mission crashing down and end with Kazi taking Jenna.

The man barked at her in poor English. "Where is Jenna Hamilton?"

She had to buy time. "*I* am Jenna Hamilton."

He called someone, spoke in Dari, which, fortunately, was one of Elizabeth's languages. "She's not on this plane. Ground all flights."

Shit.

Elizabeth hoped that Derek and Jenna were already in the air.

If not, she had failed them.

"Come with me." The man took hold of Elizabeth's arm, dragged her out of her seat. "Where is Jenna Hamilton?"

"I am Jenna. Are you blind? Look at my passport."

He ripped off her burka, pain exploding on her cheek as he backhanded her. "American bitch. You are a Cobra spy."

QUINN MCMANUS HEARD the command to ground all flights. "They've figured it out. We've got to get Shields out of there."

Javier Corbray, one of the co-owners of Cobra, held up a hand to silence him, as Tower's voice came over the radio, bringing worse news.

A group of hostiles was approaching Cobra's private jet.

Fuck.

Quinn listened as Tower evacuated Jenna to a vehicle and headed with her and the rest of Team Two toward Cobra's hangar.

"Cobra, this is Team Two. Four vics and at least twenty fighters with small arms and an RPG are coming our way, over."

"Son of a bitch!" Corbray called Team One, the group of

armored vehicles that had accompanied Elizabeth. "Team One, this is Cobra. Leave current position, head north down the highway to the end of the runway. Punch a hole in that perimeter fence to make an escape route and cover Team Two, how copy, over?"

That was it.

McManus stood, headed for the door.

"Where the fuck are you going?" Corbray asked.

"Shields is alone. Team One is no longer in a position to keep her safe. I'm getting her out of there."

Corbray motioned toward the door. "Watch your six."

Quinn dashed to the lift, made his way to the weapons locker, threw on body armor, and grabbed an M4 rifle and several loaded magazines. Then he ran to the garage, climbed into an armored vehicle, and set out, passing through the warped and damaged front gate.

It was a five-kilometer drive to the airport, McManus listening as the situation went from bad to worse. Cruz was down. O'Neal was down. Jones was down.

Corbray sent in Helo One with reinforcements and to evacuate the wounded, but it would take them a while to reach the tarmac. When they did, there was no guarantee they'd arrive in time to save lives. Then came word that Tower was down, too.

Jesus sufferin' fuck!

Cobra had never lost men on a mission, but this was becoming a blood bath. Three operatives and one of the owners down.

Kazi must want Jenna very badly. Then again, her father was a wealthy US Senator. Taking her prisoner meant money in the bank.

McManus pulled up to the terminal, double parking near the entrance, and pushing his way through. A security guard tried to stop him, so he punched the guy in the face, knocking him to the floor.

She'd gone through Gate 4, off to his left.

People moved out of his way now, women gasping from behind their burkas.

Hold on, Elizabeth.

"Cobra, this is ... O'Neal. They've ... got her. They've got Jenna ... and Tower."

Four armed men appeared at Gate 4, Elizabeth between them, her lip bleeding. Her eyes went wide when she saw Quinn.

Och, she was terrified.

The men saw Quinn, too, and stopped, one pointing his AK at Elizabeth's head.

Quinn raised his M4, focused on the forehead of the man aiming at her. "Tell them to release you—now. Tell them you're going with me."

She translated his words into Dari.

The man glared at Quinn, rattled off his answer.

"He says that unless you leave, he'll kill us both. Quinn, don't risk yourself—"

"Tell him that if he harms you, I'll cut his dick and balls off and feed them to my dog. You might be dead, but he'll live the rest of his life as a woman."

Elizabeth translated again, people around them gasping.

But Quinn wasn't finished. "When I'm done, I'll kill the rest of these pig-fuckers and leave their guts for the vultures. No burial. No prayers."

Elizabeth translated once again.

More gasps.

Quinn moved forward, let his rage show. "Drop your fuckin' weapons!"

Elizabeth translated.

One by one, the bastards dropped their AKs to the tile floor.

Quinn reached out, grabbed Elizabeth's wrist and jerked her toward him. "I've got you, Lilibet Go. The vehicle is double parked outside the door. Stop for nothin'."

She ran.

Quinn kept his rifle aimed at Kazi's men, then tossed a smoke grenade, and ran for the front door.

Elizabeth was already climbing into the vehicle when he reached it.

He launched himself into the driver's seat, started the engine, and sped out of the car park, heading for the airport's front gate.

Beside him, Elizabeth was quaking like a leaf. "Th-thank you. Thank you. I can't believe you scared them into letting me go. They were taking me to Kazi. Th-they said he was going to rape me and then sell me or behead me."

Quinn reached over, took her hand. "I'm sorry I didnae get here sooner. The entire operation has gone to hell. Let's get you back to the compound."

WHAT THE HELL did Quinn mean by that?

"Is Jenna...?"

A voice came over the radio.

"Cobra this is Helo One. We're en route to Kabul with three casualties, all critical. Tower and Hamilton are confirmed missing. Tower is believed to be wounded."

Jenna's heart sank. "Oh, my God. They got her. I blew it, and they got her. Now, she and Derek are missing and the others are wounded."

"It's no' your fault, Elizabeth. Kazi is a smart bastard. Somehow, he figured it out. That's no' your doin'."

"I tried to stall. I kept telling them I was Jenna, even after they knew I wasn't."

"You did all you could do. Dinnae blame yourself."

The drive back to the compound was surreal, Elizabeth listening as Cobra operators and staff did everything they could to save the wounded men's lives and launch a rescue operation for Tower and Jenna.

When they got back to the compound, Quinn called the ops room via his radio to let them know he and Elizabeth were safely back. Then he helped Elizabeth out of the vehicle. "Let's get you to Doc Sullivan, have him check you out. It looks like they struck you pretty hard."

Elizabeth shook her head. "I'm fine. I don't want to waste—"

"You've got a bloody lip and a bruised cheek. You need to be seen." He shepherded her to the elevator. The moment the doors closed, he drew her into his arms. "It's okay, Lilibet. You're safe now."

His body armor was unyielding, but his embrace was warm, a sanctuary.

"I don't want to know what would've happened if you hadn't come for me."

"Do you think we would let those fuckers take you to that bastard Kazi?"

"I can't believe you intimidated them into letting me go." Quinn had seemed absolutely fearless. "You were outnumbered. You could have been killed."

"Kazi's men are bullies, and bullies are cowards. When they know you're no' goin' to back off, that you mean what you say, they buckle. There's no way I'd have let them kill you. I had that bastard's forehead in my sites. I'd have blown his head wide open afore he could squeeze off a shot."

She smiled, touched by his gory attempt to comfort her. "You always know just what to say to a woman."

He led her to medical and left her with Doc Sullivan, his blue eyes telling her that he wished he could stay. "You're in good hands now."

She wished he could stay, too.

"Quinn!" she called after him.

He stopped. "Aye?"

"Thank you."

Her words were woefully inadequate. The man had risked his life to rescue her, forcing four armed fighters to let her go.

He grinned, his smile giving her belly flutters. "Always."

1

————

Quinn McManus unlocked his gear cage and walked inside, the Scottish flag hanging on the back wall, marking the space as his. He set his duffel on the bench, that familiar gloominess rising inside him. He felt this way at the end of every deployment and had learned to ignore it—with the help of Bell's whisky.

You're no' right in the heid, man.

What reason did he have to feel dour? The team had gotten the senator to and from his meeting with Afghan military leaders, and not a shot had been fired. It had been a textbook operation, the kind of mission that had earned Cobra International Security its reputation as a top-of-the-line private military company.

"Home, sweet home," said Nick Andris, whose cage stood next to Quinn's. Andris had been with Cobra since it began operations, joining after a career with Delta Force and the Central Intelligence Agency.

"I bet you can't wait to get back to your sweet baby girl," said Malik Jones, a former Army Ranger.

"Or her mother," added Dylan Cruz, who'd served with the Navy SEALs.

"You got that right."

If Quinn were married to Holly Andris, he'd want to get home, too. A former CIA officer, she could have been a movie star with that face. Aye, she was quality, so she was— both smart and bonnie.

She's not Lilibet.

Elizabeth, with her sharp mind, strawberry-blond hair and sweet face, worked for Cobra, too, and that meant she was off limits. Cobra had strict rules about employees getting together. It was all a load of shite as far as Quinn was concerned. His kissing her square on her smart mouth posed no risk to operational security that he could see.

Still, it was probably for the better. At thirty-six, Quinn lived alone. It's not that he didn't want a woman in his life. Aye, he'd had his share of lovers and had hoped one day to have a family. But there was an ugliness inside him, proof that the apple hadn't fallen far from the tree. No woman deserved that.

Quinn let the men's conversation drift over him, unzipped his duffel, and began to unpack, tossing dirty clothes onto the floor and stowing his gear in his locker. Body armor. Safety glasses. Helmet. Night vision goggles. Knife in its ankle rig. His personal Browning Hi-Power pistol with loaded magazines. First-aid kit. Cook stove and fuel pellets. Emergency blanket. Mess kit. Enamel cup for tea. Tin of teabags.

He never went on a mission without tea. He wasn't a barbarian.

He shoved his pistol back into the duffel along with his dirty laundry. Their duty weapons had been packed onto pallets when they'd left Kabul and would be taken to

Cobra's full-time armorer, who cleaned and inspected each firearm after every mission.

"McManus, you in?" Jones asked.

Quinn hadn't been listening, but the single men always went out to their favorite bar to let off steam after an operation. "Aye, I'm up for gettin' rat-arsed."

Thor Isaksen, who'd served with Denmark's Sirius Patrol, snorted. "Rat-arsed? You Scots have a million ways of saying *drunk*."

Quinn couldn't help but grin. "Aye, that we do."

And you're proud of that, are you?

Derek Tower, one of the co-owners of Cobra, a former Green Beret, entered the room wearing a tailored suit, a smile on his face. "Welcome back. Good work. I wish all assignments were this easy."

Quinn was about to say he'd be bored out of his fucking mind if that were the case when his personal mobile phone rang.

Andrew Lewis.

Lewis had been Quinn's lieutenant in his first few years with the SAS—Britain's Special Air Service. He'd been a bloody good officer, and Quinn would have followed him straight into hell had he but asked.

Quinn answered. "Lewis, man, what's happenin'?"

"I'm sorry to bring you bad news. Murray's dead."

"Jack Murray? Dead? Och, yer arse! He left me a message a few days back. I couldnae call him back because—"

"He was attacked two nights past in Glasgow, his throat slit. The police think it was a robbery. I know this must come as a shock. What an awful business. We're all terribly upset. I wanted to tell you myself. I didn't want you reading about this in the papers or finding out some other way. With social media and all—"

"Jack's ... *dead*?" The blood rushed from Quinn's head, his ears ringing.

"He is, mate. I'm dreadfully sorry. I know how close you two were—the two Glaswegians in our unit. He was a good man, an outstanding soldier."

"Aye, that he was." Quinn swallowed. "When is the service?"

"I don't know. The Procurator Fiscal has ruled the death a culpable homicide, and police are investigating. They won't release his body until they're certain they've got all the evidence. Some of us are pitching in to pay for military honors."

"Count me in."

Jack was dead.

Grief hit Quinn square in the chest. "Do they have any suspects?"

Jesus!

"Not that I've heard."

Quinn thought of Jack's wife and his two wee daughters, his throat growing tight. "How are Ava and the girls?"

"I went to see her this morning, offered my condolences. She's managing as well as anyone can expect. Victim Support has been round to see her. I'm not sure the children understand. They're quite young."

"Aye, they are."

Olivia was four. Isla wasn't yet two.

They wouldn't even remember their father.

"I've a few more calls to make. I'm terribly sorry, McManus."

Quinn fought to push aside his shock and grief. "Thanks for lettin' me know, man. That took balls. I'll be there for the service."

"Good man. Let me know when you get here." Lewis ended the call.

Quinn sank to the bench, legless with shock and sick to his soul.

Jack was dead.

It took him a moment to realize that the room had fallen silent around him. He glanced about, saw that his fellow Cobra operatives were watching him.

Tower broke the silence. "Bad news?"

Somehow Quinn found the words to answer. "My best pal was killed two nights past—his throat slit. We served together for the better part of ten years. He's got a wife and two wee ones."

"Jesus."

"God, I'm sorry, man."

"Fuck."

Quinn looked over, saw understanding on the men's faces. Combat created a bond that was stronger than blood, a bond only someone who had served could understand. "I need to take some time."

"Take all the time you need," Tower said. "Don't worry about paperwork. We'll deal with it."

"Thanks."

Quinn was going home to Glasgow.

ELIZABETH SHIELDS WAS LATE JOINING the others at the Pony Express—the dive bar that served as the official Cobra hangout. What she really wanted was to go home, sink into a hot bath with a glass of wine, and then go to bed. She hadn't slept much on the flight from Kabul and had spent most of the afternoon in an intel briefing with Cobra's owners—

Javier Corbray and Derek Tower—about a possible mission to Saudi Arabia.

But as one of the few women employed by Cobra, she couldn't let the place turn into a boys' club. When the men went out together, she went with them. She might be an intel analyst and not a fighter, but she was as much a part of the team as they were. She wouldn't let them forget that.

She walked through the entrance, the steady rhythm of the Eagles' *One of These Nights* coming from the juke box inside. "Hey, Evan."

The big bouncer's stern expression became a wide smile. "Hey, Elizabeth. Those losers you hang with are sitting at the bar."

"Thanks."

The guys weren't hard to find. Taller and more muscular than most men, they moved with that swagger she'd come to associate with special forces operators. They were some of the best fighters in the world—and, yeah, they knew it.

She threaded her way through the crowded room and squeezed in next to Dylan, Thor, and Malik. "Hey, guys."

She glanced around, looking for Quinn, but didn't see him. With that beard and a head of thick, red hair, he stood out no matter where he was. The two of them danced together from time to time.

Okay, so they flirted, too. But who could blame her? His Scottish accent made everything he said sound sexy. She could admit to herself that she was drawn to him—in no small part because he had rescued her from Abdul Jawad Kazi's men—but it was nothing serious. As long as they both worked for Cobra, it could never be serious. Not only were those the rules, but Elizabeth had learned the hard way what could happen when a woman slept with a coworker.

"Hey, Shields. They finally let you out for a breath of air?" Malik asked.

"Finally." She motioned for the bartender. "A glass of merlot, please."

She must have been tired because it took her a moment to realize that something was wrong. The men weren't ribbing one another like they usually did, their expressions grave. "What is it? What happened?"

It was Malik who answered. "McManus got a call. His best buddy from SAS was murdered a couple nights ago, his throat slit."

"Oh, God. How awful!"

"He looked pretty torn up, man." Dylan asked for another beer.

Elizabeth searched the crowd for Quinn once more.

"He's on his way to Glasgow," Malik said. "He flew with Corbray to D.C. and is catching the red-eye to London."

"Oh." Elizabeth wished she'd known. She would have said something and offered to drive him to the airport. "He'll want to be there for the funeral."

"The guy had a wife and two little kids," Thor said. "Imagine surviving a decade at war and then being murdered on the streets of your hometown."

"Awful," Elizabeth said again, at a loss for words.

She had watched on satellite and drone feeds as good men and women were cut down. She'd flown home with heroes, their coffins draped with American flags, and had witnessed the heartbreak and grief of their families. She'd done her best to offer comfort, knowing that nothing she said would make a difference.

That was war.

But losing your husband to a robbery after he'd made it

through years of combat... That was a different kind of tragedy.

She took her glass of wine from the bartender. "Do they know who did it?"

Malik shook his head. "Nah, I don't think so. McManus said something about them not releasing the body yet because they're still investigating."

That added another layer of pain for the man's family. They'd lost him, but they couldn't yet mourn him or lay him to rest.

Lev Segal, who had joined Cobra after a career with Israel's Sayeret Matkal, came up behind them, taking a seat next to Malik. "You all hear about McManus?"

Heads nodded.

Lev ordered a Fat Tire. "I hope they find the bastard who did it."

"They should string him up by his nuts." Dylan took a sip. "That's what I would do if anyone murdered one of you. Kill one of my brothers—or sisters—and I'll make a necklace out of your teeth."

"Hell, yeah."

"Damn straight."

"What a sweet thing to say." Elizabeth couldn't help but smile.

She appreciated Dylan including her. For most of her career, she'd felt left out, a woman in a world of men—special operators, military brass, and politicians. No, she hadn't gone into combat like they had. Her life had rarely been at risk. But her work had been essential for the success of their missions. She'd done the research and analysis that resulted in US forces being sent into action—and then watched them carry out their orders via satellite feed, barely able to breathe at times.

The guys at Cobra were different, perhaps because it was a private company. There were no alphabet soup agencies or generals vying for control and glory, no politicians looking for photo ops, no one fighting over budgets. They were a team.

Then Elizabeth remembered. "Anyone want some good news?"

No one looked particularly excited by this.

"Of course," Thor said at last.

Elizabeth had gotten an email from Shanti O'Neal but had forgotten about it the moment she'd heard about Quinn's friend. "Connor made the Dean's List."

"What? O'Neal?" Malik laughed. "No way, man."

Dylan raised his beer. "Way to go, college boy."

"I guess he wasn't the idiot we thought he was," Lev teased.

Thor was more polite. "That's good to hear."

Shanti had been a Cobra client a little more than a year ago. Connor, a Cobra operative, had been the head of her security detail. The fact that the two of them ended up getting married afterward was a bit of a scandal, though Connor's decision to leave Cobra to go to college had prevented him from answering any thorny questions. That had been a harrowing mission, though certainly not the roughest for Elizabeth. She'd come to respect Shanti, a human-rights attorney, and they were now good friends.

The conversation drifted after that, but Elizabeth's thoughts stayed with Quinn. She took out her phone, sent him a quick text message.

I just heard the terrible news. I'm so sorry. Please let me know if you need anything.

She waited for a moment, hoping he'd respond, wanting to know she'd reached him. Cobra's planes were equipped with wi-fi. But after a few minutes with no answer, she tucked her phone away.

Glasgow

It was almost nine in the morning when Quinn arrived in Glasgow. He rented a black Vauxhall Crossland X and drove down the M8 toward Stepps to Jack and Ava's place off Cumbernauld Road, rain drumming on the windshield.

It was a typical dreich day—cold, wet, gray.

Och, he hated this city. Memories rushed back at him, but he pushed them from his mind. He'd left that life behind long ago. It had no hold on him now.

He took the A80 exit and soon found himself in front of the house. Jack had done well for himself after leaving the service. He'd gone to work as private security for some MSP in Holyrood. He and Ava had bought this place—a respectable villa made of proper stone—when she'd fallen pregnant with their first. Quinn had helped them move.

Och, who needs all these bloody books?

Those are Ava's. She loves to read, so she does.

Quinn parked, sat in the car. He'd spent twelve hours in the air trying to come to grips with the truth, but some part of him still couldn't believe it.

Jack. Dead.

Nothing about it made sense.

He re-read Elizabeth's text. He'd already sent her a reply.

Thank you.

What else was there to say?

Quinn glanced over, saw that the blinds were closed. He hadn't warned Ava he was coming. It had been midnight in Glasgow when he'd left Denver, and he'd been certain she and the wee ones were sleeping.

How would she feel about him showing up at her door?

He was about to call her when the front door opened and Ava appeared, Olivia and Isla behind her. He climbed out of the car, left his duffel in the boot, and walked up the footpath to the door.

Ava stared at him, clearly surprised to see him. Her eyes were red from crying, dark circles beneath them, her blond hair pulled back in a messy ponytail. "I'm so glad you're here."

He wished he'd been here a few days ago to stop this from happening. "I'm so bloody sorry, Ava."

She stepped into his embrace, her body trembling as she wept. "He's gone."

Quinn held her, wishing he could cry, too. Instead, he felt only rage.

After a moment, Ava drew back. "I apologize. I'm a mess. You've come such a long way. Can I make you some tea?"

Quinn hadn't had a proper brew since breakfast yesterday. "Aye, I'd be grateful."

"Olivia, do you remember your Uncle Quinn?" Ava shepherded her daughters inside while Quinn held the door for them.

Olivia looked up at Quinn through wide blue eyes, nodded.

He walked inside and closed the door, shutting out the damp. There on a small mat sat four pairs of wellies, the largest belonging to Jack. Jack's coat hung from its hook, his brolly in the stand.

God almighty, Jack. How the fuck can you be dead?

"I'm embarrassed by how untidy the place is." Ava's English accent sounded formal to Quinn's Glaswegian ears, especially after five years of living in the United States. "I do apologize."

"Never you mind about that."

They moved to the kitchen, where the rubbish bin overflowed and dishes sat piled high in the sink.

Ava filled the kettle and put it on to boil. "Have you had breakfast?"

"I had a bite at the airport." He didn't want her fretting about him.

She turned to the sink. "I'll do the washing up while that boils."

Quinn stood. "Ava, come and sit. I'll do that."

"Oh, I couldn't ask you—"

"You're no' askin'. I'm offerin'." He knew how to load a dishwasher.

She turned, met his gaze, her control crumbling, despair in her blue eyes. "It's been only three days—just three days —and it's been a living hell. I didn't know a person could feel this much pain. How am I supposed to get through the rest of my life?"

It was an honest question, one that came from her heart. Christ Jesus, he wished he knew what to say—or whose head to bash.

He led Ava to a seat at the table, knelt down in front of her, and looked into her eyes, trying not to let his emotions show. "You'll take it one day at a time, aye?"

2

Quinn sipped his tea, while he and Ava talked, the two wee ones playing in the next room. "He called last week, but I was in Afghanistan. I didnae call him back. We were busy, and by day's end I was pure knackered. I shoulda taken the time."

He would never have the chance to speak with Jack again.

"Don't feel guilty about that. It wasn't your fault."

"Have the police told you anythin'?"

"A little." She drew a breath, as if to steel herself. "The post-mortem said he died quickly of a single slash wound to the left side of his throat that severed his carotid artery and trachea, but I could see that for myself. They asked me to identify his body and..."

Ava's face crumpled, and she began to sob.

Rage sheared through Quinn at the sight of her suffering.

"I would have done anything to put life back into his body. He ... he was blue and... so still. God, I want him back."

Quinn had seen death, had carried the corpses of friends from the battlefield. "Try not to remember him that way. I know from experience that it disnae help."

"Yes. Quite right." She nodded, sniffed. "The autopsy found no signs that he'd been in a fight—no bruising or cuts. The toxicology tests aren't back yet. The detective says it looks like a robbery. The killer left the car but took Jack's watch, wallet, and his mobile phones—both his personal phone and his work phone. Police said they could use the phones to track the killer, but so far..."

The killer would have to be daft not to think of that, but Quinn didn't say so. "Give the police time. There are a fair few ways to track a mobile phone."

Ava's lips curved in a wobbly smile. "He'd only had that new phone for a few weeks. He lost the other one while he was working. I had his old number memorized, but not this one. Not yet. The phone isn't even paid off. God, this can't be real."

This brought fresh tears, her grief breaking whatever heart Quinn had left. He'd never felt so helpless. "I'm sorry, so I am."

When she'd regained her composure, she told Quinn how Andrew Lewis and Alastair Whitehall, the MSP who'd been Jack's employer, had stopped in with flowers to offer their condolences in person. "Whitehall said such nice things about Jack to the press. Wasn't that kind?"

"Aye." Quinn thought it was the least Whitehall could do. "Do you have kin nearby, someone to help wi' the girls, make meals, get the messages... er... do the shoppin'?"

He didn't know anything about Ava's family, but Jack's parents were gone—his mother in a car crash, his father of a stroke.

"I've lived here long enough to know what 'get the

messages' means." Ava smiled. "My mum and sister live in London. My mum has Alzheimer's, and my sister is her full-time carer. She's looking for someone to relieve her so she can stay with us for a few days. Jack's sister, Hannah, is coming this afternoon to take us to Paisley. I'll stay with her and her husband and their boys for a while."

"That's good. You shouldnae be alone at a time like this."

"I don't understand. What was Jack doing in that alley? Andrew said he was no longer on duty. The police have no idea—or they won't tell me." She reached for a tissue. "Yesterday, the detective asked me whether Jack had behaved strangely of late. I told him he'd seemed tense but nothing too unusual. Then he asked whether Jack had ever used or sold *controlled substances*. My Jack?"

"They're only doin' their job. We both know Jack would never touch that shite. He was a good and honest man, so he was."

Unlike Quinn, Jack had come from honest poverty, his mother a widow on the breadline with four wee ones to raise. Jack had joined the army because he'd believed it was his duty to serve his country. Quinn had thought him a proper bampot at first, the sort of idiot easily lured into the military by lies about honor and glory. It had taken Quinn most of a year to realize that Jack was the real thing—a truly good man.

Everything Quinn knew about honor and decency he'd learned from Jack Murray.

"What if they've found evidence, a reason to suspect him?" Ava dabbed her eyes. "During the six years we were married, I never doubted him."

"Then don't start doubtin' him now."

Yet, it *was* strange.

What had Jack been doing in that alley so late at night?

How could anyone have gotten the better of him? Jack had been a skilled trooper, a warrior who could kill as efficiently with his hands as any weapon. But somehow, he'd died from a single slash of a blade—without so much as throwing a punch.

Ava went on. "If he'd died at war, if he'd been killed in the line of duty, I could at least say he died a hero, giving his life for his country. I might learn to live with that. But to lose him like this... He died for *nothing*."

"In all the years I've known Jack, he never did anythin' wi'out a good reason." Quinn poured more tea into Ava's cup. "The police are still investigatin'. When they've done their job, we'll likely find that Jack was in that alley because he thought someone needed help or saw an injured dog."

She nodded through her tears. "He was wearing a stab vest. If only the killer had tried to stab him in the chest or back instead, he would have had time to react and fight back. He might still be here."

"That's a piece of bad bloody luck."

That kind of knife wound meant that whoever had stabbed Jack wasn't just trying to get him to hand over his money. The killer had meant for him to die.

The bell rang.

"Oh, God, I hope it's not the press again."

Quinn stood. "You stay here. If it's reporters, I'll tell 'em to bolt."

Reporters weren't the only people that worried Quinn, and he found himself wishing he'd brought his concealed carry piece rather than leaving it in his hotel room. It wasn't legal here, but he didn't care. It troubled him that police hadn't placed a watch on the house. Whoever had murdered Jack and taken his wallet had surely gotten his address from his driving license. That could bring the bastard here.

A murderer capable of bringing down a man like Jack in one move would make short work of a woman and two wee girls.

He glanced outside, saw a man in a tan trench coat, a yellow-and-blue police car parked just behind his rental.

"It's the police," he called to Ava.

He opened the door, hoping to fuck there was news.

The man in the trench coat introduced himself as Detective Sergeant Wilson, sizing Quinn up through expressionless brown eyes. "And you are ...?"

"Quinn McManus, a friend of the family." Quinn stepped back, let the man enter. "I hope you've brought answers, detective. Mrs. Murray is in the kitchen."

Elizabeth sipped her coffee and read reports about known threats to the Saudi royal family, some in English, some in Arabic. The list of potential dangers wasn't short. The royal family had around ten thousand members, with forty-three potential heirs to the throne, some of whom hated the current king and crown prince.

Then there was Iran and the Iran-backed Houthi fighters in Yemen. There were also escaped al-Qaeda and ISIL/ISIS cells hiding inside the Saudi homeland. If that weren't enough, Libya, Syria, Hezbollah, Bangladesh, Afghanistan, Israel, Thailand, North Korea, and Russia all had scores to settle with the kingdom and its ruling family.

If Cobra accepted this job, she would be leading a team to audit Saudi Arabian security. Shaken up by an attack on their oil fields, the Saudi government wanted a second opinion on how best to protect its assets and ruling family. It would be an interesting mission and a chance to use her

Arabic, but Saudi Arabia wasn't her favorite destination. Why couldn't Cobra send her on a mission to Tahiti or Bali?

She was reading an account of a Houthi attack on a Saudi border checkpoint when Tower stuck his head through her door.

"Got a minute?"

"You're the boss. I have all the time you need."

He sat in the chair across from her, dressed as always in a tailored suit. "Corbray spent the morning on the phone with Riyadh. We've turned down the job."

"We turned it down?" She tried not to look relieved. "Why?"

"It seems the minister in charge of the audit didn't want a woman leading the team. Corbray explained that we assign the best people to each task and that the best person in this case was a woman. They couldn't accept that, so we told them we weren't interested."

Elizabeth gaped at Tower. "That must have been a million-dollar contract."

"Almost two million, actually." Tower didn't seem bothered by this. "This company won't let bigotry or sexism determine who's part of a mission and who isn't. It's not fair to our staff, and it's not who we are as a company, no matter how big the payday."

Warmth blossomed in Elizabeth's chest. "Thanks. I appreciate that."

She'd spent her entire adult life working in a heavily male-dominated field, dealing with everything from subtle chauvinism to groping. She'd learned to fight for herself, to be a woman no one dared to abuse—or ignore. She wasn't used to others standing up for her.

Tower stood. "Have you heard anything from McManus?"

Now why would he ask Elizabeth that question?

"Not a word." Okay, so she'd gotten one word from Quinn — two words, in fact.

Thank You.

That's all he'd said.

Not that she'd expected more. Quinn was dealing with a big loss and was home among friends. Yes, he enjoyed flirting with her and teasing her, but in the end, she was just a coworker.

"I guess you don't have to read all of that." Tower pointed to the stack of reports. "Go play in the snow. You must have lots of personal time after this last mission."

Being on a job site often entailed twelve- to eighteen-hour days with occasional all-nighters. The company balanced that out with liberal vacation and personal time in an effort to prevent burnout and maintain peak performance.

"Thanks, but I'm still going to read it all. I like to stay current, and, believe it or not, I find it interesting."

Tower nodded. "I guess that's why you're one of the best."

He left her to her work.

QUINN SAT on the sofa of his hotel room, a bottle in his hand, images from the day turning over in his mind. Ava in tears. Jack's wee ones playing, unable to understand that their da was forever gone. The police detective asking Ava's permission to search Jack's belongings.

"Not without a warrant," Ava had said, getting to her

feet, her cheeks flushing with anger. "You're supposed to find the man who murdered my husband, not treat him like a suspect!"

Then the detective had turned to Quinn and pelted him with questions. What was his relationship with the deceased? Where was he the night Jack was murdered? When was the last time he'd spoken with Jack? Had he ever known Jack to use drugs?

It had taken great restraint for Quinn to answer without resorting to profanity. He and Jack had been best pals since their army days. He'd been in Afghanistan on U.S. government business the night Jack died. He'd last spoken to Jack almost a month past. Naw, Jack was *not* the sort of man to use drugs.

"Jack Murray was an honorable man, so he was. If you're tryin' to prove otherwise, you're off your heid."

You bastard.

The detective had asked for Quinn's address and phone number and then left, his visit leaving Ava done in. Quinn had tried to comfort her, making another pot of tea, listening to her rage. Then he'd helped her pack for her stay in Paisley, waiting with her until Hannah, Jack's sister, had arrived.

Hannah hadn't forgotten him. "Jack would be glad to know you're here."

"I wouldnae be anywhere else."

Quinn had carried Ava's bags to Hannah's car. "If you need me, you just call. I'll stay in Scotland as long as I can and come back for the service if I must."

Ava had taken his hand. "Thank you, Quinn. I don't know what I would have done this morning without you."

Quinn had watched them drive away before climbing into the Crossland and heading off to meet Lewis for a late lunch. He and Andrew had stopped for a drink and a bite, the two of them talking about arranging military honors for the funeral and sharing memories of Jack. The way Jack's hand had always shot up when Lewis asked for volunteers. The time they'd come under fire in the middle of Jack's shower and he'd run outside naked with his rifle. The way he'd removed a tick from Couper's anus when they'd been on a ten-day reconnoiter together.

"I can't believe he's gone." Lewis had raised his beer. "He was the best of us."

"Aye, that he was. Cheers."

Quinn had stopped at a whisky shop and then booked a room at a hotel—the Dakota, one of the poshest hotels in the city. He didn't care about luxury, but he'd wanted to show the town that had almost broken him that he was no longer the poor boy who'd joined the army just to have a bite to eat and a roof over his head.

Beyond the room's floor-to-ceiling windows, the sky was beginning to darken. He'd forgotten how short the days were here. In Colorado, the sun wouldn't set until around eighteen-hundred hours. Then again, he was still jet-lagged from all the bloody flying he'd done—Kabul to Denver, Denver to D.C., D.C. to London, London to Glasgow. He didn't know what time it was anyway.

He set the bottle on the end table and, before he knew it, fell asleep.

When he woke, it was dark—and he was famished.

He ordered a steak and chips from room service and ate while watching the news. Another Brexit extension. A cyclist injured in a hit-and-run in Aberdeen. The body of a missing teenage girl found in a ditch at a construction site outside Edinburgh. Then an image of Jack filled the screen.

"Investigators are no closer to an arrest tonight in the

homicide of Jack Murray, a decorated veteran of the SAS who worked as a private security guard for Scottish Conservatives MSP Alastair Whitehall. Murray's body was found in a Glasgow alley near his car. Police refused to comment, citing the ongoing investigation, but a source close to Police Scotland said drugs might have been involved."

Quinn was on his feet, rage pounding in his chest. "Jesus sufferin' fuck!"

How could they do that? How could they say that on the television without proof? They were dragging Jack's name through the mire—and he wasn't yet in his grave.

Had Ava seen this?

Christ, Quinn hoped not.

Och, Jack, what the bloody hell happened that night?

Quinn reached for the remote, turned off the telly. He had half a mind to ring up DS Wilson and ask him which bastard at Police Scotland had leaked those details.

He must have evidence that points to drugs or he wouldnae keep pursuin' this.

The first inkling of doubt washed through Quinn, leaving guilt in its wake.

No. Never. Not a chance.

Jack Murray could drink until he was steamin', aye, but never in all the years Quinn had known him had he touched drugs. It was a load of shite—all of it.

Quinn reached for his mobile phone, navigated to his voicemail, and listened to Jack's message again, as if listening would help him understand.

Hey, McManus, it's Jack. Ring me when you get this, aye?

After almost two decades of friendship, those were the last words Jack had spoken to him. How could that be? How could those dozen ordinary, everyday words be the last?

Quinn had lost friends in combat, but this was different.

Grief cut him off at the knees, left an ache in his chest. Sweet Jesus, he would give anything to have gotten that call, to have had a chance for a right good blether—and a proper goodbye.

Or maybe it wouldn't have mattered. Neither of them would have known it was to be their last conversation.

Quinn reached for the whisky and tried to drink away his sorrow. It was after midnight when he gave up, set the half-empty bottle aside, and went to bed.

He held up his phone in the darkness, listened to the message once more. There was something about it, but he couldn't say what, his thoughts clouded by drink. Worry pushed at the edges of his mind, niggled at him. So, he listened again and again.

Something wasn't right, but he couldn't put a finger on it. *You're off your heid, man.*

He set the phone aside and drifted into a restless sleep.

3

Elizabeth had just hit her snooze button when her cell rang. She fumbled for it in the dark, saw that it was Quinn.

She answered. "It's six in the morning here, you know."

"I need your help."

The tone of his voice made Elizabeth sit up. "Are you okay?"

"Aye, I'm well, but there's somethin' goin' on here. I cannae say whit just yet, but it disnae add up."

Elizabeth could tell he was upset because his accent always got thicker when he was under stress. She was about to ask him what he meant, but there was no point in discussing anything until she'd had at least one cup of coffee. "Can you call me back in a half hour? If you want me to think, I need a shower and some caffeine."

"Aye. Talk to you then."

Elizabeth turned off her alarm, took a hot shower, and went to the kitchen to make coffee, still in her bathrobe, her hair damp. She'd just finished her first cup when her phone rang again. Quinn was right on time.

"Hey." She grabbed a notebook and a pen. "Okay, start from the beginning."

While he explained, she took notes. His friend, Jack, had been found dead in an alley. He'd been wearing body armor, but the killer had slashed his throat. There were no bruises, lacerations, or other signs of a physical altercation on the body. The murder had taken place at about three in the morning. Someone, ostensibly the killer, had taken Jack's work and personal cell phones, watch, and wallet, but had left his car. No one knew why Jack had gone into that alley. He'd left his job working as security for a member of the Scottish Parliament three hours earlier, so he hadn't been on duty.

"Police have been askin' his wife, Ava, whether he had a history of usin' or sellin' drugs, but Jack Murray would never do that."

Elizabeth could understand why investigators had moved in that direction. People didn't drive into back alleys for the scenery. "How can I help?"

"Last night, I had a feelin' that somethin' wisnae right, but I'd had a wee swally of whisky, and I couldnae make sense of it."

Meaning that he'd been drunk—again.

Quinn went on. "But this mornin', it struck me. Ava told me that Jack had lost his personal mobile a few weeks back while on the job and that the killer stole the new one. But when Jack called me a few days afore he was murdered, he called on his old personal phone, the one Ava thinks he lost a few weeks ago."

"Are you sure?"

"Aye. There's no mistake. Ava said the new mobile came wi' a new number. He called me from the old number."

Okay, that *was* strange.

"So, he lied to his wife." That certainly wouldn't lessen police suspicions. Secret cell phones were exactly the thing you'd expect to find associated with selling drugs. "I know he was your best friend, but it's possible that he's changed. Maybe he had problems with post-traumatic stress or—"

"I cannae believe it. If you had known Jack... I need to find that mobile."

"What makes you think the police don't already have it? I don't know the laws in Scotland, but I'm sure investigators are able to access the phone records of homicide victims. Wherever that phone is, they'll be able to track it."

"I need to find it first."

"Quinn, I know you want to help Jack, but if you were to find that phone and keep it to stop police from uncovering ties to drug dealing, you'd be guilty of obstruction or interfering with a police investigation."

"I'm no' doin' this to keep Jack's secrets. I want to find the killer."

"So do the police."

"Aye, but I dinnae trust the police. The detective, Wilson, is a smug bastard, so he is. The way he spoke to Ava... There's a leak in his office. Some fucker told the news that police think there might be a tie to drugs. Jack isnae here to defend himself—or Ava and the wee ones."

"And you think that's your job."

That was one thing about Quinn. He was loyal to a fault.

"Aye."

"How can I help?"

"If I give you his number, can you track the mobile or look at his phone records to see where he's been and who he's called?"

Elizabeth couldn't have heard Quinn right. "You want me to track his phone or hack his service provider?"

She wasn't a cryptographer, but she'd taken all the training the Agency had offered and had some skill with the computer side of intelligence work. She'd put those skills to work for Cobra on many occasions, monitoring enemy communications, tracking GPS signals, even hijacking a drone or two.

"You've done it many times afore."

She laughed. "Yes—with the proper authorization. Hacking into his phone records without permission would be a *crime*. You know that. I want to help, Quinn, but I'm not going to spend the next twenty years in a Scottish prison."

"But you *can* track it, aye?"

"I'd need the number associated with its SIM card or the IMEI number, but the service provider isn't going to give them to me just because I ask nicely. If Ava has them on file somewhere, I can give it a try. If not—"

"I dinnae want to ask her. I cannae find it in me to tell her that he lied about his mobile. I dinnae think she could bear that just now."

"Then there's nothing I can do. I'm really sorry, Quinn."

"I understand." There was disappointment in his voice. She hated letting him down. "If you think of anythin' or get any ideas, you'll ring me, aye?"

"Of course. Just promise me you won't do anything illegal or stupid."

"Och, you know me."

She did—and that's what scared her.

QUINN LEFT his hotel later that afternoon, bought a few things he'd need from a tool shop, and dropped a few quid on a supper of bangers and mash at a pub near his hotel.

Knowing he'd need his wits, he kept himself to one wee pint. Then, when it was dark, he made the drive back to Jack and Ava's house.

Och, he had to be mental to have asked Elizabeth to hack into Jack's phone records. She wasn't the kind of person to bend the law, much less break it. Quinn didn't want her to end up in the nick for his sake. He would have to manage this on his own.

Aye, he'd done intelligence work in the past. After leaving the SAS, he'd gotten retrained and spent two years analyzing satellite and drone images for MI6, something he did for Cobra when needed. But he didn't have Elizabeth's skills with electronic gadgets—computers, phones, tablets. For that matter, he didn't have her facility with languages or people, either. She was trained for sophisticated intelligence work, while he was little more than an expert killer.

But a well-paid killer, aye?

He turned onto Cumbernauld Road, parked down the street, then grabbed the small paper bag of tools, and started up the walk, a sense of guilt niggling at him. Ava hadn't wanted police to search the place, and she likely wouldn't be pleased if she learned that Quinn had broken in and poked about. But it was either this—or tell her about the phone.

That he just couldn't do.

She need never know he was here. He would jimmy the door lock, bypass the security system, and search for records that might have the SIM or IMEI number for Jack's mobile. If he were lucky, he might even find the phone. Then he'd leave the place just like he'd found—

A flash of light.

It had come from the upstairs bedroom.

Quinn stopped, saw a beam of blue light moving in the darkness.

Someone was up there.

In a heartbeat, Quinn's training kicked in. He moved soundlessly toward the door, saw that someone had broken the lock. He nudged the door open, found the house dark and the control panel for the security system forced open.

Bloody hell.

A wee pair of night vision goggles just now would have been brilliant, not to mention body armor and his Glock. At least he'd brought his knife. He set the paper bag of tools aside, bent down, drew the knife out of its ankle rig. Holding the blade, he moved down the hallway toward the stairs.

He took the stairs quickly, quietly, the sound of footsteps and rustling coming from Jack and Ava's bedroom.

Squeeeeeeek!

The sound could have woken the dead.

Fuckin' hell!

In the dark, he'd stepped on a fucking toy.

Whoever was up there now knew he was here. There was no doubt about that. The rustling stopped, and the house fell silent.

Aye, Quinn would give his bollocks for a firearm right now.

Keeping his gaze on the bedroom door, he backed down the stairs, not wanting to get caught by an armed assailant in such a narrow space.

A dark shape emerged from the bedroom.

"Who the fuck are you?" Quinn flicked on the light. "What's your business here?"

The man was dressed entirely in black, a balaclava covering his face. He flew down the stairs straight at Quinn, hurling something as he ran.

Quinn ducked, a metal torch grazing his cheek before crashing to the floor behind him. It was just a distraction, a way of trying to take Quinn's attention off the blade in the fucker's right hand. But Quinn saw the knife and blocked the blow with his left arm. He thrust with his right, chibbed the bastard in the face.

The attacker grunted, staggered back, and fled, gloved hand raised to his left cheek. It was only then Quinn noticed the black bag hanging over the man's right shoulder, something heavy inside.

"What are you stealin'?" Quinn ran after him, but the bastard disappeared through the hedge in the neighbor's front garden. If Quinn followed, he might end up with his throat slit, too. "You fuckin' bastard!"

Rage thrumming in his veins, Quinn walked back inside, shut the door, glanced about. In the light, he saw that the place had been ransacked. Whoever the man was, he'd been here for a good while before Quinn had arrived. He'd gone through everything—DVDs, kitchen drawers, the pantry, the refrigerator.

Then Quinn saw it.

Blood.

A trail of crimson drops led to the door.

Quinn must have got him good.

Naw, ya eejit. That's your blood.

The prick's knife had cut deep into his left forearm.

He walked to the kitchen, grabbed a bit of kitchen roll, pressed it against the gash to staunch the bleeding. He needed to call the police. But before he did that, he would have to hide his knife and the ankle rig, as well as the lock-pick tools he'd bought. He couldn't risk rousing the suspicion of investigators, who might search him.

He wiped the blade, sheathed it, and stuck it in Jack's

tool box with the lockpick tools beneath the kitchen sink, then took out his mobile and dialed 101.

What the hell would he tell the police? What would he tell Ava?

I came here to break into the place, but someone had beaten me to it.

He would tell them that he'd come to check on the house because he'd worried that the killer might have the address. From there, he could just tell the truth. He'd noticed a light moving in the upstairs bedroom, walked to the door, and found that someone had broken in. He'd been jumped by a man, who'd swung at him with a knife before running off into the neighbor's yard with something in a pack.

That's what he'd tell Ava, too. The police would notify her. She'd be afraid and face the added trouble of cleaning up this mess.

"This is Quinn McManus calling to report a burglary." He gave the woman on the other end Jack and Ava's address. "I'm a friend of the family come to check on the house. I saw a light movin' about inside and walked up to the door to find that someone had broken in. I guess I startled the gobshite because he ran, but no' afore slashin' my arm wi' his blade."

As he recounted the confrontation, one thing stood out for him.

Whoever he was, the bastard moved with uncanny speed and knew well how to wield a knife.

I<small>T WAS ALMOST</small> noon in Glasgow when Elizabeth checked into Quinn's hotel. For all her expertise in predicting human behavior, she often didn't understand herself. She'd wanted to spend her vacation relaxing on a tropical beach. Instead, she'd flown to Scotland where it was dark and rainy and cold because she knew Quinn would end up in trouble without her.

Damn it, Quinn!

Her one shot at a beach vacation this year, and she was going to spend it babysitting a rough, hard-charging operative whose big heart might land him in prison. Instead of drinking daiquiris, soaking up the sun, and watching the waves roll in, she'd be freezing her butt off and not understanding a single word anybody said.

She was fluent in four languages, but Glaswegian wasn't one of them.

Leaving her computer and other electronics in their suitcase, she unpacked her clothes and took a shower to refresh herself. The hot water didn't help as much as she would have liked, but then she hadn't yet gotten over the long flight home from Kabul. She blew her hair dry and put on a little mascara and lip gloss, ignoring the dark circles beneath her eyes. Then she dressed in jeans and her black V-neck cashmere sweater.

Feeling a little more human, she tucked her room key into her pocket, took a notebook and pen, crossed the hall to his door, and knocked. She hadn't told him she was coming, perhaps because she couldn't believe it herself. But here she was.

She heard his footfalls, saw a shadow move over the peephole in his door.

He opened it, wearing only a pair of jeans, astonishment on his handsome face. "*Lilibet?* What in God's name are you doin' here?"

A jolt of heat shot through her, her pulse picking up.

Holy freaking heaven.

Defined pecs dusted with freckles and auburn curls. Flat tan nipples. A trail of curls bisecting his six-pack. Broad, strong shoulders. Thick biceps. Scars.

"I...um..." She'd never seen him without a shirt before and was so distracted that it took her a moment to notice the dark bruise on his face and the bandage on his left arm. "I came to keep you out of trouble. It looks like I'm late."

He motioned her into his suite, locking the door behind her. A half-empty bottle of whisky sat on the coffee table, the TV muted on some news channel, a bloody T-shirt hanging on the door handle to the bathroom.

"Tea?"

She turned to face him, willed herself to keep her gaze on his eyes and not to ogle him. "Tell me what happened."

"I'm brewin' myself a cuppa, so it's no' trouble."

"Okay. Fine. Tea. Thanks. What happened?"

While he brewed the tea in the room's kitchenette, he told her how he'd gone to break into Jack and Ava's house to search for information on the phone, only to find someone already there. Rather than calling the police, he'd gone inside alone—of course, he had—to confront the culprit. He'd stepped on a squeak toy, alerting the intruder, who had run at him down the stairs, thrown a flashlight at his head, and tried to stab him before running off, a bag over one shoulder.

Chills skittered down Elizabeth's spine. "He had a knife?"

"Aye, but I caught the blow wi' my left arm and got him in the face wi' my blade." Quinn grinned, held up his left arm. "The police made me to go A&E—Accident and Emergency—afterward. Six stitches."

Elizabeth gaped at him. "Quinn, he might have *killed* you."

"Och, well, he didnae, did he?"

Dear God, give me patience.

"Not this time." She'd worked with special operators all of her adult life. Their confidence in their own abilities was well-founded, but sometimes it got them into trouble. "You should have called the police and waited for them to arrive. They might have been able to arrest him, and we'd know who he was and why he was there. What if by rushing in you let Jack's killer escape?"

Quinn carried two cups of tea to the coffee table, his expression troubled. "Aye, I've thought of that. There's sugar if you'd like."

"No, thanks. What did the police say?"

"Mostly, they yelled at me and asked questions."

"I can't blame them." Elizabeth wanted to yell at him, too.

"They asked why I was there. I told them I'd come to check on the house because I knew Ava wisnae home. They called Ava, asked her to come. Jack's brother-in-law, David, drove her in from Paisley. The color left her face when she saw the place. The only thing missin' as far as she could tell was Jack's laptop. She's right afraid, she is."

"Can you blame her?" Elizabeth sipped her tea. "Someone murdered her husband, and now a man with a knife broke into her home, ransacked it, and attacked her husband's *idiot* of a best friend."

"Och, I know what I did was daft, but some murderin' bastard took Jack from us." Grief mingled with rage in Quinn's eyes. "When I saw the light movin' in his room, I couldnae just stand there. I had to *do* somethin'."

Elizabeth couldn't hold that against him. It was hard-wired into his DNA to charge into danger when other people ran away. "I'm just glad you're not dead. Do you know how pissed off I would be if I'd given up a beach vacation and come all this way only to find you in the morgue?"

Quinn grinned. "Are you sayin' you care what happens to me, Lilibet?"

The way he said "Lilibet" had always made her knees weak, but the accent and the bare chest together were too much.

She kept her expression professional. "Put on a shirt, and let's get to work."

4

———

Quinn could scarce fathom that Lilibet was here in Glasgow in his hotel room.

It disnae mean what you wish it meant, man.

She lifted her cup to her lips, sipped, her red-gold hair hanging over her right shoulder. He could tell she was fighting jet lag, dark circles beneath her blue eyes, but she looked as lovely as ever to him.

She set her cup on its saucer. "I had time to think it over on the flight. The best use of my skills might be to take all the information you have on Jack's murder and start picking it apart, looking for anything investigators might have missed. We can also try to reconstruct the last few weeks of Jack's life and see what we learn."

"That's no' a relaxin' way to spend your holiday."

"You can make up for that by showing me around Glasgow."

"Aye, I can do that."

"Just remember I was a counterterrorism analyst, not a detective. I've never tried to solve a crime. I'm not sure I'll be any help."

"I trust you afore I'll trust that bampot Wilson."

A smile tugged at her lips. "You're sweet to say that, but what's a 'bampot'?"

Quinn couldn't help but laugh. "A bampot is an eejit, a numpty, a stupid person."

She smiled. "So, I could say that you were a bampot last night when you went into that house alone, right?"

There was that smart mouth again, the one he'd imagined kissing.

"Aye, so you could." He changed the subject. "Where do we start?"

She stood. "We have to go to an office supply store. I need something to write on, something to use as a whiteboard."

"We can do that, but I promised I'd help Ava and Hannah clean up the house this afternoon. Ava said she'd feel safer wi' me there. Also, I need to get my knife back. I hid it with my lockpicking tools under their sink in Jack's toolbox."

"That's fine. I'll help, too. It will give me a chance to meet Ava."

When Elizabeth had retrieved her raincoat, they rode the lift down to the main floor and retrieved the Crossland from the car park. Quinn drove her to Alba Office Supply, amused by her gasp when he turned right into the left lane.

"Dinnae worry yourself. I learned to drive this way."

"I'd crash in the first five minutes."

They bought some dry-erase markers and a small, portable whiteboard that folded and just managed to fit in the back, stopping at a florist shop along the way so Elizabeth could buy flowers for Ava. Then they made the drive to Jack and Ava's house, going over everything Quinn knew about the murder once again.

"Tell me about Ava."

Quinn shared what he knew. Ava was English. She and Jack had met when she was assigned to him as his physical therapist after he injured his shoulder in combat. They'd gotten together when they ran into each other two years later and had been together since. She had an older sister, who was caring for their ailing mother. Both she and Jack had wanted children, so Olivia and Isla had come along quickly.

"Somehow, she brought Jack back to earth, brought him home from the battlefield. He stopped drinkin' so much and became a family man." Quinn glanced over at Elizabeth, who seemed to be taking all of this in, a thoughtful frown on her face. "Have you ruled her out as a suspect?"

Elizabeth shot him a look. "You bampot. The more I understand about her, the more I'll be able to see this through her eyes."

Quinn turned onto Jack and Ava's street. "She's devastated, she is. Jack loved her wi' all of his heart, and she loved him. She told me she disnae know how she's goin' to live the rest of her life wi'out him. She wants answers. She wants justice."

"Those answers might not bring her the peace she wants."

Even as he understood Elizabeth's meaning, Quinn rejected that thought. "I know what it looks like wi' him lyin' to her about his mobile, but I cannae believe he'd sell or use drugs."

Would you bet your life on that?

Aye, so help him God, he would.

"Dinnae you say a word about that phone to Ava, aye?"

"I promise."

They arrived at the house to find Ava and Hannah

already there, Ava standing in her kitchen, looking overwhelmed, while Hannah made tea.

Quinn introduced Elizabeth, who gave Ava the flowers.

"I'm so very sorry for your loss—and for this latest upheaval in your life."

"Thank you. These are lovely." Ava took the flowers, sniffed them, and handed them to Hannah, who rummaged under the sink for a vase. "You work with Quinn?"

"I used to be a counterterrorism analyst with the CIA. I've come to help him see if he can unravel what happened to your husband."

"The CIA?" Ava stared at her. "I'm so grateful. Quinn has always been such a good friend."

"Would you mind if I asked you some questions?"

"Anything to get justice for Jack."

While Quinn and Hannah cleaned up in the kitchen, Elizabeth sat down with Ava, taking notes as Ava answered her questions.

"Was she really wi' the CIA?" Hannah whispered.

"Aye, she was. She's one of the cleverest people I know."

"I'm happy she's on our side."

So was Quinn.

Ava sat across from Elizabeth on the sofa. "I hope you're not going to ask me whether my husband was dealing drugs. I know what they said on the news last night. I've had a half-dozen *friends* call to tell me about it and ask how I'm coping. Jack and I didn't keep secrets from each other."

Elizabeth hurt for Ava, knowing that this wasn't true. "I'm so sorry—and, no, I wasn't going to ask you any of that."

Ava answered anyway. "Jack used to drink, but he never

touched drugs. He refused to take anything stronger than ibuprofen when they operated on his shoulder. I couldn't believe his pain tolerance."

"Quinn has already vouched for Jack's character, so I believe you." Elizabeth moved on. "Quinn says you told the police that Jack seemed tense lately. Can you tell me more about that?"

"Jack was always very closed about his work, and I understand that. As a physiotherapist, I had to maintain patient confidentiality. When you're in the military or working for the government, you can't share everything about your job. If you have a bad day, you can't come home and unload."

Elizabeth knew all about that. "You think he had a bad day?"

"A few weeks ago, he came home late—that is to say very early in the morning. I woke when he got into bed. I asked if he was all right. He didn't answer. He just held me—held me as if..." Ava's words trailed off, fresh tears in her eyes. "... as if his life depended on it. I asked again if he was all right. He said, 'The world is an ugly place.' Then he kissed me and told me to go back to sleep."

"Was that the end of it?"

Ava shook her head. "He seemed troubled at breakfast and left for work early."

"When you say 'troubled,' what does that mean?"

"He was quiet, lost in his own thoughts, tense. For days afterward, he seemed worried, pensive."

Elizabeth wrote that down. "Do you remember what night that was—the night he came home late? I know this is difficult. I'm sorry to ask so many questions."

"Don't apologize. I know you're trying to help." Ava drew out her cell phone, and looked at her calendar app. "It was a

Friday night. He often worked late on Fridays. That was the same week Hannah's oldest broke his wrist skateboarding. It must have been October eighteenth."

Elizabeth wrote that down, too. "About three weeks ago, then?"

Ava nodded. "Yes."

"Why did he work late on Friday nights?"

"Alastair Whitehall—that's the Member of Scottish Parliament, or MSP, who employed Jack—is quite wealthy. He gets invited to a lot of political and social events. Jack said it came with the job."

"That makes sense." Elizabeth had yet to meet a politician who didn't love the limelight. "How long had Jack worked for Mr. Whitehall?"

"It's been a few months. Andrew Lewis, another SAS veteran, helped him land a job as a security guard at Holyrood when he left the service, but Alastair took a liking to him and hired him to be part of his personal security team a few months ago. Jack was chuffed because it came with a big pay rise."

"I'm not familiar with the laws in Scotland, but in the United States, you might have access to some of the information about this investigation—a case file. It would be really helpful for me to have that file."

"Hannah's husband, David, is a solicitor. I'll ask him to look into it."

"I appreciate that." Elizabeth took a moment to glance through her notes. She wasn't Sherlock Holmes, and she was probably overlooking something. "Do you have the serial number for the stolen laptop?"

"Not that I know. I'm sorry."

"Did he have any conflicts with people at work?"

"Jack was the kind of man who got on well with most

people, but I did think of a couple of things. This past August, a man confronted Alastair outside Holyrood. Jack said he was drunk or off his nut on drugs. It was Jack who fought him to the ground and held him until police arrived. The man kept shouting about abortion and threatening to kill Alastair and Jack, too, if Jack didn't release him. Police arrested him, but I don't know what became of him after that. Jack laughed about it."

"I'll look into it." Oh, how Elizabeth wished she could ask Ava for the SIM and IMEI numbers for Jack's phones, but she'd made a promise. "How about acquaintances, friends—people outside of work?"

"He was in a gang for a time as a teenager—the Young Boys—but that was such a long time ago. He lost touch with most of them, though he and Leo Grant stayed in contact. They had a falling out about a month ago."

"Tell me about Leo."

"Leo was Jack's best pal growing up. Leo thought Jack should stop working for Alastair and come to work as a security guard for him. He offered Jack double what he was making. When Jack declined, Leo flew into a rage and accused him of turning his back on his roots and Scotland. Leo supports Scottish independence, and Alastair favors the union."

That was interesting. "What kind of business does Leo operate?"

"I think he runs a shipping firm. He owns warehouses and ships that dock in Troon. Jack thought his business dealings were suspicious and wanted no part of it."

"Do the police know this?"

"I told them, but I have no idea whether they'll investigate."

"Thank you, Ava. I know this can't have been easy for you—especially talking with someone you don't know."

Ava wiped tears from her cheeks, her emotions naked in her eyes—grief, gratitude, fear. "If Quinn trusts you, I trust you, too. He and Jack were like brothers. They met in the army, but they both had a rough time of it as children, growing up on the breadline here in Glasgow. They used to joke that if they hadn't both joined the army, they might have met in prison."

Ava laughed, so Elizabeth laughed, too, though she wasn't sure what Ava meant by that. Quinn had never talked about his childhood. Still, Elizabeth had no difficulty imagining him as a troublemaker.

Ava grew serious again, worry in her eyes. "May I ask you something?"

"Of course."

"Do you think the man who broke into our home, the man who tried to stab Quinn, is the same person who killed my husband?"

"I've asked myself the same thing. It seems suspicious, but knife crimes are hardly rare here." On her flight, Elizabeth had read that Glasgow had once been the stabbing capital of Western Europe. Though the city's Violence Reduction Unit had brought about a steep decrease in the number of violent crimes, it was still among the higher crime areas in Scotland. "There's certainly a possibility that it was the same man. I just don't have enough information to make a reliable assessment."

Ava looked disappointed. "So many unknowns."

Elizabeth reached over, rested her hand on Ava's. "Quinn and I will do all we can to get to the truth—I promise."

"Thank you."

After that, Elizabeth helped clean up, sweeping floors

and sorting through papers that lay strewn across Jack's home office. Quinn joined her, the two of them making quick work of it.

"Did you get your knife and tools back?"

"Aye."

"Good." She bent down to pick up a few papers that had slipped beneath a bookcase when her fingers bumped something hard—a box.

She drew it out, saw that it was an Apple iPhone box. "Quinn."

"It must be the box for his new phone."

She pulled off the top, located the SIM number and IMEI numbers on the packaging, and took a photo with her cell.

A shadow fell across the floor, and Elizabeth looked up to see Ava standing in the doorway. Elizabeth was about to make up an explanation for what she'd just done, but it was clear that Ava hadn't noticed.

She stood there, her arms crossed protectively over her chest. "It doesn't look like he took anything besides the laptop, but then we don't have many valuables. Why would he take Jack's computer? It wasn't new or fancy."

"Och, Ava." Quinn stood, hugged her, his compassion putting a lump in Elizabeth's throat. "Some people will do anythin' for a few quid, aye?"

As Ava walked away, Elizabeth met Quinn's gaze and knew that he didn't believe what he'd just said, either.

Quinn drove through traffic toward his favorite pub. "Can we track the laptop?"

"She doesn't have the serial number, and I doubt he

installed any tracking software. The only other option is to hack his Gmail account and check the security log to see whether anyone signed in from a new IP address."

"But the thief would have to be an idiot to leave tracks like that, aye?"

"Yes, exactly. I doubt the laptop will lead us anywhere. Besides, I'm ... not... hacking." Her words trailed off and became a yawn.

"Jet lag catchin' up wi' you?"

"With a vengeance."

"The fish and chips at the Bonnie Prince are the best in Glasgow. They've got a good selection of whisky, too."

She yawned again. "Don't drink too much because I'm sure as hell not driving."

"I'll keep that in mind."

They were a bit ahead of the supper crowd, so Quinn found parking on the street. They walked through a light drizzle into the pub, Quinn holding the door for her. Och, it made him feel special to walk in with Elizabeth at his side. Every straight man here would envy him.

She's no' your woman, and you're no' on a date.

Aye, but no one else knew that.

He glanced about for familiar faces but saw no one he knew, the mingled scents of whisky and food making his stomach growl. A young woman led them to a quiet table in the back corner and left them with menus. They both ordered the fish and chips, while Elizabeth asked for a Coke and Quinn ordered a pint and a shot of Bell's.

"Cheers." He raised his shot glass.

"Cheers." She took a sip of her Coke. "Have you ever heard of the Young Boys?"

"Aye, the Young Boys. That's the gang Jack ran wi' in his younger days. I dinnae think they're still a force. Twenty years ago, those boys were full of piss and whisky, running about the town, lookin' to pick fights wi' other boys."

"Were you ever part of a gang?"

"Aye. There wisnae much else to do besides drink, fight, and fuck." Most of the time, Quinn tried not to think about those days. "We were the South Bank Boys."

Elizabeth's lips curved in a teasing smile that made his pulse spike. "Were the South Bank Boys full of piss and whisky and running around picking fights?"

"We had to defend our territory. Mostly that meant getting drunk on stolen booze and talkin' about whose arse we were goin' to thrash."

"All bark and no bite."

"We did get into a few fights but nothin' serious." Then it hit him. "Are you thinkin' there's a connection between Jack's murder and the Young Boys?"

"I really can't say. I was just trying to be thorough." She glanced down, frowned. "I left my notebook in the car. Can I have the keys? I'll run and get it."

"Leave it. Enjoy your supper. Life shouldnae always be work."

She smiled, her sweet face lighting up. "That's right. I'm on vacation."

Quinn steered the conversation away from his childhood, asking Elizabeth what she'd like to see in Glasgow.

"Are there any castles or Roman ruins?"

"We've got castles—Crookston Castle and Dumbarton up north. There's also the Antonine Wall and the Bearsden Bath."

She picked up her mobile. "Crookstone?"

"Crookston." Quinn spelled it for her then watched as she read about the castle's history, something stirring in his chest at the sight of her—the play of light on her skin, the excitement in her delicate features, the smile on those sweet lips.

Och, she was bonnie.

She looked up. "What was the other one?"

The other one?

Castles, you eejit.

"Dumbarton Castle. D-U-M-B-A-R-T-O-N."

She typed the letters into her phone and scrolled through photos, reading some of the history. "Mary Queen of Scots was there?"

Quinn couldn't take his gaze off her. He was so transfixed that he didn't notice the server standing beside the table with their food until she spoke.

"Fish and chips?"

Elizabeth looked up. "Oh, wonderful. I'm starving."

They made plans while they ate, Quinn promising himself that he wouldn't waste her entire holiday on Jack's murder.

"Are you going to show me where you grew up?"

The question took Quinn by surprise. "Naw. The place was demolished."

Och, he would have loved to have seen that. He would have cheered as the building collapsed into a pile of dust and rot.

Quinn insisted on paying, given that she'd flown here to help him.

"Thank you. Those might well be the best fish and chips I've ever had."

He helped her into her jacket. "I told you so."

They walked outside and made their way back to the car.

Elizabeth looked up. "The rain has stopped."

"For now." Quinn wanted to take her hand, to wrap an

arm around her shoulder, but crossing that line could have serious consequences for them both.

"It must have been incredible to grow up surrounded by so much history," she said. "Crookston Castle has stood there since the twelfth century. The most historic building in my hometown is only a hundred and fifty years old."

Quinn had never had time to think about the history of Glasgow. He'd been too busy trying to survive. "Aye, the city is rich in history, so it is."

They reached the car, Elizabeth mistakenly walking to the driver's side.

"The other side, aye?" He took her shoulders and guided her out into the street, unlocking and opening her door for her. "You're knackered."

"If by that you mean tired, then, yes, I am." She climbed in, put on her seatbelt, leaned her head back, and closed her eyes.

Quinn got into the driver's seat, started the engine, and merged with traffic, heading back to the hotel. "Are you cold?"

"A little."

He turned on the heater and the seat warmer then turned left.

"Mmm. That feels good."

Her little moan might have made him crash had his attention not shifted to the car behind him—a black Corsa. It had pulled away from the curb at the same time that he had. Two turns later, it was still behind him.

You're imaginin' things.

With Elizabeth half asleep in the seat beside him, he decided to test that theory, turning right and heading north.

The Corsa did the same.

Quinn locked the doors, drove another kilometer down the street, and pulled over in front of a nightclub.

The Corsa slowed, stopped, giving Quinn a clear view of its plate number in the brief moment before its driver pulled to the side of the road, too.

Elizabeth's eyes opened. "Are we stopping?"

"Nay." He headed north again. "I'm just conductin' an experiment."

The Corsa waited for him to get a block ahead then did the same.

"An experiment?"

"I think we're bein' followed."

5

"Followed?" Elizabeth's drowsiness vanished.

"The Corsa a few cars back. He's been wi' us since the pub, turnin' whenever I turn. He pulled over when I stopped in front of the nightclub and then followed me back into traffic. He's bein' clever, keepin' his distance, lettin' other cars come between us."

"I see him." Elizabeth watched the vehicle in her side-view mirror, thinking through the possibilities in her mind. Maybe law enforcement had taken an interest in Quinn after last night. Or perhaps the man who'd tried to stab him had waited outside Jack and Ava's house and then followed them into the city.

"I'm goin' to try to lose him." Quinn changed into the right lane.

"No, don't. You'll tip him off. We need to know who he is."

The Corsa waited a few seconds, then changed lanes, too, coming to a stop behind them at the red light.

Prickles of foreboding rose along Elizabeth's spine. "I don't like this."

She'd seen too many snatch-and-grabs and read too many reports about street shootings that started like this. Car stops at red light. Assailants climb out of next car over and riddle the target vehicle with bullets—or grab someone and drag them away. US special forces employed the same technique when necessary.

"Who are you, you fucker?" Quinn grumbled.

Elizabeth reached inside her handbag for her phone. "I'm calling the police."

"What if they *are* the bloody police?"

So, he'd thought of that, too. "This is one way to find out, isn't it?"

"I'll do it." Quinn's phone was already sitting in its holder on the dash. He tapped it to activate it. "Call one-oh-one."

Police Scotland dispatch answered.

"This is Quinn McManus. We spoke last night when some bastard tried to stab me. I'm bein' followed through the city by a black Corsa." He gave them the license plate number and their current location.

"What makes you think you're bein' followed?" the woman on the other end asked, sounding bored.

"I'm a veteran of the SAS, for fuck's sake. If I say I'm bein' followed, then I'm bein' followed. Get DS Wilson. No, I dinnae know his division or his station name. He knows what's goin' on."

That seemed to get the dispatcher's attention. She cautioned Quinn not to evade the other vehicle but instead to drive as if he were oblivious, following her directions to a place where two police cars would intercept the Corsa.

Elizabeth spoke quietly so as not to be overheard by dispatch. "I guess that answers our question."

It wasn't the police following them.

The dispatcher guided them along a simple route with a few turns that took them toward the center of the city. "At the light, turn left. Two police cars will come up behind you there."

Quinn made the turn, the Corsa following. "I see them."

Elizabeth saw them, too—two police cars, coming up fast behind them, lights flashing blue and white. Then she heard an engine roar. "He's going to run. Shit!"

The Corsa sped up, flew through the intersection, and disappeared.

Quinn slammed a closed fist against the steering wheel. "Fuckin' hell!"

One of the police cars sped after the Corsa while the other pulled up behind them.

Elizabeth sympathized with his fury. For Quinn, this wasn't just about some creep following them. It was about his best friend's murder.

She tried to offer support, touching a hand to his arm, the contact electric as always. "They might still catch him."

"We'll escort you to the police station now," said a voice from Quinn's phone.

"Och, hell." He ended the call. "*This* is why you dinnae call the police. It's goin' to be a long night."

They followed the other police car to the station, the bright lights making Elizabeth blink. A woman who introduced herself as PC Patel took contact information and a statement from each of them. She also asked to see Elizabeth's passport. Then she showed them where the coffee was and asked them to wait.

Quinn poured them each a cup, anger and frustration making his features hard. "They're no' goin' to catch that bastard."

"You don't have much confidence in the police."

He met her gaze, and his expression softened, his lips curving in a lopsided grin that sent a trill of excitement shivering through her. "I spent too many years runnin' from them myself."

What was it about the way he looked at her? She'd met lots of ripped, handsome men in her years working with special forces guys, but none of them had made her feel the way Quinn did.

She was about to say that she wanted to hear more about his days as a delinquent when a man in a tan trench coat strode toward them looking annoyed.

"Wilson." Quinn's dislike for the man was obvious.

"McManus, why am I no' surprised to see you?"

"Perhaps because the control room told you I was here." Quinn could be *such* a smart-ass. "Did you catch the bastard?"

"Let's talk. Your friend, too."

He led them to an interview room, a small space with a table and a few chairs. He shut the door behind him—and laid into Quinn. "If you're after findin' the person who killed Jack Murray, you'd best think again. This is a police matter."

"Why in God's name are you angry wi' me? I take a woman out to the pub, some bastard follows us, and I'm to blame?"

"By confrontin' the burglar last night, you've drawn unwanted attention to yourself. I want to know where you've been today, what you've been doin'."

"You ought to be lookin' into who's leakin' details about this case to the media, not worryin' about us. Aye, you've a leak in this office."

While the two men argued, Elizabeth watched DS Wilson closely. There was nothing in his body language to indicate that he was hiding something or being less than truthful with Quinn. At the same time, it was clear that he didn't trust Quinn.

Well, Quinn did have a talent for rubbing people the wrong way.

"Gentlemen!" Elizabeth interrupted them, eager to get back to the hotel and anything that resembled a bed. "While I agree it was stupid for Quinn to enter the house alone with a possible killer inside, that's water under the bridge. Now, it's late, and I'm jet lagged. This conversation is going nowhere."

Both men shut their mouths.

Elizabeth asked the obvious question. "Did they catch the guy who followed us?"

Wilson shook his head. "The driver evaded us long enough to abandon the car on a side road. The car matches one that was stolen in Edinburgh this mornin'."

Elizabeth gave Quinn's hand a squeeze to keep him from going off on Wilson again. "Are we free to go?"

Wilson nodded. "Try not to get yourselves killed, aye?"

QUINN DROVE BACK to the hotel, glancing in his rearview mirror every so often. "Surveillance cameras? What for? The hotel has security guards and surveillance cameras in the lobby and all the entrances. You can't use the elevator wi'out a keycard."

"All of that can be hacked or bypassed. You know that. You've seen me do it."

"You think we're dealin' wi' someone who's capable of that?"

"I don't know." She yawned. "The guy who followed us tonight—he was savvy enough to use a stolen car and to elude the police. What's his next move? Does he give up, or does he try something different—like putting a listening device in your room?"

"You're thinkin' he'll try to get at me at the hotel."

But Elizabeth was lost in her own musings and didn't answer. "I wish I understood his motivation. Was he trying to find out who you are and where you're staying? Is he trying to keep tabs on you or find out how you're connected to Jack? Was he hoping to get a second chance at you with that knife?"

"Let him try." After tonight, Quinn would like a crack at the bastard.

"I'll do a threat assessment tomorrow." Elizabeth yawned again. "But if this were a Cobra job, I would insist that we install some kind of surveillance in our rooms. You don't want to walk in on this guy—or leave yourself open to being bugged."

None of those possibilities had crossed Quinn's mind.

That's why she's the brains and you're the brawn.

"I don't suppose you borrowed any surveillance equipment from Cobra."

She laughed. "I could get into big trouble for that. We can get what we need from an electronics store in the morning."

Quinn turned into the car park adjacent to the hotel, keeping an eye on their surroundings as he walked inside with Elizabeth. The lobby was empty, apart from a couple drinking together at the bar.

They rode the lift to the fifth floor.

"Would you like me to clear your room afore you sleep?"

"Sure. Thanks." She pulled her key card out of her handbag, followed him out of the elevator to her room, and swiped her card.

At the green light, Quinn opened the door, flicked on the light, and stepped inside, wishing once again that he'd thought to bring his Glock.

Elizabeth took off her jacket, tossed it onto the sofa. "Thanks for dinner."

"You're welcome." Quinn cleared the bedroom, her closet, and the bathroom. "You get some sleep and ... Lilibet?"

He found her fully clothed and already sound asleep on the bed.

For a moment, he stood there, watching, a strange tenderness swelling in his chest. Then he took a throw blanket from the foot of her bed and draped it over her. "Sleep sweet, Lilibet."

He turned off the lights and let himself out, checking the door behind him.

Inside his own suite, he walked to the bedroom, reached inside the closet for one of his boots, and pulled out the Glock 42 and holster hidden inside. Twice now, he'd wished he had it with him. He wouldn't leave it behind again. He couldn't legally possess or carry it in Scotland, but he'd be damned if he'd let the killer harm Elizabeth or get a second chance at him.

He checked it—six rounds of .380 hollow-point ammunition in the magazine and one round in the chamber, enough to stop Jack's killer if it came to it.

Enough to keep Lilibet safe.

Elizabeth woke early the next morning and showered, details from yesterday running through her mind. She'd been so exhausted by the time they'd gotten back to the hotel that she didn't remember getting into bed. Oh, the joys of jet lag.

She toweled off, blew her hair dry, and dressed in jeans, a T-shirt, and a blue fleece jacket. She didn't want the hotel's housekeeping staff entering her suite, so she put out the Do Not Disturb sign and made her own bed. Then she called room service for a pot of coffee and some toast.

While she waited for her breakfast, she unpacked her UK plug adaptor and power converter so that she could hook up her computer. She would be able to create a secure connection with her computer at Cobra, which had the various frameworks and applications she would need for almost anything—tracking cell phones, organizing intelligence, and even cracking encrypted security.

Not that she had any intention of hacking.

By the time her coffee and toast arrived, she was set up and ready to work. Quinn would probably want her to go straight to tracking the SIM and IMEI numbers they'd gotten off that box yesterday, but after last night, her first task was to do a threat assessment for the two of them.

Being followed last night had changed things.

This wasn't like any threat assessment she'd done before. There were no satellite or communications feeds to analyze, no regional history to study, no cultural or religious forces to consider, and no long list of potential players to complicate matters. There was simply an unsolved murder, the unknown attacker who'd stolen Jack's laptop, and someone with unknown motives who had followed them in a stolen car.

She nibbled her toast and sipped her coffee, thinking through all she knew about the murder. In the end, it came down to two things—

A knock.

She set down her coffee, walked to her door, and looked out the peephole to see Quinn. She opened the door for him —and had to fight not to stare.

He stood there, looking impossibly sexy in a dark gray cable knit sweater and butter soft jeans, his thick red hair damp, his beard trimmed short, the bruise on his cheek beginning to fade. "Mornin'."

Seriously? He was one man she couldn't touch and he just had to show up at her door looking like a Celtic god, all rugged and manly. He even smelled good, damn it, the herbal scent of his soap and shampoo mingling with the salt of his skin.

She struggled for words, pheromones having apparently short-circuited her brain. "Er ... good morning."

He entered, saw her computer. "Hard at work, I see. Have you had breakfast?"

"I've had some toast."

"Och, that'll no' get you through the day. It's time you had a proper fry up."

"A fry up?"

"A full Scottish. Come. It's time for a wee bit of culture."

Elizabeth went with Quinn to the restaurant downstairs. A young man in a white shirt led them to a table, where Quinn ordered breakfast for both of them.

"Coffee, please," Elizabeth added.

"Tea for me." Quinn waited until the server had walked away. "You want to get surveillance cameras?"

She nodded. "I started doing a threat assessment for us this morning. Two things stood out for me. The first is that whoever killed Jack is truly dangerous. Jack served in special forces and worked as a security guard, but he died without a fight."

Quinn's jaw tightened. "Aye. I cannae fathom it."

"The second involves the guy who followed us. If Jack's murder were a random event, what motivation would the thief or thieves have to follow you? Their best bet would be to hole up somewhere, not to chase you through Glasgow." Elizabeth changed the subject as the server approached with their beverages. "Does it always rain here?"

"Near enough." Quinn waited until the server had walked away. "You're thinkin' there's more to it."

"It's all about motivation." She tried to explain. "Let's assume that the killer, the man who broke into Jack and Ava's house, and the guy who followed us last night are all the same person. If Jack's murder were random, why would the killer risk being caught just to ransack his house and steal his laptop? He's looking for something. Why else would he risk a confrontation with police by stealing a car and following his victim's best friend through town?"

"Criminals are stupid. Trust me on that."

Elizabeth leaned in. "Does a man who killed an SAS veteran with one slash, rushed you on the stairs, and escaped both you and the police seem stupid?"

Quinn's brow bent in a frown. "Naw."

A family of four sat at the table beside theirs, forcing them to talk about other things—sight-seeing, Scottish history, and whether Elizabeth should get herself a proper pair of wellies, which, she learned, were what Americans called rain boots.

"It's no' goin' to stop rainin', and if we're out muckin' about at Dumbarton Castle, you'll want dry feet, aye?"

"Aye," Elizabeth said, mimicking his accent to tease him —a small and insufficient way of getting back at him for looking so damned hot.

Then the server brought their food.

"*This* is a fry up." Quinn pointed to the different things

on her plate. "Sausage, bacon, tomato, black puddin', tattie scones, grilled mushrooms, beans, and eggs."

"So, 'fry up' is slang for 'heart attack on a plate'?" The mingled scents made Elizabeth's mouth water. "What is black pudding?"

"It's blood sausage."

Elizabeth stared with revulsion at the two dark patties beside her eggs, her expression seeming to amuse Quinn. "Is there actual blood in it?"

"Aye, pork blood, oats, barley, spices..." He chuckled. "You've never heard of blood sausage?"

She couldn't conceal her revulsion. "Would you like to eat mine?"

"Aye, thanks." He jabbed the two patties with his fork, shifting them from her plate to his. "You know what this means?"

She shook her head.

He leaned closer, a teasing glint in his eyes. "No haggis for you."

6

Q uinn stuck the small camera into place with a strip of adhesive. The hotel's management wasn't going to like this, but they would deal with that later. He turned the unit on, pointed the lens toward the door where Elizabeth stood. "Ready."

She did a little dance to set off the motion detector, her gaze on her phone.

Quinn heard her mobile buzz. "So, it works, does it?"

She smiled. "I'm looking at myself on the screen, so it's working perfectly."

If anyone entered their rooms while the cameras were operational, the devices would notify both phones using the hotel's wireless system and send an image of the intruder to their screens. If the bastard tried to break in while they were in their rooms, Quinn would be ready with the Glock 42.

He hadn't told Elizabeth he had the pistol. He didn't want to make her complicit if he was forced to use it and faced prosecution. It was small enough that he could carry it in its holster inside the waistband of his jeans. She need never know it was there.

With cameras in both rooms, Quinn helped Elizabeth set up the white board, watching for the next five minutes while she cleared space for her computer and then arranged her pencils and notebook.

"I'd no idea that intelligence work demanded such precision. Does it make a difference to national security if the pencils point this way instead of that?"

She shot him a look, a smile tugging at her lips. "I like to be organized."

"Aye, I can see that."

When she was satisfied, she picked up a dry erase marker and her notebook. "Let's write down the facts—no guessing or assumptions. Just facts."

Quinn sat on the back of the sofa. "Jack is dead, murdered."

She turned to the board and began to write.

JACK MURRAY MURDERED — TIME OF DEATH ca. 3 A.M. 2 NOV.

God almighty, had Jack truly been dead for almost a week now? Last Friday at this time, Quinn was in Afghanistan, and Jack was living his last day on this earth.

It didn't seem real. It wasn't right.

I'll find the bastard, Jack, and I'll make him pay. I swear it.

"We don't have toxicology tests yet. Who identified the body?" Elizabeth turned, met Quinn's gaze, stopped.

She set the marker aside, walked over to him, and wrapped her arms around him, her head resting against his chest. "I'm so sorry, Quinn. This won't be easy for you. I'll seem like I'm being cold and analytical. I'm probably going to throw out ideas that are upsetting. But I'm here because I care. Don't forget that."

Quinn held her, the feel of her precious in his arms. He wasn't used to accepting comfort from others. For most of his life, physical contact had come in two forms—sex and violence. Her kindness touched him more than he could say. "Thanks."

She stepped back, looked up at him, sympathy shining through her blue eyes. "You were Jack's best friend. I never met him. I'm going to do my best to be objective, and you won't always like it."

"Fair enough." He felt an urge to kiss her but knew it would drive her away. He'd always been careful during their wee flirtations not to cross the line. Elizabeth took her work seriously. She wasn't about to risk her career over a kiss—or a man.

She turned back to the board. "Who identified the body?"

"Ava did."

Working off her notes, Elizabeth wrote down all the facts they had about Jack's murder and the events that had followed. "Is that everything? Am I missing something?"

"He rang me."

"Oh, right! He called on his original phone. When was that?"

Quinn drew his mobile from his pocket, looked at the date on Jack's message. "He rang on October twenty-eighth. It was almost nineteen-hundred hours in Afghanistan. That's fourteen-thirty Glasgow time."

Elizabeth turned back to the board, marker in hand, and wrote that down. "Let's start there—with his phones. We've got the SIM and IMEI for the new one. I'm sure the police do, too, but let's see what we find."

She sat on the sofa, her laptop on the coffee table in front of her, and logged in to her computer at Cobra via VPN—their virtual personal network.

"Will the system detect you doin' this?"

"I log in from overseas all the time and from home. There shouldn't be any reason for the system to flag me." She hit return. "There. I'm in."

Quinn read the SIM and IMEI numbers from the photo she'd taken yesterday while Elizabeth entered them into the tracking framework. He had no idea how it worked. He only knew that the framework had been developed by the NSA— National Security Agency—and leased to Cobra. "Now what happens?"

"I'll tell you what's *not* going to happen. If we get a fix on this phone, you are *not* going to go charging out there. You're staying right here. I'll send an anonymous email to Wilson so the police can handle it. Are we agreed?"

Quinn wanted to object but knew she was right. "Aye, agreed."

"It shouldn't take long." She explained how the framework was actually a global network of cellular service providers that had agreed to share data with the NSA. "The program sifts through literally billions of numbers looking for a match and then connects with the GPS in that device or nearby cell towers to give us a location."

"Is this what the police are usin'?"

"No, it's far ahead of that. The police go directly to the service provider, and the service provider..." Her words trailed off. "It's gone."

"What's gone?"

"His new cell phone. It's not showing up anywhere. The search came up empty." She doubled-checked the SIM and IMEI numbers and ran the search again, ending up with the same results. "Nada."

"I dinnae understand. It must be somewhere."

Elizabeth looked up at him, "Either the phone is being kept in a place that blocks EM energy—"

"Aye, like a Faraday cage?"

She nodded. "—or someone has destroyed it."

"Now we know why the police haven't said anything about the stolen phones." Elizabeth logged out of the VPN and closed her laptop. "They haven't found them."

"Ava disnae know that."

"If I were you, I wouldn't tell her." Elizabeth stood, stretched. "You don't want to add to her worries, and if she mentions it to Wilson…"

"Aye. I've no desire to stand there while that numpty shouts in my face." Quinn stood, too. "Are you hungry? I hope the hotel serves Scotch pie."

She couldn't even think about food. "I'll never be hungry again after that breakfast. You go ahead and eat without me. I should probably go to the gym. Running helps me think."

"I'll get a bite and meet you there."

While Quinn went downstairs to the restaurant, she put on a pair of leggings, a jog bra, and a T-shirt, turned on her security camera, and took the elevator to the third floor in search of the gym. It was the middle of a workday, so the room was almost empty. She walked over to a treadmill, keyed in her usual workout, and started her three-mile run.

Televisions hung at strategic points throughout the room, offering distraction. She focused on the news channel, letting her mind relax.

Preparations for Remembrance Day across the UK.

Lest we forget.

Five members of a dog-fighting ring in Aberdeenshire sentenced to twenty months in prison each.

Good riddance.

Toxicology tests on the body of a teenage girl found in a ditch three days ago show that the cause of death was a drug overdose.

Poor thing. Awful.

Elizabeth waited to see whether they'd give an update on Jack's murder, but they moved to sports, which held no interest for her at all. She turned her mind to the whiteboard, let random thoughts trickle through her head.

The phone had been a dead end, but why would someone steal a phone and then destroy it? Most people who stole cell phones tried to sell them.

Ava had mentioned two men. There was the man who had tried to attack MSP Whitehall, threatening to kill him and Jack and shouting incoherently about abortion. What had happened with him? Then there was Leo Grant, Jack's former gang buddy, who had gotten angry when Jack had refused to work for him. Ava said Jack had had doubts about Leo's business dealings. The man must make good money to be able to afford private security and double Jack's pay.

There was also Jack's past involvement with gangs.

The toxicology results from Jack's post-mortem weren't back yet, so she...

Elizabeth's gaze snapped back to the television, and she tried to remember the report about the teenage overdose victim verbatim.

Katie Cameron, the fourteen-year-old teenager whose body was found three days ago in a ditch outside Edinburgh, died of a drug overdose it has been revealed. Tests showed alcohol, cocaine, and heroin in her body at the time of her death.

They'd found the girl three days ago and already had her results. They'd had Jack's body for twice that long and had told Ava the results weren't back yet.

They found something.

That's why they were focused on drugs.

Elizabeth's heart sank. If she was right, both Quinn and Ava would take the news hard. Maybe she could make it easier for Quinn at least if she shared her suspicions. Then again, maybe she was wrong. Maybe Scotland placed a priority on toxicology results for murdered minors. In most places in the US, murders and rapes had higher priority when it came to toxicology and DNA testing.

Quinn walked in wearing a T-shirt and gym pants that rode low on his hips. He flashed her a smile and walked over to the free weights, setting up the chest press.

Damn.

Elizabeth had seen him work out before—all that muscle in action. Cobra had a gym in the basement that most of the employees used to stay fit. The difference between Cobra's gym and this place was that they were on vacation now—and they were alone.

It would be *so* easy to give in and let her hormones win. She'd danced with Quinn and knew he was good with his body. He'd probably be as lethal in bed as he was out of it. But she'd hooked up with a coworker once before and had paid a terrible price for it. She'd sworn to herself never to make that mistake again.

Still, she was on vacation. It didn't hurt to ogle him—just a little.

Bench press. Bicep curls. Triceps. Incline press.

He got to his feet, raised the hem of his T-shirt to wipe the sweat from his face, exposing that delicious six-pack.

Elizabeth didn't realize she'd stopped running until the machine tossed her onto the floor. She toppled with a shriek, landing flat on her butt.

"Are you hurt?" Quinn jogged over, held out a big hand to help her up.

Heat rushed into her cheeks. "I'm fine."

She took his hand, stood, coming face to face with him —or face to sternum. He smelled like salt and sweat and soap, the warm scents filling her head, leaving her intoxicated.

Pheromone alert.

"Did you forget you were runnin'?" The gleam in his blue eyes told her he found all of this funny.

She couldn't tell him the truth, so she lied. "I'm not sure what I did."

She was *such* an idiot.

He leaned down, bringing his gaze level with hers. "Next time you're wantin' to watch me at the weights, turn off the machine first, and come pull up a chair."

QUINN SAW Elizabeth's eyes go wide, her cheeks flaming scarlet.

"You!" She glared at him, gave him a wee shove.

"Me?" He fought not to laugh. Och, she was adorable when she was angry. "It was you gawpin' at me and you who fell. What did *I* do?"

"Oh, like you've never stared at my ass before." Furious now, she gave herself a slap on the bum and then cupped her breasts through her T-shirt. "Or ogled my tits."

The sight of her cupping her own breasts sent blood rushing to his groin and brought his gaze to the exact place it should not be.

Sweet blazin' hell!

"Aye, I'll no' deny it. We're both adults. What's the harm in lookin'?"

His words seemed to make her angrier. She opened her

mouth as if to blister his ears—then leapt into his arms and kissed him.

Quinn caught her, drew her hard against him, his shock washed away by a rush of lust. He forgot about Jack's murder. He forgot they were in the hotel gym. He forgot that they shouldn't be doing this, because, *sweet Jesus*, they ought to have done it years ago. He forgot everything but Lilibet— her taste, the soft feel of her body against his, the sweet scent of her skin.

Och, the woman could kiss. She took everything he could give her and demanded more, her tongue teasing his, her teeth nipping his lips—

"Is this man harassin' you, miss?"

Elizabeth went stiff in Quinn's arms, the two of them opening their eyes to find a young security guard walking toward them.

Quinn set Elizabeth on her feet, trying not to laugh at the absurdity of the situation. "We're just havin' a wee snog, aye?"

"Miss?" The man didn't seem to believe Quinn, but waited for Elizabeth to answer. "It didnae look like snoggin'."

It took Quinn a moment to understand the accusation— a measure of how distracted he was just now. The guard must have seen Elizabeth shove him on the surveillance feed and had gotten the wrong idea.

Fuck.

Elizabeth gave the man that beautiful smile of hers. "I'm fine. Thank you. I fell off the machine. He helped me up and teased me about it, so I gave him a shove and, um, kissed him. I guess we forgot where we were. I'm so sorry we worried you, but I do appreciate your concern for my safety."

"If you're certain, miss…"

"Yes, thank you."

Quinn couldn't fault the guard for watching out for women, but the thought that anyone could believe him capable of abusing Elizabeth set his temper on edge. He wasn't that sort of man. No matter what anyone said, he was nothing like his father. Some part of him wanted an apology, but that would make him a right prick.

The guard was just doin' his job, aye?

Elizabeth turned to Quinn. "I'm done with my run. I'll see you upstairs."

"Aye, I'm comin', too."

The security guard walked out of the gym with them. "Enjoy your stay wi' us."

"Thank you." Elizabeth made small talk with Quinn until the lift doors closed behind them, giving them privacy. Her smile vanished, her gaze dropping to the floor. "I'm sorry. That was my fault. I…"

"Dinnae apologize unless you truly regret it. You kissed me, and, from what I could tell, you liked it as much as I did."

Her head snapped up, her gaze locking with his. "It shouldn't have happened."

He couldn't resist. "So, next time you come at me, I should fend you off, aye?"

She rolled her eyes. "There can't be a next time."

The lift doors opened onto their floor.

Elizabeth walked quickly down the hallway toward her room, Quinn beside her. "I don't want to risk our friendship, and I don't want to lose my job."

"Why did you do it?"

She swiped her keycard, but it didn't work.

Lilibet was flustered, so she was.

Quinn took the card, turned it around, and swiped it for her. "Why, Lilibet?"

She opened the door. "Can we please not talk about this in the hallway?"

Both of their cell phones buzzed, proof that their surveillance cameras worked.

Quinn walked over to the device and turned it off. "I'm listenin'."

She sank onto the sofa, ran her fingers through her hair. "I was embarrassed, and you were so ... *smug*."

"And your solution was to throw yourself into my arms and kiss me? I should be smug more often."

Her cheeks flushed pink. "What do you want me to say?"

"Admit that you're attracted to me, just as I'm attracted to you."

She shot to her feet. "Okay, fine! I'm attracted to you. I think you're hot. I'd love to rip your clothes off and fuck your brains out. Everything about you turns me on—all those muscles, that sexy accent, your red hair. Are you satisfied now?"

"Aye." Quinn had never seen Elizabeth so rattled before —and he liked it. He liked what she'd just admitted, too. He plopped onto the sofa, folded his arms behind his head, a grin on his face. "Well, now that's out in the open."

She wanted to rip his clothes off and fuck his brains out, did she? She was pure gaggin' for it, and so was he.

"It doesn't change anything, Quinn. I know what happens when you get involved with a coworker. I won't go through that again."

7

Elizabeth didn't know what was worse—her mortification over what she'd admitted just now or the unsatisfied ache inside her. She had kissed Quinn, and he was right. She *had* liked it.

The taste of him. The press of his lips on hers. His hard body. The feel of his arms around her. She couldn't remember a kiss that had affected her so intensely, setting her body on fire, making her want to get him naked right then and there.

It can't happen again.

She tried to move on, ignoring both her embarrassment —and the fact that she was now distractingly horny. "Where did we leave off?"

Quinn stood, walked over to her, concern on his face. "Did somethin' happen at the Agency?"

Shit.

She'd said too much, and now he was curious. She sat again, resigned to telling him. "In my second year with the Agency, I started dating a fellow analyst, a jerk named Jason. I knew pretty quickly that it wouldn't work out and ended it.

He was unhappy with that and came close to getting me fired."

She'd given him a simple answer and hoped that was enough.

Quinn sat in the armchair across from her, his concern now an angry frown. "What did he do, this fuckin' gobshite?"

She knew that look. She had aroused Quinn's protective side, the one that had brought him to the brink of violence more than once at the Pony Express when a man had been rude to her or grabbed her butt. "It doesn't matter now."

"It matters to me."

Elizabeth could see in Quinn's eyes that he meant what he said. Maybe it was best if he knew. Then maybe he'd understand. "I dated Jason for less than a month. We had sex once. I knew then that it wouldn't work out."

Quinn arched an auburn brow. "That bad?"

She nodded. "We weren't really a couple, but I ended it. Jason got angry and threatened to destroy my reputation. He started spreading rumors that I was trying to sleep my way to the top. Men I didn't know started hitting on me in the elevator and outside the bathrooms. One touched my butt. Another grabbed my crotch. I got encrypted emails with dick pics, photoshopped images of me having sex with terrorists and politicians, and vulgar messages. 'Lizzy ain't a lezzy. She loves to suck dick.' I was afraid to walk to my car alone at night."

"Fuckin' bawbags, the lot of them. Did you report them?"

"Of course! I saved the emails and the photos and all the computer data and gave my supervisor his name and the names of the men who'd assaulted me. I was assured that the Agency takes sexual harassment seriously, but nothing was done. I felt betrayed."

"You *were* betrayed."

"When the Agency refused to act, I went on the offensive. I stood up in a meeting where the rat bastard was present, showed the photos, read some of the emails—and almost got fired. They accused me of breaking rules against fraternizing and behaving unprofessionally."

"*You*? He was the bastard they needed to terminate. Is he still there?"

"Oh, yes." Elizabeth told Quinn how she'd refused to leave and had focused instead on becoming impervious to the insults. "I put all of my energy into being the best analyst I could be and supporting the other women, especially the younger ones. They watched out for me, and I watched out for them."

"I'm sorry, Lilibet. That wisnae right or just."

"Thanks." She couldn't help but smile at the sympathy in Quinn's eyes. He might be hell with a rifle in his hands, but he was such a softie when it came to women. "In the end, I was promoted, and he was transferred to another division. When I resigned to work for Cobra, the same people who'd refused to help me asked me to stay. That's some sort of justice, I suppose."

"No' the kind I'd like to give him."

"Your kind of justice might land you in prison. But now you know why I will never date a coworker again."

A look of hurt came over his face. "You think I'd treat you like that?"

"God, no, not at all!" She hadn't meant to suggest that. "It's not that I don't trust you, Quinn. It's the contract we both signed, the rules we both agreed to follow. There aren't a lot of organizations in the world where you and I can do the kind of work we do. Anyway, that's the past, and you and I need to focus on the present."

Quinn didn't look pleased with this. "Aye, all right."

Then she remembered. "Oh, yes! We should check with Ava about the toxicology tests. There was a report about a girl whose body was pulled from a ditch a couple of days ago. Police already have her toxicology results. It made me wonder why Ava hasn't gotten Jack's. Maybe they're using a different lab or perhaps the teen's tests had priority because she was a minor. Or maybe they've gotten the report and just haven't told us."

"Why would they do that?"

She said it as gently as she could. "Maybe they found something and don't want it to be public for fear of compromising their investigation."

"That cannae be it." He took out his phone. "I'll text Ava and see if she's heard."

The answer came almost immediately.

Quinn glared at his phone. "She still disnae have the results."

Elizabeth wasn't surprised.

She got to her feet, went to stand before the whiteboard, studied the bullet points. "What we need are actionable leads, and all we've got are the two men Ava mentioned."

"That bastard who threatened to kill Jack and that MSP —he sounds like he was off his heid."

"Ava didn't know his name, but surely the papers covered the incident." Elizabeth settled on the sofa and picked up her laptop. "He shouldn't be too hard to find."

Quinn moved to sit beside her, heat seeming to radiate off his body.

Focus, Shields.

It took Elizabeth less than a minute.

"Clive James MacDonald of Thurston Tower, Muir-house, Edinburgh." She wrote down the address, handed it to Quinn. "How do you feel about having a friendly chat with Mr. MacDonald?"

"Friendly?"

"Yes, friendly. That means no punching."

Quinn scowled. "I bloody well know what it means."

IT WAS dark by the time they reached Edinburgh. Quinn parked on the street, getting as close as he could to the high-rise known as Thurston Tower. He'd never been here, but the neighborhood was one of the poorest in the UK and had a reputation for shabbiness and violence.

"This isnae the safest part of town. Stay close by me, aye?"

"I understand."

They walked the short distance to Thurston Tower, coming to a big grassy area with paths and a playground—not the sort of place he would have brought Elizabeth at night if he'd had any choice. But the weather was chilly, and few people were about. A drunk in a thick woolen hat. A group of teenage boys huddled together near the swings. An old man walking a wee dog.

"It seems nice enough to me."

"Does it now? When I was a boy, people called it Terror Tower. I hear it's scheduled to be demolished."

They reached the entrance to the high-rise, the lock on its security door broken, enabling anyone to walk in off the streets. They stepped into the lobby, memories rushing back at him. He hadn't set foot in social housing since the night his father had thrown him out on the streets.

Elizabeth glanced at her cell phone. "He should be on the sixth floor."

Quinn pushed the button for the lift. "What if this bastard willnae talk wi' us?"

"Then we leave. We don't have police authority or any official status here."

Quinn was used to arriving with overwhelming force—armed to the teeth and authorized to kill. He felt naked showing up with nothing but a wee Glock 42.

The lift arrived, its doors gliding open to reveal a filthy, dingy interior, the fluorescent light fixture hanging down on one side by its wires, the reek of piss strong.

Elizabeth wrinkled her nose as they entered, but she said nothing.

The four walls pressed in on Quinn.

Get oot ma hoose, ya fuckin' bastard! Yer nae son o' mine. Dinnae be comin' back or I'll beat the life oot o' ye, so I will. This is yer hame nae mair, ya worthless fuck!

The lift stopped, bringing him back to the present, the doors opening on a filthy hallway—dirty vinyl dotted with rat droppings, the walls and ceiling stained black with mold, used syringes mere feet from a child's pram. The thrum of hip hop. A baby's cry. A man and woman arguing.

Quinn willed himself to breathe, the familiar stench of mold overwhelming.

Elizabeth took it all in, seemed to hesitate. "Number Six-Ten."

"This way." Quinn pointed.

A rat scurried past their feet, making Elizabeth jump.

"Sorry." She looked up at Quinn, clearly embarrassed. "It just surprised me. That's all."

"You've no need to apologize." He didn't like her seeing this.

What would she think if she knew he'd grown up in such squalor?

Clive MacDonald's flat was at the end of the hallway, a shabby gray door that didn't stop the sound of the telly from coming through.

Elizabeth knocked. "I'll ask the questions, okay?"

Quinn nodded. "You're the intel expert."

A pretty teenage girl with blond hair and wide green eyes opened the door, her gaze darting warily from Quinn to Elizabeth. "What is it?"

Elizabeth gave the girl a warm, calming smile. "I'm Elizabeth, and this is Quinn. We'd like to speak with Clive if he's at home."

"You're American."

"Is it that obvious?" Even Elizabeth's tone of voice was soothing.

"Aye. The accent." The girl smiled.

"It's my first time in Scotland. What's your name?"

"Nicola."

"May we come in, Nicola?"

"He's been drinkin'," Nicola said in a warning tone of voice. She opened the door to let them in. "Da, there's some people to speak wi' you."

Quinn followed Elizabeth inside. The flat was small and cluttered but not filthy, its ceiling sagging in places and stained with mold, the cloying odor permeating everything. They found Clive MacDonald sitting in his underwear in a battered recliner, a bottle in his hand. Pale and balding, his belly bloated from a lifetime of drinking, he wasn't the man who'd attacked Quinn at Jack and Ava's house.

"I'll no' speak wi' police. Get the fuck oot!"

The girl looked over at Elizabeth. "You're no' the police, are ya?"

"No, we're not. We're friends of Jack Murray." Elizabeth's gaze was on MacDonald when she spoke. "He's the bodyguard who was found murdered a week ago in Glasgow."

Quinn saw no sign of recognition on MacDonald's face or his daughter's, but then he wasn't the expert. Elizabeth was.

"Jack Murray? I dinnae know the man," MacDonald grumbled.

Quinn fought to keep his gob shut.

"That's strange." Elizabeth held out her phone. "Here's a photo of you with Jack. He stopped you when you ran at Alastair Whitehall. He held you down. He said you were shouting about abortion and that you threatened to kill him and Alastair."

MacDonald's expression turned to rage. "I told you they were police. Lyin' bastards. Get the fuck oot!"

"We're no' police, man." Quinn knew he'd agreed to let Elizabeth ask the questions, but he wanted answers. "Jack Murray was my best friend, and now he's dead and gone, and I'm tryin' to understand."

MacDonald looked straight into Quinn's eyes. "It wisnae me who killed him. I didnae know that bastard's name till the police came and asked me aboot him."

So, MacDonald had just lied. He *did* know who Jack was.

Elizabeth pressed him. "Why did you threaten to kill him and Mr. Whitehall?"

"If I threatened yer friend it was only because he had me pinned to the bloody ground, aye?"

"What about MSP Whitehall?"

MacDonald's gaze shifted to the TV. "I cannae recall."

"He was drunk." Nicola spoke in a rush, fear on her face. "You were oot of your hied, aye, Da? Ravin' drunk and angry about the babies. Da disnae think we should have abortion in Scotland."

MacDonald nodded, met Elizabeth's gaze. "Aye, I was mad wi' it. Have you never been so drunk that you couldnae remember a thing after?"

Elizabeth shook her head. "No, I haven't."

MacDonald grinned. "You're a right prim little cunt, you are."

Quinn's fists clenched, but he stayed where he was. "You'll keep a civil tongue in your heid, or I'll rip it out."

MacDonald had the good sense to apologize. "I didnae mean offense. Go and leave me in peace."

Nicola led them to the front door, an apologetic look on her face. "I'm sorry for yer friend, so I am, but my da knows nothin'. I know how it must seem, but he's no' a bad man, really."

"You've no need to apologize for your da," Quinn said. "What he says and does is on him alone. It disnae reflect on you."

His words seemed to touch Nicola. "Thanks."

"Thank you for your help, Nicola." Elizabeth reached into her handbag and drew out a business card. "If you hear anything or just want to talk, this is my email address."

Nicola took the card—and shut the door in their faces.

ELIZABETH PUSHED her way out the front door and hurried toward the street, inhaling the fresh night air, letting it wash away the terrible stench of mold, urine, and despair. She had never seen anything like that before. "How can they live like that? The smell is terrible."

Quinn fell in beside her. "No' everyone is born into an easy life."

He sounded defensive. Had she offended him?

"I'm not judging them. I just can't believe they live with all of that black mold. The whole building reeks of it. It's a health hazard."

Quinn said nothing but walked faster.

Elizabeth changed the subject, sharing what she'd gleaned from that brief encounter with Clive MacDonald and Nicola. "He's lying. He knows something."

"MacDonald's no' the man who killed Jack. I knew that the moment I saw him."

"I agree. He couldn't have killed Jack. But he knows something. When I first mentioned Jack's name, he had an adrenaline reaction."

"He thought you were the police, aye?"

That might have been it, but Elizabeth didn't think so. "Nicola was afraid."

Quinn was walking so fast now that Elizabeth almost had to run to keep up. "She's got reason to be afraid, livin' wi' an alcoholic. Maybe he beats her when he's rat-arsed. Who's to say?"

"That's not what I meant. She hurried to explain away her father's behavior when all he could say was that he didn't remember. He's lying about that, too, I'm sure."

Elizabeth stopped chasing after Quinn, walked at her own pace, confused by this change in him. Then again, he'd been tense since they left Glasgow. She'd thought it had to do with the reality of investigating Jack's murder. But now...

"Is something wrong, McManus? And remember—I can tell when you're lying."

He stopped, turned to face her, his expression obscured

by the darkness. "*I* grew up in a place just like this wi' a da much like him."

Oh, God, Quinn.

She felt a rush of sympathy for him, his defensive response making sense now.

Shit.

"I'm sorry for what I said. I don't blame—"

"It wisnae anythin' you said. It's just this place. It brings back ... memories."

She could understand that. "Then how about we get the hell out of here and go somewhere fun for dinner?"

"Somewhere fun?" He seemed to consider this. "Aye, we could do that."

They hurried to the rental car, Elizabeth once again going to the wrong side. "The news articles repeated what Jack said. MacDonald was shouting about abortion. Does Scotland have an anti-abortion movement?"

"There are some who would like to change the laws, but they're in the minority. No one here is harassin' women, killin' doctors, or burnin' clinics to the ground."

"Clive doesn't strike me as an activist."

"He was probably off his heid wi' drink, saw somethin' on the news that upset him, and went off."

Elizabeth's intuition told her there was more to it than that.

Twenty minutes later, Elizabeth found herself seated at a window staring out at Edinburgh Castle, floodlights playing over its stone walls. "I love how they've lighted it."

It loomed over the city, ancient and massive.

Quinn's lips curved in a lopsided grin that made her belly flutter. "There wouldnae be much to see otherwise, aye?"

She had kissed those lips today. God, it had been hot. "I wish it were open."

"The castle? We can come back later in the week."

They server came with their drinks. Quinn ordered the shepherd's pie, and Elizabeth ordered the roasted duck breast.

After the server walked away, Quinn grew quiet, his brow furrowed. "Sorry about earlier. I was just havin' a wee bitch."

Elizabeth reached across the table, took his hand, awareness arcing between them. "You don't have to apologize, Quinn. I'm grateful that you explained. I didn't know you'd had such a rough childhood."

Then again, she couldn't remember him ever talking about his childhood or his family. Now she understood why. Poverty left its mark on a person.

"Others had it worse." Quinn took a sip of his scotch. "Thank you for trustin' me with what happened at the Agency. I'll crush that bastard's balls if I meet him."

"You say the sweetest things." Elizabeth sipped her wine, Quinn watching her through smoky blue eyes. "I guess we both learned something new about each other today."

"Aye, so we did." His lips curved in a smug and sexy grin. "I learned that the restrained and self-possessed Ms. Shields can be very ... *impulsive*."

Elizabeth's cheeks burned.

8

Q uinn poured the whisky in the sink, tears blurring his vision, his hands shaking. If his da wanted to drink himself to death, that was fine. But drinking made him angry and mean, and Quinn wouldn't let the bastard strike him again.

He'd told the other boys that he'd gotten his black eye in a fight against another gang and that the boy who'd hit him had paid dearly. He couldn't bear to tell them that it was his own da who'd struck him.

"What the fuck do ye think yer doin'?"

Quinn turned on the spot, heart in his throat, the half-empty bottle falling to the floor, spilling whisky on the chipped and dirty tile. He stood his ground. "I dumped it—all of it. You're mean when you drink, Da. I'll never let you work me over again. You already drove Ma and Paige away. You—"

"Fuckin' bastard!"

Quinn blocked the first blow and the next. "I'm bigger than you now. I'm no' just a wee boy you can thrash."

"I'll break you, boy." His da left the kitchen.

Quinn reached for a bit of kitchen roll to wipe up the spilled *whisky unaware that his da had returned until a shadow fell across the floor.*

The blow of the belt took him by surprise, pain lashing across his back.

"You're nae so big now, are ye?" His da glared down at him. "You think you're better than I am, all high and mighty, but you're the same. That's why your ma left you wi' me. You didn't know?"

White hot fury and adrenaline had Quinn on his feet. He jerked the belt out of his da's hands and slammed the bastard in the face with his fist, splitting his lip and sending him staggering. "Shut your fuckin' gob!"

Christ, it felt good to hit back, so Quinn did it again and again, until blood flowed from his da's nose and the bastard looked dazed.

Da stepped away, wiping blood from his face. He glared at Quinn with undisguised hatred. "Get oot ma hoose, ye fuckin' bastard! Yer nae son o' mine. Dinnae be comin' back or I'll beat the life oot o' ye, so I will. This is yer hame nae mair, ya worthless fuck!"

Quinn jerked awake, the nightmare leaving a tangle of emotions inside him. He threw off the duvet, glanced at the hotel alarm clock. It was oh-six-forty.

Knowing he wouldn't be able to go back to sleep, he switched on his security camera and went to the gym to lift weights, working his muscles hard, trying to burn off the dream. He was no longer the boy who'd lived in fear of his old man. He wasn't helpless and dependent. That night had been a new beginning for him. He'd turned the tables, made his da bleed.

It was only what he deserved.

If his da were still alive, he would have rung him up and thanked him for throwing him out. That night had been the start of a new life. Quinn had worked hard to make something of himself after that, to turn himself into the kind of man his da would have no choice but to respect—and fear.

In the end, it hadn't mattered. His da had died soon after he'd joined the army, his liver eaten through by drink.

Forget him.

When Quinn had finished three sets of reps for each muscle group, he made his way back to his room, shed his clothes, and went straight into the shower, his mind turning to better things.

Lilibet. The kiss.

He had imagined kissing her hundreds of times, but the experience, as brief as it had been, had far surpassed his fantasies. He relived it, trying to remember all of the sweet details. The heat of her body against his. Her soft curves. The press of her lips. Her scent. Her taste. She'd kissed him as if she truly meant it, as if she were starving for him, as if she wanted him as much as he wanted her.

The memory left him with a raging stonner. Not one to turn down that invitation, he took matters into his own hands, his mind on Lilibet as he came.

Wankin' is a poor substitute for the real, live woman.

Aye, but the real, live woman was off-limits, and he'd best remember that.

He dried off, put a clean bandage over his stitches, and walked naked back to the bedroom to dress.

A buzz.

His mobile.

He searched for the bloody thing, found it in the living area stuck between two cushions on the sofa. It must have fallen there when he'd been watching the news last night. There was a notification from his security camera, and a text message from Elizabeth.

He opened the security notification first.

There on his screen was an image of him standing stark naked exactly where he was, his tadger and balls hanging out.

Och, shite.

Fighting laughter, he walked over, turned the device off.

Then he opened Elizabeth's text message.

`Shut off your camera!`

Chuckling, he was about to send her a humorous reply, something like, "Stop looking." Then he remembered the dick pics and the harassment she had endured at the Agency. Would she think he'd done this on purpose?

Fuck.

He tapped out his reply.

`I'm right sorry I am.`

~

ELIZABETH STARED at the screen on her phone where the image of Quinn had just disappeared and then read his apology, her conscience pricking her.

Good. Freaking. Heaven.

She'd been asleep when her phone had buzzed. She'd seen it was an alert from the security camera in Quinn's room and had been halfway out of bed when he'd suddenly appeared, buck naked, on her screen. He'd vanished into the bathroom to take a shower and had emerged ten minutes later, his hair wet, his body gloriously exposed. She knew it was almost exactly ten minutes later because she'd stared at her screen the entire time.

She'd finally tipped him off—but not before she'd gotten a very good look.

You're terrible, Shields.

But, dear Lord, who could blame her?

Elizabeth had seen her share of naked men, but she'd never seen a man who looked like Quinn. His butt didn't bounce, it shifted, twin globes of moving muscle. His abs ended in the beautiful V of his obliques, her favorite muscle on a man.

And his cock...

He hadn't even had an erection.

She squirmed, the ache between her thighs making her wish she'd brought her vibrator. She never traveled with it for fear that some customs agent would think it was an explosive and pull it out of her luggage with the Cobra guys there.

She ought to apologize to Quinn, but what would she say?

Sorry I didn't tip you off sooner, but I couldn't quit staring at your dick.

That didn't carry quite the professional tone she hoped to convey.

She laid back on her pillows, reached down between her thighs, and touched herself, her mind mingling the sight of Quinn's naked body with yesterday's catastrophic, wonderful, amazing kiss. She let herself imagine him sliding, hard and thick, inside her, his big body moving over hers, deep thrusts carrying her higher and high—

A buzz on her phone.

Have you had breakfast?

Damn it, Quinn.

Give me 10 minutes.

She tried to go back to her fantasy, but couldn't, not knowing she had to be done and dressed in ten minutes. "Hell."

With a moan, she threw off the covers and marched into the bathroom, the unsatisfied ache between her thighs leaving her grumpy. She took a quick shower, brushed her teeth, and put on makeup. Then she stomped back into the bedroom to dress, choosing a peasant blouse and a pair of faded jeans.

By the time her ten minutes were up, she was ready to go —and frustrated as hell.

She met Quinn in the hallway, her irritation growing at the clean, fresh scent of his skin. Seriously, could he be any more attractive?

"Did ye sleep well?"

"No." She set off for the elevator.

"I'm sorry to hear it. Are you ready for another full Scottish?"

She pushed the elevator call button. "No, thanks. I'll stick with toast or yogurt."

"Are you angry wi' me?"

She didn't dare meet his gaze, or he'd see guilt written all over her. "No."

"Aye, you are. I'm sorry. I forgot about the camera."

"It's okay, Quinn. I know you didn't flash me on purpose. Besides, I'm thirty-three. Yours is *not* the first penis I've seen."

The elevator car arrived. Elizabeth hoped it would be full of people so that this conversation would end. No such luck.

"Then why are you so upset? I can see it on your face. You're ready to explode."

Jesus fried chicken!

Elizabeth drew a deep breath, tried to come up with an excuse. She looked up at the security camera, not sure whether it had a mic. "Let's not talk about it here."

They rode the rest of the way to the ground floor in silence, giving Elizabeth time to come up with an excuse. By the time they were seated, she was ready.

"I'm frustrated because I've used up four days of my two weeks here, and we haven't gotten anywhere. I'm working with both hands tied behind my back. I'm not used to being ineffective."

That was at least true, if not the truth.

"Och, you shouldnae be so hard on yourself. We're workin' blind here. If we had those phone records…"

"Can't we ask Ava to request them on our behalf?"

Quinn shook his head. "What if she looks at them herself and discovers that Jack didnae really lose the old mobile?"

Even Quinn's compassion was sexy.

Damn him.

"Then I guess we support her through that. Whatever the truth is, she'll have to face it eventually. Better sooner than later."

"Aye, it's true, but I dinnae want to be the one to hurt her."

"It might be better coming from you than Wilson."

"Aye."

"Let's not get ahead of ourselves. We have no idea what's in those phone records. But I *do* know what will happen if we don't get them."

"What?"

"Nothing."

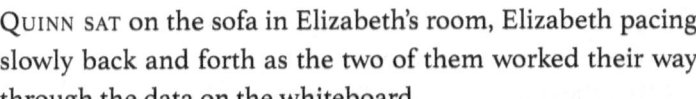

QUINN SAT on the sofa in Elizabeth's room, Elizabeth pacing slowly back and forth as the two of them worked their way through the data on the whiteboard.

"It's three in the morning. He drives into the alley for some reason. He gets out of the vehicle—or is forced to get out." She shook her head. "No, he gets out voluntarily. If someone forced him to get out, he would have known something was going to happen."

"What if the killer pointed a firearm at him?"

Gun crimes were rare in Scotland, but they did happen.

"If the killer had a firearm, why didn't he just shoot Jack? Why risk getting close to him to cut his throat when he could end it with a bullet?"

Aye, that didn't make sense.

Elizabeth moved on. "He gets out of the car for whatever reason, and someone cuts the right side of his throat. Okay, combat expert, let's try it."

"Try killin' a man?"

"Aye, killin' a man." She mimicked his accent—not bad, really, but then she was a linguist. "I want to do a walk-through."

Quinn got to his feet. "You want me to pretend to be the killer, aye?"

"Exactly." She motioned him forward. "Stab me."

He'd like to penetrate her all right. "Where should I stand?"

Keep your mind on the job.

"That's part of what we're figuring out. Are you right-handed or left-handed?"

"Right-handed. So was the man who broke into Jack and Ava's place."

"Where would you stand to stab a man in the left side of the throat?"

Quinn thought through the motions. "I'd have to be standin' in front of him, aye?"

"Wouldn't Jack see the knife coming?"

"Aye, but no' necessarily in time to react." Quinn moved lightning-fast, his hand stopping millimeters away from Elizabeth's throat.

Her pupils went wide. "Wow. Okay. What if he stood on Jack's right side?"

Quinn moved to stand beside her, putting about an arm's length of space between them. "It's awkward. He'd need a bit of room to get up the necessary momentum even with a sharp blade. It's no' easy to sink a knife into a man's body. It takes force to penetrate skin and tissue, and if you strike bone..."

He feigned drawing a blade, driving it into her throat. "Aye, that might work. I cannae say whether Jack would have seen it."

"And from behind?"

Quinn walked behind her, rested a hand on the slender curve of her shoulder, and pressed a finger to her neck, the scent of her skin filling his head. "The thrust of a blade *here* would instantly sever a man's carotid."

Her eyes drifted shut. "And ... his trachea, too."

"If the killer cuts hard and deep enough." Quinn knew he shouldn't, and yet he couldn't seem to stop himself. He ducked down, brushed feather-light kisses over the sensitive skin beneath her ear.

She gasped but didn't pull away. "I-if the attacker was behind him, wouldn't Jack have .... heard ... him ... coming?"

"Possibly." He nipped his way along her throat, felt the frantic rush of her pulse. "It wouldnae have been easy to sneak up on Jack."

She sank against him, her head resting against his chest, her eyes still closed. "We shouldn't do this."

"Aye, I know." He nibbled her earlobe and reached around to cup her breasts, their weight filling his hands, making him hard. "I want you, Lilibet."

She arched into his hands. "What about our jobs, our contracts?"

Quinn didn't give a damn, not when touching her like this felt so right. Besides, how would Corbray or Tower find out? "Are you goin' to grass on us?"

"*No.*" She took one of his hands, moved it down between her thighs.

He cupped her through her jeans, groaned as she ground herself against his hand. She was as passionate as he had imagined she'd be, her body pliant beneath his touch.

He slid one hand beneath her blouse, teasing the tight bud of her nipple through the lace of her bra while his other hand slid inside her panties.

Och, she was already wet.

She moaned, rocked her hips forward, urging him on.

He stroked her clit, letting her responses guide him—the little shudder of breath when he got it just right, the involuntary jerk of her hips, her attempt to part her thighs. "I want to undress you, kiss every inch of you, and fuck you until you scream my name."

"*Yes.*"

He scooped her into his arms, carried her to the bedroom, and set her on her feet at the foot of the bed. Then he reached over and flicked on the light. "I want to see you."

She started to take off her blouse, but he stopped her.

"Let me." He drew her blouse over her head, her nipples just visible through the lace of her bra. He reached behind her, and unfastened the clasp, hungry to have those nipples in his mouth. "Perfect."

He cupped her breasts, ducked down, licked each puckered bud, thrilled by her reaction, each flick of his tongue making the rosy tips draw tighter and summoning a little gasp. But he needed more.

He reached down, yanked off her jeans and panties, and tossed them aside. Then he stepped back and let his gaze rove over her from her full breasts to the flare of her hips to the auburn curls between her thighs, lust and tenderness washing through him in equal measure, leaving an ache in his chest—and his groin.

"Och, Lilibet, you're beautiful."

She smiled. "I bet you say that to all the naked lasses."

He chuckled. "And how many women do you imagine that to be?"

"Hundreds at least."

He teased her. "Thousands."

She helped him undress, but seemed to get distracted the moment his shirt came off, her hands sliding over the muscles of his chest and belly, tracing his scars, her breathing rapid, her pupils dark. Then she took his erection in hand, stroked him, making him harder. "I guess now I'll be able to decide whether size matters."

Quinn chuckled, though he couldn't deny feeling a wee bit of pride. "If all a man has goin' for him is a big cock, he's probably a lousy lover."

She sat on the bed, scooted backward, then lay back and let her legs fall open, giving him the most erotic view. Her gaze met his once again. "I want you inside me."

Och, Jesus!

He stretched out beside her, his cock straining for her, his heart pounding. "You're protected, aye?"

He knew Cobra paid for contraception for female staff sent to regions of the world where there was a risk of sexual assault.

She nodded. "An IUD, courtesy of our bosses. *Fuck me.*"

But Quinn was in no hurry. "If this is the only chance I get to make love wi' you, Lilibet, then I'm goin' to make it last."

9

Quinn's words sent a shiver through Elizabeth. He gazed down at her as if she were precious, his brow furrowed, the intensity in his dark eyes stealing her breath. Then he cupped her cheek and lowered his mouth to hers.

This was nothing like yesterday's impulsive kiss in the gym. It was sweet and slow and achingly tender. He teased her with soft butterfly kisses until her lips tingled, then traced the curve of her lower lip with his tongue. "I feel like I've waited a hundred years for this."

"So have I." Years of working side by side, dozens of dangerous missions, and through all of it, she had wanted him. "*Quinn.*"

She slid her fingers into the thickness of his hair, drew him back into a kiss, caressing his tongue with hers, nipping his lower lip.

In a heartbeat, the kiss transformed from gentle to fierce. Quinn took control, plundering her mouth, his tongue sparring with hers, demanding her surrender. She yielded gladly, desire lancing through her, his kisses and the heat of his naked body igniting her unspent arousal from this morning.

Oh, God, she had dreamed of kissing him like this. The hard press of his lips. The rasp of his beard against her skin. The skilled strokes of his tongue.

He tore his mouth from hers, trailed fiery kisses across her cheeks and along the sensitive skin of her throat to the divot between her collar bones. Then he cupped her breast in a big, callused hand, lowered his mouth to her aching nipple, and sucked it into the heat of his mouth.

She whimpered, arched to meet him, her fingers clenching in his hair, little darts of pleasure shooting straight to her belly with every tug of his lips and flick of his tongue. He went from one breast to the other and back again until she squirmed beneath him, her body aching for release.

But Quinn had clearly meant what he'd said. He wasn't going to rush this.

He moved slowly over her body, driving her crazy with his mouth and hands, kissing and caressing her breastbone, licking and nipping her belly and the curve of her hips. He teased the sensitive skin of her inner thighs and the backs of her knees, chuckling at her response.

"I'm ticklish."

"Aye, you are." He nudged her legs wider apart with his knee then slid his hand between her thighs, his gaze fixed on hers. "Och, you're so wet. Show me what you like."

She reached down to guide him, the intimacy of looking into his eyes as he explored her and gave her pleasure startling. But, *sweet heaven*, it didn't take him long to get it right, his fingers stroking her clit just the way she liked it. "Just... like... *that*."

It felt good, *so* good, Elizabeth's eyes drifting shut, her breath coming in pants, her body rushing headlong toward orgasm. She fought to hold her hips still, the nails of one hand digging into the hard curve of his shoulder, the other hand fisted in her sheets.

Quinn kept up a relentless rhythm, kissing her, whispering nonsense against her skin "Lilibet. Sweet Lilibet. *Mo ribhinn.*"

Then he lowered his mouth to her breasts once again and suckled.

She came with a cry, climax washing through her, a tide of molten bliss.

He stayed with her until her peak had passed, pressing kisses to her breasts, her throat, her lips. Then he raised himself above her, all man and muscle, and settled his hips between her thighs, his erection resting against her. "Do you want this?"

The big, sweet Scot was giving her one last chance to turn him down.

As if.

"Yes." She reached down and took hold of his cock to guide him.

His gaze fixed on hers, he nudged himself into her, going a little deeper each time, until she ached for him again.

"Och, you're tight." He took one of her legs, rested her calf against his shoulder, opening her more fully. Then with a single slow thrust, he buried himself to the hilt, Elizabeth's delighted gasp becoming a moan.

"Are you okay?" He held himself still inside her for a moment, a muscle clenching in his jaw, the look in his eyes as he gazed down at her making her pulse skip.

"Hell, yes." She was better than okay.

His lips quirked in a grin—and he began to move.

He went slowly at first, deep, unhurried strokes that

enabled her to savor every sweet inch of him—the slick glide, the piercing stretch, the satisfying fullness.

"That feels ... *so* good." Hungry for him, she slid her hands along his pecs, his shoulders, his biceps, the shifting muscles of his ass, the feel of him an aphrodisiac.

But as incredible as it was, she'd never been able to climax from penetration alone. She was about to reach down to give herself a hand when he shifted his hips. With his next thrust, the base of his cock rubbed against her clit.

She gasped and stared up at him, astonished.

He chuckled, adjusted his position, and thrust again, falling into a rhythm, stroking her inside and out, driving her out of her mind.

She was lost, beyond all control now, her eyes closed, her nails digging into his forearms as she fought to hold on. Panting ... sweating... needing him... needing more. Then she shattered, crying out his name, orgasm singing through her, sweet and pure and bright, his thrusts driving her pleasure home. "*Quinn.*"

He stayed with her until the quaking inside her subsided, then adjusted his hips again and drove into her hard, his body shaking in her arms as he came at last.

Still breathing hard, she opened her eyes, looked up at him, an unfamiliar ache in her chest. She reached up, cupped his cheek.

He rolled off her, drew her against him, pillowing her head against his chest, where she could hear the rapid beating of his heart. He pressed a kiss to her hair. "Thank God I've lived to see that."

"See what?"

"How bonnie your face is when you come."

Elizabeth's heart melted.

QUINN TRACED Elizabeth's spine with his fingertips, his body replete, a strange sadness taking hold in his chest. He'd been with his share of women, but he'd never felt like this afterward, as if he were somehow changed.

Aye, he'd wanted Elizabeth for years. He'd watched her work, come to respect her abilities, laughed at her smart mouth. He'd known she would be passionate and that sex with her would blow his mind. But he hadn't known that it would hit him like this.

Every part of him down to his DNA wanted to claim Lilibet as his lover, but he knew that couldn't happen. She'd worked hard to get where she was. She wouldn't sacrifice her career for a bit of sex and romance. By the time they were fully dressed, she would tell him how this could never happen again and how they needed to maintain a professional distance.

Aye, he could tell her that he felt more for her than friendship, that he wanted her in his life, but he didn't want to come across like that fuckwit at the Agency. That bastard hadn't cared for her at all.

Quinn did.

And that's why you'll let her go, aye?

It was better this way. Though Quinn had never struck a woman, he couldn't be all that different from his da. He'd beaten the bastard bloody—and then he'd gone off to kill for a living. What woman could love a man who'd beaten his own da?

She stirred, ran her fingers through his chest hair, spoke in a sleepy voice. "Was that Scottish Gaelic?"

It took Quinn a moment to figure out what she was talking about. "Aye."

"What does that mean?"

He had no idea how she'd react, but he told her anyway. "It means somethin' like 'sweetheart.'"

She made a little purring noise, and for a while neither of them spoke.

Then her body tensed.

"What is it?"

She turned in his arms and looked up at him. "Jack was murdered by someone who knew him."

"That's what's goin' through your mind—Jack's murder?"

You're no' as good in bed as you think you are, man.

She smiled. "Nothing was going through my mind, and then the pieces just clicked. But I don't want to talk about that now. I just mentioned it because I'm about to slip into a sex coma and didn't want to forget. You're amazing, Quinn McManus."

She snuggled against him again, and soon they were both sound asleep.

QUINN WAS HAVING a delicious dream about fucking Lilibet only to wake and find her kneeling between his thighs, giving him head. "*Jesus!*"

She moved her mouth and hand together up and down his length, her tongue doing something incredible. She lifted her mouth from him, gave him a pouty look. "I woke up hungry. I hope this is okay."

Och, she was too much.

"Feel free to go down on me any time you..." His words unraveled as she took him into the heat of her mouth again.

He moved her hair aside so he could watch, the sight of

her devouring him making his cock jerk in her hand. "More pressure ... aye, like that."

Pleasure uncoiled at the base of his spine, the first hint of climax making his balls draw tight. She kept up the pace, down to the base and up again, her tongue swirling around the aching head, her gaze fixed on his.

After that, it didn't last long. Quinn clenched his teeth, arching as orgasm ripped through him, Elizabeth finishing him with her hand, cum spilling onto his belly.

He lay there, stunned. "If only I could wake up like this every day..."

"I'll take that as a compliment." She hopped out of the bed naked, walked to the bathroom, and came back with a warm washcloth to wipe him clean.

"Now, that's service," he teased, some part of him still unable to believe they'd slept together.

"You are the best sex I've ever had, Quinn, and that was the best sex nap ever." She pressed a kiss to his solar plexus. "But now I really *am* starving."

Quinn glanced at the bedside alarm clock to see that it was almost suppertime. How bloody long had they slept?

She jumped up again and bustled around, getting dressed, brushing her hair, perusing the room service menu. She glanced over at him. "Aren't you going to get up?"

Quinn's mind was willing, but his body was still coming down from somewhere in the stratosphere. Besides, he could have watched her all day. "Give me a minute."

She read out the choices from the room service menu and ordered. By the time the food arrived—roast chicken and wine for her and venison and whisky for him—Quinn was upright and dressed.

While they ate, Elizabeth explained what she'd tried to tell him earlier.

"They found no sign of a struggle on Jack's body. Whoever killed him had to be standing within arm's length of him, either in front of him or off to the side. Whatever brought him to that alley must have been unusual, and that means he likely would have been on his guard."

"Aye, true enough."

"This morning, you told me that the best way to kill a man with a knife is to sneak up behind him and slit his throat."

"Aye. You take him by surprise, sever his vocal cords and trachea and carotid in one motion. He can't cry for help and alert others, and he bleeds out quickly."

Killing was a gruesome business.

She took a sip of her wine, a thoughtful frown on her face. "I don't think a man like Jack would stand side-by-side with a stranger in an alley in the middle of the night. It's too sketchy. He probably wouldn't let a stranger walk right up to him, either. He would maintain some distance. That's what you're trained to do, right?"

"Aye." Quinn saw where she was going with this. "You're sayin' the killer had to be someone he knew to get close to him in that environment."

She nodded. "The killer got close to him and managed to slash at him without giving a seasoned warrior like Jack any sense he was in danger in a situation where most of us would be on edge. I assess that this person was someone he knew, someone who had experience fighting with knives— perhaps someone who knew Jack was wearing body armor that night."

Ava's words came back to Quinn, prickles rising along his nape.

If only the killer had tried to stab him in the chest or back instead, he would have had time to react and fight back.

"Aye, the bastard knew right where to sink his blade."

Elizabeth set her tray aside, leaned back with her glass of wine, her gaze meeting Quinn's. "I can understand why Wilson is focused on the drug angle. This wasn't a random robbery and stabbing. It was premeditated. It was personal."

ELIZABETH WATCHED Quinn's face as what she'd said sank in —anger followed by acceptance.

He sipped his whisky. "When I heard how he'd died, where he'd been stabbed, I knew that whoever had killed him hadn't just meant to incapacitate him and take his money. They wanted him dead. I guess I was right."

"Yes." Her heart hurt for him.

"But who would want to kill him?"

"That's the question, isn't it?"

Quinn's cell phone buzzed. "It's Ava."

Elizabeth went into the bathroom to brush her teeth and to give Quinn some privacy. She could still hear his side of the conversation. The news wasn't good.

"Thanks for tryin'. Naw, nothin' yet. Och, Ava, I'm so sorry. There's got to be an explanation. We'll do our best to find it—I promise. We spoke wi' the man who threatened to kill Jack, but he couldnae have done it. She's certain the killer is someone who knew him. Aye, we will. Thanks."

Elizabeth left the bathroom to find Quinn staring at the ceiling. "Bad news?"

"The police willnae share information from the investigation wi' Ava. There's no file for her to request, no public information."

"Damn." But Elizabeth knew that wasn't all of it. "What else did she say?"

Quinn looked up at Elizabeth, despair in his eyes. "She demanded to know about the toxicology tests. There were no drugs in his system, but they found cocaine and heroin residue on his hands, in his car, and in his jacket pocket."

"Then it *was* drug-related. I'm so sorry, Quinn." Elizabeth could only imagine how difficult this was for him.

Nothing hurt more than being disappointed by those you loved.

"I dinnae believe it. There must be an explanation." Quinn's faith in his friend touched Elizabeth. "I know how it seems, but Jack wouldnae sell drugs."

She wouldn't argue with Quinn, not today anyway. He was grieving. She couldn't expect him to be objective. That was her job.

She turned to the whiteboard. "Ava said Jack and Leo Grant had a falling out this summer. If the police talked to Clive, they've almost certainly paid Leo a visit. That doesn't necessarily mean they've ruled him out. I'd like to talk with him, too."

Ports and dockyards were a natural setting for drug smuggling, ships going in and out all day with cargo. She had no idea where Leo's operation was located or which ports in Scotland were hotspots for drugs, but that would be easy enough to research.

"I'm no' takin' you to the docks at night. It's no' safe there."

All at once, the situation seemed futile.

She sank onto the sofa beside Quinn. "This is getting us nowhere. The police are ten steps ahead of us. If I'm going to help at all, I need something to go on."

"We can pay Leo a visit on Monday.

"Why not tomorrow morning?"

"Tomorrow, I'm takin' you to see the sights." Quinn drew

her into his arms, resting her head against his chest as they talked about places they might visit.

It felt so natural to be held like this by him. She kept waiting for the post-sex awkwardness to strike, but it hadn't. She hadn't been exaggerating when she'd told Quinn he was the best sex she'd ever had. He had blown her mind. She had no regrets.

Still, they needed to talk. She needed to make it clear that once they got back to the US, everything would go back to the way it had been.

Are you sure you want that?

It was either that—or one of them had to give up their job.

Then it hit her. "I know where we should go tonight."

"Where?"

She sat upright. "The alley where Jack was killed. I want to see what it's like in the dark."

Quinn scowled. "Naw, we're no' goin' there, no' at night. We should wait until daylight."

"I want to see what it's like at night, how well-lighted it is." She stood, went for her shoes. "It's not like the killer is going to be hanging out there, waiting for us. You don't have to come if you don't want to. I can catch a cab."

He glared at her, got to his feet. "You're no' goin' alone."

She'd known he would say that. "I'll look up the crime scene in the papers and meet you in the hallway in five minutes. Don't forget to arm your security camera."

10

Quinn stepped with Elizabeth into the elevator, the loaded Glock 42 tucked into its holster and concealed in the waistband of his jeans. It was time to lay out the rules. "If we get there, and I think it's unsafe, I willnae let you get out of the car. If I tell you we're goin', they'll be no argie-bargie."

"What's an argie—?"

He cut her off with a kiss. "You're the intel expert, but if it comes to fightin', it's my problem. You'll do what I tell you to do, aye?"

She nodded. "Right. Okay."

They retrieved the rental from the car park and set out.

Elizabeth had looked up the location of the crime scene in the newspapers. "It's an alley off Topmast Lane between Howard and Clyde. Do you want me to use GPS—"

"Naw, I know where it is." He turned right. "What are you expectin' to find? The police have already searched the area and cleaned away the mess."

"I just want to see what Jack would have seen. Maybe the alley is near a busy place like a nightclub where we might find witnesses. Maybe there's something about the location that explains why Jack was there. Maybe there are cams, and the police have the whole thing on video and haven't told anyone. I don't know. Maybe we won't learn anything."

The knot that had been in Quinn's stomach since Elizabeth had mentioned going to the alley drew tighter, and it took him a moment to fathom why.

It's where Jack died.

He wasn't sure he was ready for this.

It took them ten minutes to reach Topmast Lane. Quinn drove slowly, looking for the opening to an alley.

Elizabeth pointed to a gap between buildings. "There."

"Aye, I see it." He turned left, steering the rental vehicle between the buildings.

The alley turned out to be more of a courtyard than a true alley. There were no exits apart from the one by which they'd just entered. The space was surrounded by three-story-high brick buildings, all of which appeared to be businesses. A few large rubbish bins sat along the walls, concrete steps leading to backdoors that were closed, all the windows dark.

"May I get out?"

There was no one around.

"Aye." He parked but left the car running.

"Turn off the lights."

Quinn did as she asked, and they both stepped out of the vehicle.

"It's so dark." Elizabeth moved to stand an arm's length in front of Quinn. "He would have been able to see his killer's face, but I'm not sure he would have seen a knife in anyone's hand."

Quinn stood where he could see the entrance to the alley, his gaze moving over the ground searching for the place Jack's body had been found. There were, of course, no chalk marks like on American TV shows, no police tape left behind, nothing to show that a good man—a husband, a father, a warrior, a brother—had breathed his last here.

Grief, dark and heavy, hit Quinn square in the chest.

Jack, you bastard. What the fuck were you doin' here, man?

It didn't seem possible that Jack's life could have ended on this meaningless patch of asphalt, this nothing of a space, not after he'd survived Iraq and Afghanistan.

"There aren't any street cams here." Elizabeth's voice brought him back.

A flash.

He turned to see her taking photos with her phone. "What are you doin'?"

"I want the names of all these businesses. Some of them are painted on the doors. I can look them up later, see if they're associated with anyone who knew Jack. There has to be a reason why he was killed here of all places."

The reason seemed obvious to Quinn. "No one walkin' or drivin' by could have seen from the street. If they had, they wouldnae ask questions. It's near the red-light district and the casino."

"Yes, it's a good place for a murder, but why would Jack come here? His car was here, and there was no sign of a struggle. He drove here himself."

This was a good place for a drug deal, but Quinn couldn't imagine Jack getting involved in something like that.

The bleep of a siren. Blue and white flashing lights.

Fuck.

Elizabeth walked over to Quinn, put her mobile away. "Have we broken the law?"

That bastard Wilson stepped out of one of the vehicles.

"How the bloody hell did he know where we were?"

"He's got us under surveillance somehow." Elizabeth spoke quickly. "We're here because you want to pay your respects at the place where Jack died. Nothing more."

"Aye."

Wilson strolled up to them. "Have you been gone from home for so long that you've gotten lost, Mr. McManus? Or perhaps you and Ms. Shields are waitin' for someone."

"We came so I could see for myself the place where Jack was murdered. Is that against the law now?"

"No, but interferin' with a police investigation is. So is dealing heroin and cocaine."

Quinn laughed. "It's us you're after now? No wonder you cannae catch Jack's killer. No one is interferin' by standin' here, and neither of us have touched drugs."

"I heard you paid a visit to Clive MacDonald and asked him questions about Jack Murray. Some might wonder why. Now, if you'd get back in your car and follow me back to the station."

"Are we under arrest?" Elizabeth asked.

"Not yet." Wilson turned his back on them and walked back to his car.

ELIZABETH SAT in an interview room with PC Patel, who asked questions, while pretending the two of them were just having a conversation. Was she enjoying her holiday? Where did she work? How long had she and Quinn known each other? Why go all the way to Edinburgh to talk to Clive MacDonald when there were better things to do and see there? What did she think of legalized marijuana in

Colorado? Did she or Quinn smoke pot or take edibles? Never? Had she ever tried anything harder—like cocaine or heroin? Had she ever brought heroin back from Afghanistan?

None of this fazed Elizabeth at all. She knew all the games interrogators played. She'd mastered them working for the Agency. Because she and Quinn had nothing to hide, she told the truth. Yes, she was enjoying her time in Scotland. She and Quinn met at Cobra. They'd gone out to eat in Edinburgh, but they'd stopped to see if MacDonald was willing to explain why he'd threatened to kill Jack. Elizabeth hadn't lived in Colorado when pot had been legalized, and, no, she'd never tried it or any other illegal drug. No, really. Not once.

After the last question, Elizabeth turned the tables. "If you know I've been to Afghanistan, then why did you ask me where I work? You already know the answer."

Patel's friendly façade vanished. "Where did you work before Cobra?"

"You're not going to find that on your own." Elizabeth smiled sweetly. "I was a counterterrorism analyst and interrogator for the Central Intelligence Agency."

Patel's mouth formed an O of surprise.

Elizabeth went on. "Between you and me, Wilson is wasting his time if he thinks either Quinn or I had anything to do with Jack's alleged drug dealing. Quinn can't even bring himself to believe that Jack was dealing drugs, even after getting the news about the toxicology reports. You're on a fishing expedition, but you won't find anything because there's nothing to find."

"Why did you visit the site of the murder?"

"Quinn is grieving right now. Surely, that's not hard to understand. If someone you loved were murdered, wouldn't you want answers? You might even want to go to the place that person died to pay your respects."

Patel's gaze dropped to the table. "My sister was killed in a crash. We put flowers by the side of the road where it happened every year."

"I see you understand." Elizabeth stood. "Unless you're going to arrest us, I think it's time Quinn and I were on our way."

"There's a lot to see in Scotland. You should be enjoyin' your holiday and no' playin' detective." Patel stood and opened the door. "DS Wilson *will* arrest you if he thinks you're tamperin' with his investigation."

Elizabeth stepped into the hallway then turned back to face Patel again. "Did you find the man who followed us?"

"Not yet."

"How long have you had us under surveillance?"

Patel's pupils dilated—an adrenaline response. "I don't know what you're goin' on about."

Liar.

Elizabeth smiled. "Right."

She walked down the hallway, spotted Quinn in another room with Wilson, his face almost as red as his hair. She tapped on the glass, smiled, motioned for him that it was time to go.

He stood, shouted something at Wilson, then joined her. "Are you okay?"

"I'm fine."

"The bastard wanted to know whether Jack and I were dealin' drugs together. He didnae ask it outright, but I know what he's thinkin'. Let's get the fuck out of here."

They walked through the lobby and out the door in silence, Quinn's anger palpable. Only when they were out of the building did he speak, cursing most of the way back to the car.

"Wilson dreamed up some idea about the two of us—Jack and me—bringin' drugs into the country from Afghanistan."

"Patel asked me the same thing—whether I'd ever brought back heroin from Afghanistan." As outrageous as it was, Elizabeth understood. "They must have a good reason for considering this as an angle. They have a murder to solve, and they're going where the evidence takes them."

"Bastards." Quinn took the car keys out of his pocket, unlocked the doors.

"You and I have a bigger problem."

Quinn opened her door. "What do you mean?"

She took her cellphone out of her handbag and tossed her handbag onto the seat, then got onto her knees, turned on the phone's flashlight, and looked beneath the car.

"What the bloody hell are you doin'?"

"Looking for a GPS transmitter. And there it is—near the muffler."

Quinn got down next to her, lay flat on his belly, looked. "Sweet sufferin' shite!"

He removed the device, which was held in place by magnets. "I've a mind to shove this up Wilson's tight arse."

"Probably a bad idea." Elizabeth stood, took the transmitter from Quinn, and started back toward the police station's front doors.

He got to his feet. "Where are you goin'?"

"To give this back to Wilson." She hurried inside, Quinn a step behind her, and spotted Wilson and Patel talking together. She walked over to them, dropped the device in Wilson's hands. "I think this belongs to you."

The looks on their faces almost made her laugh.

QUINN TOOK a sip of his whisky, wishing he had the bottle. "Is that what you get after servin' your country—suspicion, slander?"

Elizabeth sat on the sofa across from him, somehow unruffled by all of this. "If they'd had any evidence against us, they would have arrested us. They've got a murder to solve. They're just doing their job."

"Doin' their job? Harassing us is doin' their job?"

"They have to go where the evidence leads them. If they have reason to suspect that Jack was selling—"

"Jack wouldnae sell drugs!" Quinn all but shouted the words, his temper frayed.

He couldn't read people the way Elizabeth could, but he knew she no longer believed him.

Can you blame her?

Even Ava was beginning to doubt, Ava, whom Jack had loved with all his heart.

"Remember what I said yesterday—how some of what I say could be upsetting?"

"Aye." Of course, he remembered.

"That's where we are now. I'm sharing my professional assessment with you."

Quinn saw the sympathy on her face, the concern in her eyes, but it didn't take the edge off his anger. Still, he didn't want to take his temper out on Elizabeth. She'd come here on what could have been a holiday to help him. None of this was her doing.

He took another swallow of whisky. "Your professional assessment is that Jack was sellin' drugs."

"The evidence so far strongly suggests that." She ran through it for him. "He was murdered in a concealed alley near his vehicle, which means he drove there himself. It's an alley you can't wander into by taking a wrong turn. You have to choose to be there. He *chose* to be there—at three in the morning."

She stood, came around the coffee table to sit on the arm of Quinn's chair. "Someone he knew got close enough to him to kill him without Jack putting up a fight. There were no drugs in his system, but there were traces of two illicit drugs on his hands, in his pocket, and in his car. We know he lied about losing his cell phone."

She let that settle, taking Quinn's left hand, which had balled into a fist, and teasing his fingers open until they threaded with hers. "I know you loved him. I know he was your best friend. I can't imagine how horrible all of this is for you. But it's not hard to see why the police believe he was somehow involved with drugs."

Despair seeped, thick and dark, into Quinn's chest. "Aye."

"I won't give up, Quinn. I won't give up on him—or you." She stood and took the tumbler from his right hand then set it on the coffee table and drew him to his feet.

"I should go." He reached for the tumbler.

She caught his hand. "Why?"

"I'm no' fit company tonight."

"You want to drink. I know. You want to forget, to make yourself go numb. You've done that before. Will it fix anything?"

"I'll sleep."

"I know how to make you sleep." She took a step back and started to undress.

Quinn's pulse skipped, his brain going blank.

She unzipped her jeans, pushed them over the curve of her hips and down her slender legs. Next, she pulled her blouse over her head and dropped it on the floor. Then she unclasped her bra, those beautiful breasts springing free.

Blood rushed to Quinn's cock. "Are you offerin' yourself to me?"

She answered by taking his hand, leading him to her bed, and helping him strip. "Lie down."

Heart thrumming, he did as she asked, watching as she crawled onto the bed and straddled his hips.

Her hands slid up his body from his obliques to his abs to his pecs, her mouth following, spreading fiery little kisses across his belly and chest, lavishing affection on each and every scar. He rested his hands on her hips, let her have her way with him, his cock aching to see how turned on she got touching and tasting him.

Her gaze met his. "I want you."

"I'm all yours."

She took his cock and guided him inside her.

It was like going home, her tight little quim closing around him like a fist, wet and hot. He held himself still, let her set the pace, reaching down to stroke her clit with one hand, palming a lush breast with the other, her nipple pebbled and hard.

"*Yes.*" Her eyes were closed now, her head tilted back, her nails digging into his pecs, her hips grinding against him.

Sexual need drummed through Quinn like a pulse, making it hard for him to hold still. She was beautiful, so beautiful. Lilibet, his Lilibet. She was the answer to every question he'd ever had. He wanted her, needed her, wasn't sure how he'd go back to a life without her, not when being inside her felt so right.

She came with a cry, her inner muscles clenching around him, driving him out of his mind. When her peak had passed, he clasped her hips and drove himself into her, hard and fast, riding her from beneath, climax rushing through him as sweet as salvation, bliss shaking him apart.

She sank against him, her head tucked beneath his chin, his cock still inside her. "I've got you, Quinn. I won't let go."

Her words hit a tender place inside him, unleashing emotions he didn't understand. He wrapped his arms around her, held onto her as the two of them drifted into sleep.

11

Elizabeth stood at the railing, looking out over the Bearsden bathhouse, the sunshine warm on her face. "It's hard to wrap my mind around the fact that this is almost two thousand years old."

"Och, well, we've got standin' stones that are older than this." Quinn stood beside her, one hand resting against her lower back, making Elizabeth feel protected and turned on all at once.

Then again, she couldn't look at Quinn now without feeling aroused. In a single day, he'd gone from the sexy friend she'd fantasized about to the man who'd given her the best sex of her life. She knew how it felt to have his cock inside her. She knew the feel of his skin. She knew his taste. They'd been friends-with-benefits for only twenty-four hours, and already she was addicted to him.

She ought to be terrified, but she wasn't. For some reason, she trusted Quinn. She trusted him in a way she hadn't trusted a man since Jason.

"Standing stones? I've always wanted to see standing stones."

"Have you now?" His smile was warm, even teasing, but it didn't reach his eyes.

They had already been to Old Kilpatrick, where they'd taken in the view from the site of the ancient Roman fort above the beautiful Firth of Clyde, and Duntocher, where they'd seen a section of the stone base of the Antonine Wall. After so many days of gray and rain, it was wonderful to see blue sky again.

Though Quinn seemed to be enjoying sight-seeing, too, Elizabeth could tell from the shadows in his blue eyes that he was hurting, whether from the nightmare he'd had last night or because of the murder investigation or all of it together. He'd refused to talk about the dream or the investigation over breakfast today, instead asking her what she wanted to see.

They strolled together through the ruins, the remnants of stone walls and floors revealing where the different pools had once stood. The frigidarium, or cold bath, had a horseshoe shape. The caldarium, or hot pool, was missing its stone floor. The tepidarium, an area like a dry sauna, still had visible ducts that had carried heated air from a furnace creating a kind of radiant heat.

"To think that the Romans had radiant heat two thousand years ago."

Elizabeth came across another sign, which she read aloud. "'When the Romans abandoned the Antonine Wall and Scotland for good in one-fifty-eight AD, they burned and destroyed their forts and buildings, including the baths.' How sad."

"They couldnae give their enemies a place to shelter or leave anythin' that might give them a tactical advantage, aye? Tribes of Picts occupyin' Roman forts along the wall would have made the emperor shite himself."

She smiled up at him. "I guess your ancestors were one group the Romans couldn't conquer."

It felt good to be with him. It felt natural to share the day with him.

He grinned. "Aye, it's true. That job was left to the bloody English."

After that, they made a short drive south to Crookston Castle, Elizabeth reading about it on her phone. "It says the first castle was built there in the eleven-hundreds. What remains today was built in fourteen-hundred. Mary Queen of Scots was betrothed to Lord Darnley there."

"A match made in hell." Quinn parked at the edge of a grassy area. "There it is."

Elizabeth stepped out of the car and looked toward the top of the hill. There, peeking out from amid the bare branches of deciduous trees, stood Crookston Castle. "It's not as big as I thought it was going to be."

Quinn grinned. "You were singin' a different tune yesterday, doll."

Had he just made a dirty joke? Yes, he had—and he'd called her *doll*.

Oh, she liked that.

She laughed. "You bampot."

But now he had her thinking about his big, gorgeous cock and all the lovely things he could do with it, namely fuck her silly.

They walked hand-in-hand up the hillside, the grass wet beneath their shoes.

An idea came to her. "Have you ever had sex in a public place?"

Quinn looked down at her, one brow arched. "Why are you askin' me that?"

"Sex in a castle might be fun."

"You're serious." He glanced around them, and she knew he was considering it. "There are people out walkin', families wi' wee ones. It's a weekend, aye?"

"I don't see anyone around the castle."

"You'll be givin' Wilson a real reason to arrest us, you will." Quinn shook his head—but he was smiling.

QUINN WAS DISAPPOINTED to discover that they weren't the only ones exploring the castle. An older couple poked about, speaking with very proper English accents.

"This is the northeast tower." Elizabeth read from her phone, pretending to be absorbed by the history of the place. "The two western towers were destroyed in the fifteenth century and never rebuilt."

But Quinn could tell what was truly on her mind.

Sex.

He hadn't been able to think of anything else since she'd brought it up, lust driving away the lingering darkness from the nightmare about his mother, taking his mind off Jack's murder. His cock was half-hard, his body hyperaware of her —every motion, every touch, every glance.

They explored the castle's prison, walked through the barrel-vaulted basement, and climbed the iron ladders up to the top of the northeast tower, her ass enticing him all the way. A fence formed a border around the edges of the tower, giving them a view of southeast Glasgow below.

"Beautiful." Elizabeth came to stand just in front of him, reaching back to rub her hand over his fly. "What's that river?"

"That's Levern Water."

At one time, he had hated this place. Growing up, he'd

thought of nothing but getting away. But the city had changed in the past decade, and so had he.

Below, the older couple walked down the hill.

She looked back at him. "They're leaving."

"I see that." Anticipation whipped through him, his jeans now uncomfortably tight. "Come."

She wanted sex in a public place, pure gaggin' for it, and he would bloody well give it to her.

He led her down the ladder to the room below. There was only one window, daylight streaming through an arched opening in the wall, the air thick with the scents of rain, moss, and the ancient echo of wood smoke.

Quinn moved in on her the moment her shoes hit the floor, backing her up against the wall, desire rushing through his veins. "You're wantin' pumped the now, aye?"

"If you're asking whether I want you to fuck me *right now*, then, hell, yes."

He kissed her hard, already on fire for her. She kissed him back, reaching down to unzip first her jeans and then his, freeing his erection, stroking the length of him. Then she did something Quinn would never have imagined.

She stepped away from him into the middle of the room, pushed her jeans down to her ankles, and dropped onto her hands and knees, giving him a glorious view of her bare ass, exposing herself to him completely.

"*Jesus!*" He took in the sight of her, his heart slamming.

He dropped to his knees behind her, grasped her bare hips, and nudged his cock into her, entering her with a single, slow thrust.

It felt so good, her quim tight and hot. He'd meant to go slowly, but the thrill of fucking her here was too much, the element of danger heightening his excitement. He pounded into her, hard and fast, but he didn't want to leave her behind.

He reached around to stroke her clit, doing his best to please her.

Her response was immediate, her moans echoing through the castle.

Then Quinn heard it—voices.

"Shhh." He clamped a hand over Elizabeth's mouth—but he kept fucking her.

When he was certain she understood, he went back to stroking her clit, still driving into her, the first hint of orgasm dragging at him, his balls tight.

The voices grew nearer.

Still, he didn't stop, thrusting into her luscious body again and again and again, the risk of being discovered very real now—and very exciting. She was getting close, her hands clawing at the stone floor, her head tilted back, her eyes squeezed shut.

She went stiff, gasped, arched, bliss like sunshine on her face as she came.

That was all he needed, his hips a piston as he finished inside her, orgasm hitting him with the force of a blast wave, the release scorching and sweet.

"I'm certain I was wearing both gloves when we climbed the tower." Quinn recognized the voice. It was the Englishman they'd seen earlier. "You stay here, dear, and I'll go up to see if it's there."

Quinn withdrew from Elizabeth's body, stuffed his half-hard cock back into his jeans, then helped her to her feet. Fighting laughter, she pulled up her jeans and had just zipped them when Quinn heard the man's shoes on the ladder.

"What year did you say it was built?" Quinn asked, pretending to be in the midst of a conversation.

"Fourteen-hundred."

The man's head popped into view.

"Aye, that's right."

They exchanged polite greetings with the man, who recognized them, then climbed down the ladders and walked back to the car, Quinn's arm around Elizabeth's shoulders, a stupid grin on his face. "I'll never look at this place the same way. You've a way of makin' history come alive."

Elizabeth laughed. "When is the last time someone had sex in that castle?"

"Probably yesterday. This *is* Scotland." Back at the car, Quinn kissed her, a gentle, slow kiss. "I didn't realize you were so fond of takin' risks."

She gave him a smile that almost stopped his heart. "Silly boy. Why do you think I joined the Agency?"

"IT GETS DARK SO EARLY HERE." Elizabeth watched the city roll past her window, the sun almost set, and it wasn't yet four in the afternoon.

"We make up for that in summer when the sun doesn't set until about ten p.m."

"That must be nice."

"That's new." Quinn looked out the windshield at an ultramodern glass building. "I barely recognize some of these streets."

"When were you last here?"

"That would have been when I helped Jack and Ava

move into their house about five years ago. Afore that, I came for their wedding."

He'd said his father was an alcoholic, but he hadn't mentioned his mother or anyone else. "Do you have family here?"

The moment the question was out, she regretted asking.

His expression darkened. "I dinnae know."

"You don't know?" That wasn't the answer she'd expected.

"My da died about six months after I joined the army, and my mother... I've no' seen her since I was fourteen. She left, took my little sister, Paige. I've never tried to find them." His voice was calm, but he was gripping the steering wheel so hard that his knuckles were white. "I dreamed about it last night—the night she left."

So that's what his nightmare had been about.

Elizabeth rested her hand on his shoulder, her heart hurting for him. "I'm sorry."

"Dinnae bother yourself. I found my true family in the army—and with Cobra."

Jack had been a part of that family—and now he was gone.

But it was clear that Quinn didn't want to talk about his family or his bad dream. It wasn't her business anyway. Having sex with him didn't entitle her to his life history. Still, what he'd told her raised more questions than it answered.

How could any mother walk out on her own child? Why had she taken his sister but left Quinn with his father? Had she been an alcoholic, too? How had he turned out to be such a caring man without a good male role model or a relationship with his mother?

No wonder he'd joined a gang—and the military.

Everyone needed to have someone they trusted, someone who believed in them, somewhere they belonged.

Elizabeth's life had been so ordinary and almost idyllic by contrast. She'd grown up in the suburbs with two younger sisters, Sarah and Julia, a mother who was a teacher, and a father who was an urban planner and worked for the city government. Her parents were still together. Her sisters were both married, and Sarah had a two-year-old daughter. They lived scattered around the country but stayed in touch and got together for Christmas every year.

What would it have been like to grow up without that stability and support?

"You can quit psychoanalyzin' me." Quinn glanced over at her, a grin on his lips. "Aye, I know that's what you're doin'. I dinnae fault you for it. You cannae help it."

"Actually, I was thinking how lucky I was growing up. We don't get to choose how we come into this world—or who our parents are."

"Aye, that's for damned sure."

"Somehow, despite your rough start, you became the incredible man you are. You should be proud of that, Quinn." She couldn't tell whether her words touched him.

They drove the rest of the way to the hotel in silence, then ordered room service, eating in front of Netflix and watching a BBC special on Scotland's standing stones that Quinn had found for her. She thought it was all fascinating.

"I can't believe that some of these Neolithic sites are older than the pyramids."

Quinn seemed less impressed. "What the fuck is a henge anyway?"

"I guess no one's quite sure." She turned off the TV and crawled onto his lap, facing him, her hands resting on his shoulders. "They certainly are phallic, jutting up out of the ground, hard and thick and long."

He grinned, lifted her sweater over her head. "Like I said, you've got a way of bringin' history alive. If you'd been my teacher, I might have learned a thing or two."

They made out on the sofa like a couple of teenagers, his hands and mouth on her breasts, her hands inside his jeans. Then he carried her to her bed and made long, slow love to her until they were both utterly spent.

What was she going to do without him once they got back to Denver?

She didn't want to think about that now. She didn't want to think about anything.

Quinn broke the silence. "Tomorrow when I go talk to this Leo fella, you should stay here. I'd feel better if I knew you were out of harm's way. If Jack didnae trust him, then I dinnae trust him. It could get rough."

She raised her head, looked up at him. "Oh, no. No, no. That's exactly the situation where you need me. Will you be able to tell whether he's lying?"

"If Wilson follows me, he willnae be able to arrest you for interferin'—"

"I told you I wouldn't give up on you or Jack. I meant it. It's my choice, Quinn, not yours. Besides, didn't I just prove that I enjoy taking risks?"

He made a noncommittal hmph. "I'll be callin' the shots while we're there, understand?"

"Yes, sir."

He kissed her hair. "That's more like it."

12

Quinn drove southwest on the M77 toward the port town of Troon, a light rain falling. Elizabeth had located Leo Grant's business and pulled up Google satellite images of the place for Quinn to study. From a tactical point of view, it was a tricky landscape, offering cover to potential adversaries, with a rectangular warehouse and several small cargo ships moored along the wharf. He thought he'd seen a security fence, too—a potential obstacle if they needed to leave in a hurry.

He wished Elizabeth had listened to him and stayed at the hotel. It would have given him one less worry. Though he'd brought the Glock, he hoped to fuck he didn't have to draw. He didn't enjoy killing.

As he drove, Elizabeth shared what she'd found online. "According to the website, they ship coal, lumber, aggregates, construction materials, construction and farm equipment, livestock, and other goods to the smaller ports on Scotland's west coast, the Scottish islands, and Northern Ireland."

"It wouldnae be hard for him to smuggle drugs up and down the coast."

"It's the perfect set up for any kind of smuggling—drugs, people, weapons. It says here that Leo Grant, the owner, worked for the company as a young man and then bought it four years ago when its original owner retired."

"He probably did that with money from sellin' drugs. Run a load of lumber up the coast and drop off a dozen kilos of smack along the way. That could turn a tidy profit."

"This is all speculation. Don't convict the guy before he's been arrested. For all we know, he's never smuggled a thing."

"Ava said Jack was suspicious of his business dealings. Maybe Jack knew somethin' incriminatin', and Grant wanted to make certain he didnae talk."

"If Jack knew something incriminating about Leo, why would he meet him in a dark alley in the middle of the night? I know you want to find Jack's killer, but you should at least try to be objective. You won't help yourself if you walk up to Grant angry and ready to fight."

Aye, Lilibet had a point there. But how the fuck was he supposed to be objective when a man who'd been like a brother to him was lying dead on a slab? He wanted answers, and he wanted them last week.

The rain had stopped by the time they reached Troon Port, the sun peeking out from behind the clouds.

Quinn parked next to West Scotland Shipping. His phone buzzed—a text message from Lewis saying they'd raised enough money now to pay for military honors for Jack's funeral and asking whether Quinn wanted to be part of the honor guard and a pallbearer.

Fuck. What a thought.

Of course, Quinn would do that.

"It's just Lewis workin' on the military honors part of Jack's funeral," Quinn told Elizabeth, texting his answer. He put his mobile phone away. "If I say go back to the car, you're to go wi'out arguin'. Understood?"

"Yes, sir." She saluted.

They stepped out of the car, a brisk breeze blowing in off the water, catching Elizabeth's hair, gulls crying overhead.

She closed her eyes, inhaled. "I love the smell of the sea."

But Quinn was focused on their surroundings. There was, indeed, a high security fence. There were also surveillance cameras, which meant they were being watched. A guard stood at the open gate. Quinn probably outweighed him by two stone and was a good four inches taller, but Quinn could tell that the bastard was armed, the pistol in his shoulder holster making his jacket hang unevenly. He was also wearing a radio.

Och, he should have refused to bring Elizabeth along. There was no one he respected more, but she wasn't a fighter. She shouldn't be here.

Quinn approached the guard, Elizabeth beside him. "I'm Quinn McManus here to speak wi' Leo Grant."

"Does he know you're comin'?" The guard answered with an Irish accent.

Elizabeth answered. "It's a surprise."

The guard's gaze slid over her. "American?"

The bastard

"Is my accent that obvious?" She smiled.

"I've got cousins in Chicago."

"Really? That's amazing. Where in Chicago?"

Och, she was laying on the charm, but the bastard fell for it, the two of them chatting about the weather in Chicago and how his cousin owned a pub there and how she had Irish ancestors. She was like a secret weapon, using men's vulnerabilities and expectations to disarm them.

A dark-haired man in a gray suit jacket stepped out of the warehouse and walked toward them. He was a near match for Quinn in height but slightly overweight with a pug nose and hard face. He walked with the confidence of a man used to telling others what to do. Quinn recognized him at once for what he was—a predator.

"Ryan, where are your manners?" he called to the guard. "Don't leave the lady standin' out in the damp."

"Yes, sir. These people are here to see you, sir."

Leo Grant walked through the open gate, studied Quinn's face. "Who are you?"

"I'm Quinn McManus. Jack Murray was my best friend. We served together in the Special Air Service."

"What does that have to do wi' me?"

Quinn opened his mouth to answer, but Elizabeth beat him to it.

"We're heartbroken about Jack's death. We know the two of you were friends. We're just here to see if you can shed any light on what happened."

Grant looked from Elizabeth to Quinn and back again. "If you're police, you should know I've already spoken wi' the Detective Sergeant."

"Wilson? Aye, he's an eejit. But we're no' police."

Elizabeth held out her hand. "I'm Elizabeth Shields."

Grant held her hand a little too long. "From America."

Elizabeth beamed. "Yes."

Quinn followed her lead and held out his hand, too. "Quinn McManus, Glasgow."

Grant shook his hand, motioned for them to follow him. "Let's get indoors afore it starts rainin' again."

ELIZABETH FOLLOWED Quinn and Grant into the warehouse, stopping at the front desk, where he introduced them to Dorcas, a middle-aged woman who worked as his assistant.

"Dorcas will need to see your IDs," Grant said.

They hadn't anticipated this, but Elizabeth couldn't see how it was a problem. She took her wallet from her handbag and handed Dorcas her driver's license. "I didn't bring my passport. I hope this is enough."

Quinn did the same, the two of them watching as Dorcas wrote down their names, dates of birth, and license numbers. Was Grant doing a background check?

If they'd been in the Middle East, Elizabeth might have been concerned. She didn't hide the fact that she'd worked for the CIA, and there were parts of the Middle East where any association with the Agency could be a death sentence. But they were in the UK, an allied nation.

When they'd got their licenses back, Grant led them into his office.

Elizabeth took it in at a glance. The Scottish flag in the corner. A large map of the coastlines around the Irish Sea. A poster that read, "Free Scotland. Vote YES on Indy Ref #2." Framed photos of different cargo ships on the walls. A photo of a woman and three children on a shelf beside a row of plastic binders. Cigarette butts in an ashtray. A station with a coffee pot and paper cups.

Grant gestured toward two office chairs. "What do you want?"

Elizabeth had coached Quinn on how to ask the questions he wanted to ask in hopes that a softer approach might get them more answers.

"I grew up in Glasgow, like Jack. He ran with your gang —the Young Boys. I ran with the South Bank Boys."

Grant grinned. "Och, those fuckers. We bashed their heids a time or two."

Quinn chuckled. "And we returned the favor."

Come on, guys. Let it go.

"Jack and I met during recruit training and went through the SAS selection process together. We were the only Scots in our unit, both of us from Glasgow."

"I understand why you became friends—two boys off the streets of the Dear Green Place."

"I live and work in the States now. Private security. When I got the call that Jack was dead, I couldnae believe it."

"Aye." There was grief in Grant's eyes—and anger. "I warned him not to work for that cunt—Whitehall. The fucker sold out his own country to the English. I even offered Jack a job as my chief of security, but he refused. He chose that bastard over me. Where do you stand on Scottish independence, McManus?"

Quinn met Grant's gaze straight on. "I voted for it, if that's what you're askin'."

"A true Scotsman." Grant nodded, his brow furrowing. "You're here wantin' to know if I killed Murray—or whether I know who did. The answer is no. I've no' seen him or spoken to him since the day we argued about his job. If I knew who'd killed him, the bastard would be lyin' at the bottom of the Irish Sea by now. Jack and I disagreed about Scottish independence, but he was a Young Boy and a good friend. I would never raise my hand against a brother."

There was the grief again—and the anger.

"Thank you for being so honest with us," Elizabeth said. "The police say they think Jack was dealing drugs. We find that hard to believe. Do you think that was possible? Would he do something like that?"

Grant laughed, a harsh sound. "Wilson is an eejit, so he is. Jack drank, but he never touched drugs. Even when the rest of the Young Boys were smokin' grass, he'd refuse. He was a right smug prick about it."

"Do you think he changed?"

Grant shook his head, laughed again. "If that's what the police are sayin', they're full of shite."

Elizabeth was about to ask whether Grant knew anyone who might have a grudge against Jack when Grant's phone buzzed. He answered, his gaze darting to Elizabeth for the briefest instant before moving away.

"Thanks." He hung up, stood, but something had changed. Fear. Uncertainty. Rage. It was all there in his eyes. "I've answered your questions. I'm a busy man, so I'm afraid that's all the time I have, even for friends of Jack."

The door opened, and two men in dark suits entered.

"My men will see you out."

Elizabeth stood, walked with Quinn toward the office door.

Then Quinn stopped, faced Grant again.

Oh, no.

"Do you smuggle drugs?"

Hoping to diffuse the situation, Elizabeth stepped between the two men just in time to catch the full impact of Grant's fist against her cheek.

Pain. Dancing lights. Darkness.

She fell backward into Quinn, who caught her.

"You fuckin' bastard." Quinn sounded far away—and very angry.

Quinn's going to kill him.

She tried to tell Quinn she was okay, but she couldn't form the words. She couldn't even open her eyes.

"I didnae mean to hit her." Grant sounded afraid. *He should be.* "You all saw that. This bastard insulted me, and she stepped in between us."

"Aye, boss. You want us to teach him a lesson?"

"I want you to help him get her out of here!" Grant was shouting now. "Bolt, McManus! I dinnae want to see either of you here again."

"There's nothin' lower than a man who hits innocent women."

"It's her own damned fault, ya daft bastard."

Elizabeth felt herself being carried, felt the sunshine on her face, but still couldn't open her eyes, men's voices and angry words drifting over her.

QUINN SAT on the sofa in Elizabeth's hotel room, holding the ice bag to her cheek, her head resting in his lap. She'd refused to let him drive her to A&E, certain word would get back to Wilson. So, he'd driven her to the hotel, given her some paracetamol for her headache, and settled her on the sofa. "You're goin' to have one hell of a black eye."

"We'll be a matching set." She touched her fingers to the bruise on his cheek. "We need a cover. I'll tell everyone I slipped and fell and hit my face on something."

He brushed a strand of hair off her cheek, a part of him wanting to throttle her. "You shouldnae have gotten between us. I could have taken that blow."

She glared at him. "I would have let him hit you if I'd known that's what he was going to do next."

At least her smart mouth was intact. Her silence as he'd

driven away from the wharf had scared the living shite out of him.

"Then why the hell did you do it?"

"Your question surprised me. I was looking at you, not at him. I thought I could stop the situation from escalating. I was going to tell him that you didn't mean it like it sounded, that you were just upset about Wilson accusing you—or something like that."

"I needed answers."

"We didn't learn anything that way—except that he hits really hard."

Quinn felt a hitch in his chest. "I shouldnae have let you come wi' me."

"No, it's good I came along." She sat up, took the ice bag from him, pressed it to her head. "He's grieving for Jack, too, but he's also hurt. He values loyalty above all else. When Jack chose to work for Whitehall instead of him, it felt like a betrayal."

"Do you think the bastard killed Jack over it?" Quinn trusted her judgment, her ability to read people beyond his understanding.

"That's the strange thing. Up until the moment his phone buzzed, I would have said no. He meant it when he said that he would put Jack's killer at the bottom of the Irish Sea. But then..." Her words trailed off, her brow furrowed. "Then he picked up the phone and something changed. His gaze flickered to me for just a second and—"

"I saw how he looked you up and down when you introduced yourself."

Elizabeth rolled her eyes. "That's not what I mean. That call—I think it was about me. They took our driver's license numbers and our birthdates. I figured they were running some kind of background check. He learned something he didn't like. As soon as he hung up, he ended our meeting."

"What if he found out you're former CIA?"

She moaned, closed her eyes. "That's not ideal, but why should that matter?"

Had she really just asked him that question?

"Och, he really hit you hard, doll." *The fuckin' bastard.* "You're no' yourself. You're no' thinkin' clearly. Tell me. Where are we?"

"I know where we are—the Dakota hotel in Glasgow, Scotland."

Now Quinn was truly worried. "What's just across the water from us?"

"Norway?"

"The other direction."

Her eyes flew open, her gaze meeting his. "Northern Ireland."

"Aye."

"Do you think he's mixed up somehow with the IRA?"

"I dinnae know what he's doin', but those boys workin' for him were Irish. The IRA has used Glasgow as a route to England in the past."

"I read a paper recently about how Brexit has made those tensions flare again. MI5 held a conference about it, I think." She stood, ice bag in hand, walked to her computer, and booted it up. "What if Jack's misgivings had nothing to do with drugs at all? What if he was worried that Leo was supporting terrorists?"

She sat, started to read through the document, but stopped. "I can't look at the screen. It hurts too much."

Quinn was done fucking around. "I'm calling for a doctor."

He settled her on her bed and then called the front desk,

making up a story about how they'd been walking in Troon and some bastard had tried to steal her handbag and punched her when she wouldn't let go. "Naw, she disnae want to talk to police. She disnae want to see a doctor either, but I think a doctor needs to take a look at her."

"They're going to think you did it," she said when he hung up the phone.

Quinn's stomach knotted at the thought. He'd seen his mother lie for his father a hundred times. "I'd rather face their suspicion and accusations than see you sufferin'."

A paramedic arrived almost an hour later, saw her black eye, and turned to Quinn, his gaze resting on Quinn's bruised cheek. "I'd like to examine her in private, please."

"Aye, of course." Quinn stepped into the hall, memories he wished he didn't have filling his head—his mother's screams, his da's shouting, his own terror.

If you dinnae have my meals ready on time, I'll find some other cunt to do it.

I'm sorry! I'll do better.

Stop hittin' her, Da! Stop! You're hurtin' her! Can ye no' see that?

Get out of here, boy, or you'll feel the sting of my belt.

How many times had he done nothing while his da beat his mother, leaving her bruised and battered?

No wonder she left you.

The door opened again, and Quinn was allowed to enter.

"She's got a concussion and needs rest. I've given her somethin' stronger for the headache." The paramedic went through a list of things Elizabeth should avoid along with symptoms that indicated she needed to go to A&E. "I've suggested she go in for a CT scan, but she refused."

Quinn took a card from him. "My thanks."

"She swears this isnae your doin', and I've no choice but to believe her."

"I'd never hit her or any woman. I'd have stopped the bastard if I'd seen the blow comin'. I couldnae go after him because I was holdin' her."

"It seems the two of you have had a rough time of it." The paramedic eyed his bruised face again then handed Quinn a business card. "Dinnae hesitate to call, aye?"

Quinn held the door for him then locked it and walked to the bedroom.

Elizabeth was sound asleep, a brochure about resources for victims of domestic abuse on the bed beside her. He covered her with a blanket, picked up the brochure, then crumpled it in his hand, overwhelmed by disgust. Why hadn't anyone helped his mother? Why hadn't he done more to protect her?

Then he turned off the light. "Sleep sweet."

13

———

Elizabeth woke the next morning feeling a little light-headed from the pain pill the paramedic had given her, her headache mostly gone. Her spirits sank to find herself alone. She could have sworn Quinn had been there during the night, but he wasn't beside her now. He'd been angry with her, and she supposed she couldn't blame him, though she hadn't meant to get punched in the face.

She climbed out of bed, found herself still fully clothed, and walked to the bathroom to shower and brush her teeth, glancing out at the living area as she passed.

Her heart melted.

Quinn lay, shirtless and sound asleep, on her sofa. He was a mountain of a man, and the sofa was small, his big feet sticking off the end. That couldn't be comfortable.

Then she saw it—the almost empty whisky bottle.

Oh, Quinn.

She'd never thought of his drinking as a problem because she'd never met an operator who didn't drink hard. But she'd spent enough time with Quinn now to know that he was self-medicating. Not that he didn't have good reason to want to blunt his emotions with Jack lying in the morgue. But how many times in the past few years had she heard him say that he just wanted a *wee swally*?

She walked to the bathroom, flicked on the light, and got a good look at herself for the first time. "Shit."

She'd never had a black eye before, and this was a bad one—or a good one, depending on how a person felt about it. Her left cheek was swollen, a dark bruise spreading across her temple and around her eye.

You look like a raccoon, girl.

She stripped and stepped into the shower, hot water and shampoo clearing her head, reviving her. She rinsed her hair, opened her eyes, gasped.

Quinn stood in the doorway, leaning up against the door jamb, arms crossed over his bare chest, his gaze sliding over her, a mix of concern and lust on his face. "I didnae mean to startle you. I just wanted to make sure you're okay bein' in here by yourself."

"I'm fine—and you're free to stay and watch or join me if you like."

His lips curved in a slow smile that she felt deep in her belly. "I like."

He shucked his jeans and boxers, opened the glass door, and stepped into the shower, his gaze darkening when he looked at her cheek. "I should have killed him."

"He would have killed you right back." She got her hands soapy and ran them over his wet skin, aroused by the sculpted feel of him, his chest hair rasping against her palms, his nipples tightening under her touch, his erection jutting up between them.

He did the same, lavishing attention on her breasts, belly, and ass, his hands spreading fire over her skin, fueling the blaze between her thighs. "Your skin is so soft."

It turned her on just to see how much touching her turned *him* on, his brow furrowed, his blue eyes burning as his gaze moved over her.

She squeezed a bicep. "You're so hard—all of you."

They rinsed, water sluicing over their skin.

Quinn kissed her, soft butterfly kisses. "I want to go down on you."

Her heart skipped a beat. "Don't feel like you're obligated."

"Obligated?" He laughed. "I want the taste of you on my tongue."

Shivers.

No man had ever said that before, most acting as if giving her head was just the price they had to pay for receiving, a sexual quid pro quo.

Quinn drew her hard against him and kissed her, his tongue doing wonderful things to hers. Then he turned her so that her back pressed up against the cold tile wall and knelt before her, lifting one of her thighs over his shoulder.

"God, I love the look of you—so fuckin' sexy." He parted her, explored her with a few slow licks. "Mmm."

Her fingers slid into his wet hair, and she watched as he tasted her, flicking her clit with his tongue, the sensation and the intensity on his face making her belly clench. Then he took her clit into his mouth and suckled her.

Her fingers balled into fists, the pleasure of it almost unbearable, his head moving in and out, his lips stroking her, his mouth maintaining suction. "*Fuck!*"

She fought to hold onto her self-control, but what he was doing felt so fucking good. She cursed, cried out, called his name. "*Quinn!*"

Then he slid two fingers inside her, thrusting to match the rhythm of his mouth and she couldn't speak at all, every exhale a moan, her thighs quivering, pleasure drawing tighter and tighter inside her—until it exploded.

She cried out, arching against the tile, climax flooding her, drowning her in bliss.

Quinn drew out her pleasure, making it last, staying with her until she was weak and breathless. Then he lowered her foot to the shower floor, stood, the raw emotion in his eyes making her pulse skip. "Lilibet."

He claimed her mouth in a deep, hard kiss, his lips wet with her taste. Then he cupped her ass with his hands and lifted her off her feet, bringing her face to face with him. "I cannae get enough of you."

He thrust into her, fucking her slowly, sending her over the edge again, his gaze never leaving hers, not even when he came.

～

Quinn read through the files Elizabeth had pulled up for him, all of them relating to the risk of renewed violence as a result of Brexit. "JTAC—that's the Joint Terrorism Analysis Centre—has set the threat level at severe in Northern Ireland."

"I remember seeing that." She lay on the sofa, resting to fend off a headache brought on by spending a fruitless hour online researching all the businesses surrounding the alley where Jack was killed. "We're getting ahead of ourselves again. We have no evidence that he's involved with terrorists. Leo has Irish workers? So does this hotel. He favors Scottish independence? So do you. He doesn't like the fact that I used to work for the CIA? Neither does my sweet old hippie grandma."

"Your gran is a hippie?" Quinn grinned.

"Woodstock, protests, teach-ins—you name it." Elizabeth stood, walked to the white board. "Jack has a bad night on October eighteenth. He comes home upset and seems tense to Ava. Jack calls you ten days later using a phone he told Ava he'd lost. He's found murdered the following Saturday in the early morning, killed by a single slash wound to the throat. Investigators find cocaine and heroin residue on his hands and in his suit pocket."

"Aye, but neither I nor that fucker Grant believe Jack was dealin'. If he and I agree, that has to mean somethin', aye?

"Grant might say that to deflect suspicion. How could he be selling drugs with Jack if he doesn't believe Jack sold drugs?"

"Aye, I can see that." But Jack hadn't been selling drugs.

"We've talked to Clive MacDonald, who had an adrenaline reaction when I asked about Jack but who could not have killed him. There could be reasons for his reaction."

"He disnae like the police." Of that Quinn was certain.

Elizabeth nodded. "His daughter tried to cover for him, helped him make up a story for why he'd done what he'd done. She was afraid, too."

Aye, he'd seen that. "Could she no' simply be afraid of her da?"

"Possibly. I wish I could talk to her again without him present."

"You want to go back there?"

She didn't answer, focused instead on her train of thought. "We've also met with Leo, who is grieving Jack's death and pissed off about what he saw as Jack's betrayal. But his grief doesn't necessarily mean he was sad that Jack was dead. It *could* mean he feels sad about having to kill Jack."

"What about what he said—about putting the killer at the bottom of the Irish Sea. You said he meant that."

"I did, but I could be wrong."

"I doubt it." He'd never known Elizabeth to be wrong.

She thought about this for a moment. "Leo has a history with gangs and drugs, and he tried to punch you for asking whether he was smuggling. That's a pretty clear indicator of guilt. He didn't want to punch you when he knew we'd come to ask him whether he'd killed Jack. In fact, he brought that up himself."

Aye, that was strange.

"He also got a call that I think had to do with me, a call that made him want to get us off his property immediately. We assume he found out that I used to work for the Agency and reacted to that, but it could be something else."

"Like what—your taste in music?"

She didn't seem to hear him. "I just don't see a man with Jack's training turning up in an alley at three a.m. with drugs in his pocket to chat with a man he no longer trusts—unless they were dealing drugs together and he felt he had no choice."

"What if Grant tried to push Jack into dealing drugs for him but killed Jack to silence him when he refused and then planted the drugs on him?"

"Or maybe they were conspiring together to sell drugs, and Jack somehow found out that Leo was involved with the IRA. Jack wouldn't betray the nation he'd served."

"He would have reported him." Quinn knew that for certain

"Leo said he would never harm a brother, but in that scenario, he might have felt he had no choice."

"Or maybe he no longer considered Jack a brother."

"This is pointless. We're just making things up here."

She walked over to the sofa, sank down onto a cushion, discouragement written on her bruised face. "If this were a job and I had the authority of Cobra and the Pentagon behind me or the cooperation of British Intelligence, we could get somewhere. As it is, we've got nothing on Leo and no real leads on Jack's murder—and the police are suspicious of us."

Quinn closed her laptop, went to sit beside her. "I could contact my buddies with MI6, tell them what happened wi' Grant, and see what they say. Maybe they have access to records on him."

She shook her head. "We have no evidence, not one shred of proof, no real reason to suspect him."

Then there was no other option. "I'll call Ava, explain that we're gettin' nowhere, and ask for her help getting Jack's phone records."

Elizabeth threaded her fingers through Quinn's. "I thought you were against that."

He wasn't happy about it. "We've no choice. It's like you said. Without those records, we've got nothin'."

Elizabeth's gaze was soft with sympathy. "I can speak with her if you'd like."

Quinn nodded. "Thanks."

He took out his mobile and called Ava.

WHILE QUINN WENT to get a dinner of fish and chips, Elizabeth sat in the hotel's business center, printing out all of the data from Jack's two cell phones dating back to the beginning of October—incoming and outgoing calls, text messages, data transfers, and GPS locations. Ava trusted Quinn so completely that she hadn't asked any difficult questions, except, perhaps for one.

"The police already have all of this," she'd asked on speaker. "Do you think you'll find something they haven't?"

"I won't know until I have time to analyze it," Elizabeth had answered. "I look at things differently from the police. They want evidence that will stand up in a trial. I look at patterns of behavior—what drives people."

"Please find the bastard who did this. He took Jack from us. He destroyed my life and that of my little girls."

"I'll do my best, Ava. I promise."

It had taken the rest of the morning and most of the afternoon to help Ava claim the phone account—she didn't know the password because Jack had always paid the bills—and talk her through how to access the necessary data. In the end, getting the data this way had been easier than hacking the account and one hundred percent less likely to land Elizabeth in prison.

With a month's worth of data from two phones, there were almost a hundred pages, and it took a few minutes to print. Elizabeth's gaze drifted to the nearby TV and the news broadcast. More fighting over Brexit. Strikes at universities over pensions. A man stabbed in a car park robbery.

Then Jack's face appeared on the screen. Elizabeth recognized him from the photos she'd seen when she'd spoken with Ava.

"There is evidence that illegal drugs played a role in the murder of former SAS trooper Jack Murray, it has been revealed. Murray, who was found dead in a Glasgow alley early in the mornin' of November third, worked as part of the private security team of MSP Alastair Whitehall."

Poor Ava. It must be hell on her to lose the man she loved and then watch another side of him emerge in the media. Not that Elizabeth was certain Jack had been involved with drugs. But if she'd been asked to assess the probability, she'd have put it at a solid ninety-five percent, and that was tempering it by Quinn's faith in him.

The footage cut away to an older dark-haired man in an expensive suit. So that was MSP Alastair Whitehall.

"Jack Murray was a hard-working member of my team. If he were found to have been selling illegal drugs, I would be quite surprised, indeed. My thoughts are with his family during this trying time. Thank you. No further comment."

Two things hit Elizabeth. The first was that Alastair, too, found it hard to believe that Jack could have sold drugs. The second was that the MSP's accent was completely different from Quinn's, almost more English than Scottish.

No wonder Leo hated him.

Then the image of a pretty young blond-haired girl appeared on the screen.

"Police are lookin' for anyone with information about the overdose death of fourteen-year-old Katie Cameron. Cameron, of Muirhouse, was reported missin' in October. Her body was found last week in a ditch at a construction site outside of Edinburgh."

Muirhouse.

Why did Elizabeth know that name?

Thurston Tower, where Clive MacDonald lived, was in Muirhouse.

The printer beeped to let Elizabeth know it was out of paper. She refilled it, waiting while the last handful of pages finished printing. She charged the copies to her room and was on her way back toward the bank of elevators when her phone buzzed.

She glanced at the screen. A notification from the security cam in Quinn's room. He'd probably just gotten back with their food and—

Her heart gave a hard knock, adrenaline hitting her blood stream.

The image on her screen wasn't Quinn.

Shit!

She stared as a man with a balaclava covering his face moved through the room, as if searching for something.

The man who attacked Quinn.

Chills shivered down her spine.

Her phone rang, making her jump.

Quinn. Thank God!

"Where are you?"

"I'm in the business center. There's a man—"

"I saw the bastard. That's him—the man I saw that night. I'm on my way back. Dinnae go up to the rooms. Stay in a public place. Do you hear me? He'll kill you."

"I'm not stupid enough to confront this guy." She watched as the figure on the screen prowled through the room, looking in drawers, searching Quinn's bags. Then he disappeared into the bedroom. "We should alert hotel security, call the police."

"Naw, he'll gut those poor hotel security boys."

The assailant reappeared then opened Quinn's duffel and put something inside it.

"He just put something in your duffel bag."

"Stay where you are. I'm almost there."

Elizabeth watched as the intruder left the room, disappearing from view. "He left. I'm going to position myself in the lobby where I can see the elevators."

"He'll have a wound on his left cheek where I stabbed him. Dinnae follow him. Dinnae go near him. Do you hear me? I'm on my way from the car park."

"You be careful, too. He'll recognize you."

Printed pages in hand, she ended the call, hurried to the

lobby near the fireplace, and sat where she had a clear view of the elevators, pretending to read the documents in her hands. One of the elevator cars was on its way down. Had it started at their floor? She hadn't noticed.

Elizabeth's breath caught and held as the elevator doors opened.

An older couple stepped out.

The bastard must have taken the stairs.

Damn it!

Q uinn pushed his way through the hotel's front entrance, found Elizabeth waiting for him, relief washing through him to see that she was safe. They walked together through the lobby toward the elevators, speaking in hushed tones.

"He must have taken the stairs. No one has stepped out of the elevator who could have been him—male or female. They're all too short, too old, or too overweight. I should have called the police."

"He'd have been gone afore they got here." Quinn didn't want her blaming herself. "I'm just glad you were down here and not in your room."

The idea of this murdering bastard getting anywhere close to Elizabeth turned Quinn's stomach.

"Shouldn't we report the break-in to hotel security and the police anyway?"

"I'm no' callin' them until I know what he put in my bag."

"Good point."

They rode the elevator to their floor, Quinn's hand resting near his hip in case he needed to draw.

Elizabeth's eyes went wide. "Don't tell me you're carrying a..."

Her words trailed off and she glanced up at the surveillance cameras.

"I willnae tell you, and you know nothin' about it."

It took what seemed like an eternity to reach the fifth floor, the elevator doors opening onto an empty, silent hallway.

Keeping his hand near his weapon, he walked with Elizabeth to his room, unlocked the door, and stepped inside, Elizabeth behind him. He didn't have to clear the place because she'd watched the bastard leave.

"He seemed to be searching for something."

"Aye, I saw that." Quinn walked to his duffel, nudged it open. "Fuck!"

Sitting inside was a plastic package holding something white.

Elizabeth looked. "Drugs."

"He's tryin' to frame me, so he is."

"If he's trying to frame you, it must mean the police are on their way." Elizabeth walked to the coffee table, set down the papers and the bag of food.

"What?"

"He knows you'd find that quickly, so he'll have tipped off the police right away. Thank God we have the video to prove your innocence."

"I'm no' sure it's legal to have surveillance cameras in our suites because this isnae our property." He wasn't sure about Scottish law but knew it was likely more restrictive than laws in the US. "We might face charges for vandalism or violation of privacy laws."

"Then let's get rid of the stuff. Do you have a knife?"

"Aye." He reached down, drew the blade out of his ankle rig.

"Cut it open and flush it down the toilet while I search your bedroom to make sure there's not more. Don't spill it on the floor or get it on your clothes."

Quinn hurried with the package and the knife to the bathroom, puncturing the plastic, carefully spilling whatever it was into the water, and flushing.

Elizabeth rushed in, a small plastic bag in her hands. "This was in your nightstand."

"The fucker." Quinn dumped out the smaller bag then ripped up all of the plastic and flushed it, too. "Let's hope this doesn't back up."

"Wash your hands." She washed hers also and wiped the counter dry. "When they get here, they'll search the place. You need to hide that firearm and the knife. If they have dogs..."

Then it hit Quinn. "Did you turn your camera on when you went below?"

Her eyes went wide. "Oh, God! I didn't even think of it."

They hurried across the hall to her room, stepped inside.

"My laptop is still here." She glanced around. "If he was here, he saw the white board and knows what we know."

"Check for drugs."

They split up, searched the rooms.

"There's a bunch of it here!" she called from the bedroom.

Son of a bitch!

He gave her his knife. "You start dumpin'. I'll keep searchin'."

He did his best to be thorough and found a small bag holding wee white rocks beneath her pillow and another beneath the cushions on the sofa and carried both to the bathroom. "Jesus!"

There had to be four kilos of—was it heroin or cocaine?—sitting on the floor.

"Someone is spending a fortune to try to make us look guilty," she said. "But why plant so much of it on me?"

That was easy.

"You're the brains." He dumped the other stuff into the toilet and began shredding the plastic. "If they take you out, doll, I'm fucked."

From outside came the sound of sirens.

"Police." Elizabeth's gaze met his, panic on her face as she tore open the last package. "God, I hope we found it all. You'll need to hide the firearm, too—and erase the whiteboard."

He hurried from the bathroom, used a fistful of tissues to erase the whiteboard, then sprinted out into the hallway and down to the ice machine several doors away. He hid both weapons deep in the ice then ran back to the bathroom to wash his hands—only to find Elizabeth naked and the shower running.

She smiled, reached for him, a seductress, only her eyes showing fear. "We need to look busy. This will distract them."

It distracted Quinn, too.

From out in the hallway came the sound of men's voices.

He got naked and stepped into the shower with Elizabeth.

She pressed kisses to his chest, reached down to stroke his cock. "Your heart is pounding. They'll sense our adrenaline. We have to look completely surprised when they burst in here. Back me up against the wall. Make it real."

He did as she asked, willing himself to focus on the sight

of her body, the feel of her breast in his hand, the taste of her lips.

"Police!"

Elizabeth screamed.

ELIZABETH HID her breasts and privates, doing her best to look shocked and terrified, which wasn't too hard with five police officers staring at her.

None of them had anything more lethal than a Taser.

"What the fuck are you doin' in here?" Quinn covered his half-hard cock with his hands, putting himself between Elizabeth and the other men and sounding truly furious.

"Sorry to interrupt." PC Patel walked in, looking smug and self-satisfied, her gaze meeting Elizabeth's. "Nice black eye."

"It's no big deal."

Then Patel's gaze dropped to Quinn's groin.

Poor Quinn.

Quinn didn't seem to care. He reached for a towel.

"Not so fast. Step out of the shower, Mr. McManus." Patel gestured to the men behind her. "Go with these officers. Get Nyla in here."

"You want me walkin' about, naked and wet?"

"Aye—until we've searched the towels and your clothes."

He did as she demanded. "Get these men the fuck out of here. I'll no' have them starin' at her, the bastards."

Elizabeth waited until Quinn had gone and a second female officer had arrived then stepped out of the shower, lifted her hair, and made a slow circle. "I'm assuming you've got a reason for being here—other than staring at Quinn's dick."

Patel's expression hardened, and she held out two documents for Elizabeth to see. "We've got a warrant to search your suites for drugs."

"Drugs now, is it?" Elizabeth laughed then pointed to her clothes. "Can I dress?"

Patel searched them, found nothing. "Yes."

Elizabeth stepped into her panties. "I'd like a copy of that warrant. I believe I have the right to make that request."

"If we find drugs, you might be facin' a body cavity search."

"I'm sure that would make you happy, but you need a warrant for that here just like you would in the States." Elizabeth put on her bra and then her jeans. "There are no drugs here. You're wasting your time. I already told you that neither of us is involved in anything like that. You should be hunting for Jack's killer. This is harassment."

"We'll see." Oh, Patel was smug.

Elizabeth finished dressing, hoping to God that she and Quinn had found everything. The two of them were made to sit under guard in the hallway, their feet bare, their wrists cuffed behind their backs, while their rooms were ransacked by a team of officers wearing gloves. For some reason, the police hadn't yet noticed the cameras. Then again, she and Quinn had tried to make them inconspicuous.

"Well, I didn't see this coming." Elizabeth couldn't help but laugh at the absurdity of their situation—letting themselves get caught naked in the shower together, Patel gaping at Quinn's semi-erect penis, the two of them now cuffed.

"What's funny about this?" Quinn was clearly not amused.

"All sorts of things."

"Do you think Grant is behind it?" Quinn whispered.

"He could be."

"It's quite the coincidence that we confronted him yesterday. You know I dinnae believe in coincidences."

Elizabeth had other thoughts. "What I want to know is how they got that warrant so quickly. It's like they were just waiting for his call so they could pounce. He must have a connection in the police department."

Then Wilson stepped out of the elevator, looking more than a little harried.

"What the fuck is going' on?" He glanced down at the two of them as he passed, his gaze lingering on Elizabeth's cheek before he entered Quinn's suite.

"Our food is probably cold." Elizabeth was hungry.

"Aye. Bastards."

After what seemed an eternity but was only an hour and a half, Elizabeth and Quinn were permitted to stand, and a young officer removed their handcuffs.

Wilson stepped out into the hallway, Patel behind him, the printouts of Jack's cell phone records in his hands. "What are these?"

"You know what those are." Elizabeth wouldn't play games with him. "I acquired them with the help of their rightful owner. There's nothing illegal going on here. Besides, I believe the warrant was for drugs."

"It looks like someone took a fist to you." Wilson's gaze shifted accusingly to Quinn. "Any idea who it was?"

Quinn's eyes went cold as slate. "A bastard tried to mug her yesterday when we were walking to the beach at Troon. She refused to let go of her handbag, so he swung and almost knocked her out. I'd have gone after him, but I was seein' to her. We had a visit from a paramedic last night. The front desk can confirm that."

"Why didn't you report it to the police?"

Elizabeth let her irritation show. "Right now, I'm not your biggest fan. Besides, I was pretty sure you'd try to blame Quinn."

An officer stepped out of Elizabeth's room with the blister pack of narcotic tablets the paramedic had given her. "This is the only thing we've found."

Thank God!

"Those are from the paramedic who treated me last night."

Wilson took them, turned them over, handed them to Elizabeth. "We got a tip from a trusted informant that there were drugs here. Either you knew we were comin' and got rid of the stuff, or our informant was wrong."

Quinn got in his face, crowding him. "Your informant was full of shite."

"As I'm sure you know, I'm a former counterterrorism analyst. Want my advice?" Elizabeth would give it to Wilson whether he wanted it or not. "Trace this tip carefully to its true source, and you'll be looking Jack Murray's killer in the face."

QUINN WATCHED Elizabeth's words sink into Wilson's thick skull. "I've worked with her for close to five years now. I've never known her to be wrong."

"If I brought drug dogs in, what would they find?" Wilson asked.

"I don't know." Elizabeth shrugged. "That depends on who stayed in this room before us, doesn't it? We're not drug users or dealers. Want me to pee in a cup?"

Quinn bit his cheeks to keep from laughing.

Och, she had a mouth, his Lilibet.

"Possibly." Wilson handed her back the pages she'd printed and instructed his team to move out.

Then PC Patel stepped out of Elizabeth's room, looking particularly glum.

Elizabeth gave her a frosty smile. "No body cavity search for me today, I guess."

Patel said nothing but threaded her way through the other officers and moved down the hallway.

"In case you're wondering, size really does matter," Elizabeth whispered to her as she passed.

Quinn couldn't help but grin.

When the police had gone, they returned to Quinn's suite. "Och, what a mess."

It was going to be a long evening.

They got to work in his room first, putting his clothes back on his closet shelves, calling housekeeping to change the sheets and replace the towels that had been thrown onto the floor, picking up his toiletries. Then they did the same in her room.

"You hungry?" They crossed the hallway to his room, where Quinn picked up the bag of fish and chips. "It's long since cold."

They tried reheating it in the microwave, but that left the fish tough and the breading mushy. So, they turned on their security cameras and took the bag with them down to the ground floor, where the concierge was happy to compost its contents with the kitchen scraps. They got a table in the restaurant, Quinn ordering another steak with whisky, while she had the roast chicken again with a glass of sauvignon blanc.

"Cheers."

She raised her glass, but he could see that the initial rush of relief had worn off.

"It's going to be hard to sleep tonight. He was here, Quinn. He might have been waiting and watching for us to leave the rooms. He made his way past all of this security and hacked our locks with no trouble. If you hadn't set your camera…"

Quinn took her hand. "Do you want to move to another hotel?"

She shook her head. "How would another hotel help? It took him only a handful of days to find us here. He'll just do it again. This time, maybe he'll succeed. Or maybe he'll plant drugs in your rental vehicle."

It wasn't often that Quinn saw Elizabeth shaken up. The last time had been when he'd pulled her away from that warlord's henchmen at the airport in Mazar-e-Sharif.

He ran his thumb over her knuckles. "Maybe you should fly back to the States."

She glared at him. "And leave you alone? Didn't you just say I'm the brains and you'd be screwed without me?"

Well, she had him there.

"I couldnae live wi' myself if anythin' happened to you, Lilibet."

"I couldn't live with myself if I went back to Denver and you wound up dead."

Quinn lowered his voice, leaned closer. "You're an intelligence expert. I'm an SAS veteran. We work for the best private security firm in the world."

"You think we should call Cobra."

"It's either that or we hide—stay in some cash-only hotel, dump our mobile phones and get a burner, return the rental and use the underground and buses."

She nodded. "Well, I need internet to work."

"I would rather lose my job a thousand times than risk your life."

They finished their dinner and went back up to Elizabeth's room, where Elizabeth called Corbray. She had a closer relationship with their bosses than Quinn did.

"Hey, Javier. I'm okay. Thanks. Actually, I need to have a video chat with you and Derek as soon as possible. I'm with Quinn in Scotland. I came over to help him look into the murder of his friend. The killer isn't happy about that and broke into our hotel rooms today to plant drugs on us. I brought my laptop, so I'll log into our systems via VPN. Thanks. Talk to you soon."

"What did he say?"

"He was about to go into a meeting at the Pentagon. He canceled it. He'll call Tower and be online with us in ten minutes."

15

"What the hell happened to you two?" Javier Corbray filled half of Elizabeth's computer screen, Derek Tower the other half, the former in D.C., the latter in Denver.

"I was attacked by the man who's likely responsible for the murder of my best friend." Quinn held up his arm. "He tried to knife me, but I blocked it and got him in the face wi' my blade. Shields was punched by an asshole who might be smugglin' drugs and aidin' terrorists, though we've no proof of that."

Derek remained impassive. "Could you put that into context for us?"

Corbray raised a hand. "Are you okay, Shields?"

"I've got a mild concussion, but I'll be fine." She didn't want to tell them that it was hard for her to look at computer screens. She'd deal with that later if necessary.

"And you didn't kill this asshole, McManus?"

"Och, I wanted to break his neck, but I couldnae because I was holdin' her and he had two armed goons wi' him."

"Shields?" Tower was getting impatient.

Elizabeth gave them a report as if she were checking in from the field, keeping it professional, focusing on relevant people and events—and omitting the fact that she and Quinn were sleeping together.

"Then, this evening when I was printing Jack's phone records, the man who attacked Quinn made it past the hotel's security cameras, hacked our door locks, and planted a total of six kilos of cocaine and small amounts of other drugs in our rooms. Because Quinn had turned on his security camera, we were alerted and able to get rid of the drugs before the police arrived. It was a very close call."

"Why didn't you just show them the footage?" Tower asked.

Elizabeth deferred to Quinn on that question.

"We'd likely be facin' vandalism and privacy charges if we'd done that."

"Let me make sure I understand this." Tower wasn't happy. "Two of our key operatives took vacation time following a successful but exhausting mission and are using that time, which is intended for them to rest and return to peak performance, to track down a murderer, resulting in physical injury and a threat to their freedom and their lives? Do I have that right?"

Elizabeth knew it was best for them to own it. "Yes."

"Shields is only here because I asked her—"

"Yeah, man, we got that part." Corbray seemed to mull it all over. "A guy decks Shields when you asked him about drug smuggling yesterday, and someone planted drugs on you this evening."

"Yes, sir."

"Suspicious timing," Tower said.

"Agreed." Corbray nodded. "I'm guessing neither of you

is willing to let the police handle this and come back to the US on the next flight."

Quinn shook his head. "Jack was my best friend. We fought together for ten years. You both know what that means. I promised his wife I'd do whatever I could to help catch this bastard."

"I promised Quinn I'd help with the intel side of things."

Corbray nodded. "That's what I thought. We're going to end the call now. Tower and I need to talk. We'll call you back shortly."

The screen went blank.

"Well, that wisnae so bad." Quinn stood, moved behind Elizabeth, rested his hands on her shoulders.

"They're not happy. I can tell you that much."

"Aye, but they didnae fire us."

"Not yet."

Fifteen long minutes later, Corbray and Tower were back.

Corbray spoke first. "McManus, we understand you standing by a brother like this. Shields, in your way that's what you're doing, too, standing by McManus. But the killer is onto you. You were right to call, though we wish you'd called sooner."

Elizabeth tried not to let her relief show.

"We'd like to go over parts of this in detail—the possible terrorist threat, in particular. But right now, the priority is getting the two of you to a safe location. Clearly, the hotel is not safe. We're moving you to our suite in Glasgow within the hour."

Elizabeth and Quinn looked at each other and then back at the screen.

"You've got a facility here—in Glasgow?" she asked.

It just figured.

"It's just an office with a kitchen and a few bedrooms—nothing fancy—but it's in a building owned by British Intelligence. The place is a fortress. So that's the first step."

The two men outlined the rest of the plan.

Tower had called in some favors with British Intelligence, which would return the rental vehicle and provide the two of them with Cobra's armored Land Rover. Corbray planned to file a complaint through the embassy in hopes that it would get the police to back off. In return, British Intelligence wanted to chat about Leo Grant.

"This isn't a Cobra operation, but British Intelligence has agreed to grant you a kind of provisional status. It won't keep you out of jail if you're caught breaking the law—so don't break the law. But it ought to open some doors for you."

"You arranged this in fifteen minutes?" Elizabeth was impressed—and relieved. "Thanks so much."

"Aye, you've got our thanks."

"McManus, I'm looking straight at you now," Tower said, his expression grave. "You've got the combat and tactical experience. It's your job to keep Shields—and yourself—safe. That is your first priority before any obligation to your friend or his widow. Am I being crystal clear?"

"Aye, sir."

Corbray shook his head, grinned. "You know, McManus, only you could go home for a funeral and end up fighting the murderer and then falling ass-first into a possible terrorist cell."

Quinn looked offended. "That disnae seem funny to me."

Even Tower smiled now. "I expect a report every morning. When you get back to the US, we're going to have a long talk."

"Right." Elizabeth ended the conference call, stood. "It's time to pack."

QUINN SLID his thumb over the biometric scanner again.

"Your biometric scans give you access to the front entrance, the gym, the garage, and the door to Cobra's flat," said Nigel Rhys-Jones, the security chief for the building. "The other facilities in the building remain off-limits."

Elizabeth was next. "Index finger first?"

"Yes, and then your thumb." Nigel's gaze fell on her cheek. "You've had a rough time of it here in the UK. If the bastard who gave you that black eye tries to get in here, he's going to face a rather hostile reception."

"We're very grateful." She smiled, but Quinn could see she was hurting.

"A headache?"

She nodded, swiped her index finger a second time. "It's not too bad."

"When we get settled, you need to rest, aye?"

Rhys-Jones frowned. "We've got a doctor available if you need one."

"Thanks, but all I need is sleep." She scanned her index finger for the last time then waited while Rhys-Jones reset the scanner for her thumb. "I think all the excitement today was too much."

Quinn explained. "The bastard gave her a concussion."

"Just tell me whom we need to kill, and we'll be on it."

Aye, Quinn liked this fella already.

When they were both in the system, Rhys-Jones led them to the lift, where Elizabeth pressed her finger to the scanner to call the car.

"You head up." Quinn stepped back. "I'll get our bags."

"Your bags were taken up to the flat when you arrived," Rhys-Jones said.

"Wow." Elizabeth met Quinn's gaze. "Talk about service."

Rhys-Jones grinned. "Cobra has done some big favors for British Intelligence, gotten our operatives out of some tight spots, intervened for us with the Pentagon. It's nice to be able to return the favor."

This was news to Quinn—and to Elizabeth, too, it seemed.

"Thank you. Truly. It means a lot to us."

The lift arrived, and Rhys-Jones rode with them up to the fourth floor, where they found a long hallway of black marble and burnished steel.

"This is Cobra's flat." He walked over, pointed to the biometric lock. "You can let yourselves in. We managed to get the kitchen stocked, but if you find that you need something, let us know. Is there anything else I can do for you?"

"No, thanks, man." Quinn shook his hand.

"You've been incredibly helpful."

"Get some rest." Rhys-Jones stepped back into the lift and was gone.

Elizabeth pressed her finger to the pad, and the door buzzed.

Click.

They walked through the doorway—and stared.

Black marble floors. Windows of tinted privacy glass. High ceilings.

"Yeah, nothing fancy. Good grief!" Elizabeth glanced around. "Did you know about this place?"

"Naw—but I like it."

Their bags sat on the floor just inside the door.

Quinn picked up their bags. "Let's find our rooms."

The four bedrooms, each with its own small bathroom, were down a short hallway on the north side of the flat.

Elizabeth flicked on the light in the first room to the right. "We should at least pretend to sleep in separate rooms."

"Aye." He set her bag inside, then dropped his in the room across from hers.

They explored after that—the living area with its huge flat-screen TV and leather sofas, the kitchen with its white granite counters, the office with its sleek modern desks and computer screens. It also had a huge, built-in whiteboard.

Elizabeth's face lit up the moment she saw the office. "Now we're talking."

Quinn was glad just to see her smile.

They settled into their rooms, Quinn putting a kettle on to boil for tea. Then they sat together in the living room, sipping tea and looking out at the city lights, Elizabeth leaning back against his chest.

He kissed her hair. "You saved us today. It didnae even cross my mind that the police would already be on their way. If I'd been here alone, I'd be in the nick tonight."

"You're welcome." She tilted her head to the side to look up at him. "I still can't believe we pulled it off. It was so close."

Then she laughed. "Did you see the way Patel looked at your dick?"

Quinn laughed, too. "I moved my hands, gave her the full monty. You'd think she'd never seen a naked man afore. How's your heid?"

"It's a little better." She stood, held out her hand. "We should get some sleep."

They carried their cups to the kitchen, brushed their teeth, and got ready for bed.

Then Quinn slid naked beneath the covers and drew Elizabeth against him, his chest her pillow. "Sleep, Lilibet."

Elizabeth awoke to soft kisses along her shoulder and nape, Quinn behind her, his erection pressing into her lower back. "Mmm. Good morning."

"Mornin', beautiful." He fondled her breasts, teased her nipples, bringing her fully awake—and making her ache for him.

He nibbled her earlobe, still playing with her nipples, drawing them to tight points, caressing their tips with his callused palm. Then he reached down to cup her.

He knew her body now, knew what she loved—and he made her wait for it. Instead of lavishing attention on her clit, he ran his fingertip around the entrance to her vagina, tickled her inner thighs, toyed with her lips.

She moaned in frustration, laughed. "Oh, you mean, awful man!"

He chuckled, nipped her shoulder, keeping up the torment until she was whimpering, her hands balled into fists. "Is it this you're wantin'?"

He stroked her clit, earning an "*Oooh, yes!*"

She was already so aroused that a few minutes of this had her on the brink. When he thrust his cock into her, she came, pleasure shimmering through her. "Oh... *God!*"

When the tremors inside her had ebbed, he turned her onto her belly, forcing her legs wide apart with his own, making her gasp. Then he caught her wrists, pinned them to the bed above her head, and began to move, thrusting into her from behind, going deep. "Och, you feel so good."

She'd never had sex like this before, flat and spread-eagle on her belly. Quinn completely dominated her, fucking her hard, his big, muscular body seeming to surround her, holding her in place, his cock caressing some sensitive place inside her.

She'd never come from penetration alone before, not even with Quinn, but each thrust pushed her closer and closer to the edge, until her every exhale was a cry, her fingers clenching the sheets, the ache inside her unbearable.

This time when she came, it was different, orgasm rolling through her like thunder, getting stronger with each thrust. "Quinn!"

But he was right there with her, groaning as pleasure claimed him.

He sank onto the bed beside her, drew her back against him. "I cannae get enough of you, Lilibet."

They snuggled for a while, but hunger got the better of them. They made breakfast together—scrambled eggs and toast—then showered. And then it was time to get to work.

She and Quinn sorted through the pages she'd printed, dividing the two phones' data and then separating them into piles based on content—phone calls, text messages, voice-mail, downloads and uploads, transactions, and GPS locations.

They started with the original phone. It was painstaking work, as they listed calls from contacts—his neighbor, Ava, Andrew, rugby club pals—and then looked up every number that wasn't identified.

"Another scam call."

"Aye, lots of those."

Almost all of the calls not in his contacts turned out to be scam calls, though some were legitimate. One had come from a pediatrician's office, another from the dry cleaners about his suit, and several from a dog breeder about a puppy.

Elizabeth wanted to cry. "He reserved a puppy as a surprise for Ava and the girls. The breeder has been leaving him messages. I guess she doesn't watch the news. You should call her, let her know what happened. We should tell Ava."

There was nothing unusual in his text messages or voicemails. The vast majority had come from Ava, the text messages including photos of their girls, moments from daily life for the father who couldn't be home. Olivia with lunch all over her face. Olivia and Isla asleep in a pile on the sofa. Isla sniffing a bright pink rose.

Elizabeth swallowed the lump in her throat. "These poor little girls. They won't even remember him."

A muscle clenched in Quinn's jaw. "He'll never be more than a man in a photograph to them."

Most of Jack's data uploads were images of the girls he had passed on to his sister, Hannah, though he had also sent and forwarded some emails to Ava, Hannah, Andrew Lewis, and Quinn.

Quinn read one exchange between the two men arguing about who'd been drunker after a game of rugby, chuckling to himself. "Och, there's no way that Lewis could outdrink Murray. Murray can put away a half bottle of..."

Quinn's words trailed off. "He used to..."

"I'm sorry." Elizabeth was getting to know Jack, too, watching the last few weeks of his life unfold in calls and messages, photos and emails.

They moved on to transactions, and there was only one —flowers for Ava.

Notably, there were no calls, text messages, or emails from Leo.

"Grant said he'd had no contact wi' Jack after their argument. It seems he was tellin' the truth."

Elizabeth had noticed that, too, but they still had the GPS data to analyze.

"There are no calls, no data, no texts—nothing at all—after he bought the new phone on October twenty-first, except for the call he made to you a week later." Then Elizabeth noticed something interesting. "There is still a lot of GPS data from that point on. He continued to carry the phone with him until the day he called you."

She looked at the last GPS location for the phone and checked the date and time against his last call. "The last thing he did with his original phone was call you."

16

Q uinn sat with Elizabeth in one of the offices that British Intelligence maintained in the building. "Now I know where our tax money goes."

A man who introduced himself as Agent Smith—aye, right—sat across from them. "I hear you might have something for us."

Elizabeth shook her head. "Not really. It's just circumstantial. I don't know that I would even call it intelligence."

She told them about their experience with that bastard Grant and her intuition that he'd learned something about her that worried him.

"His gaze jerked to me for just a moment. It wasn't casual. He was laser-focused on me for just a second, and he wasn't happy. The only thing I can imagine is that he somehow found out I used to be a counterterrorism analyst."

Smith frowned. "How would he learn that?"

"A few people here know. Quinn. You all. Ava Murray and her sister-in-law. Oh, yes, and PC Patel with Police Scotland. Maybe Grant has access to inside sources of information."

Smith nodded. "Interesting."

"There's a leak in the police station." Quinn knew this was outside Smith's jurisdiction, but he told Smith anyway. "Someone has been leakin' details about the investigation into Jack Murray's death to the media."

Smith listened, then shifted his attention back to Elizabeth. "I heard that Grant gave you that black eye."

Elizabeth told him what Quinn had said and how Leo had reacted. "I took the punch to be an admission of guilt about drug smuggling. Grant was sad about Jack's death. Of that I'm certain. But he also wanted us off the property the moment he got that call. Why would he be afraid of a former counterterrorism analyst?"

"I see where you're going with this. Also, why would the owner of a freight shipping company do background checks on anyone, particularly two people who aren't doing business with him? That's all highly irregular—and not something he ought to be able to do, legally speaking."

"The men workin' for him are carryin' firearms, and the ones we met are all Irish—though bein' Irish disnae prove anythin'."

Smith looked surprised. "Carrying weapons? I doubt they have permits. Did they draw on you?"

"Naw, but I could see they were carryin' pistols in concealed shoulder holsters. I do that all the time, so I know well what it looks like. Their jackets were uneven at the bottom, and the way they held their left arms..."

"I know what you mean." Then Smith went over some of the details with them. "You went to see him because you thought perhaps he was behind your friend's murder?"

"Yes." Elizabeth filled in the blanks. "He said he had no

contact with Jack after their argument, and so far, the data we've gotten from Jack's phones shows he was telling the truth. We haven't checked the GPS data yet."

"The drugs that were planted in your hotel room—that happened the day after you confronted Grant at his place in Troon?"

"Aye." It had to be Grant. *The bastard.*

Smith got to his feet. "Thank you for sharing this."

Quinn and Elizabeth stood, too.

"I wish we had something more actionable, more concrete for you. I feel a little embarrassed to be able to tell you only that he looked at me strangely and then tried to punch Quinn."

Smith smiled. "What you gave us might be more helpful than you realize. You can take the lift back up to your suite."

"Thank you, Mr. Bond," Elizabeth said, joking. "Sorry. I couldn't resist."

Smith grinned. "I'm not Bond. I'm Smith. We keep Bond in the cellar. He's rather full of himself and tends to break things."

Back up in the suite, they had a late lunch and a fresh cuppa then sat down again to work on the GPS data.

Quinn noticed it first. "The two phones—the old and the new—they went to all the same places until the old one disappeared."

Elizabeth double-checked, comparing the GPS coordinates, times, and dates. "You're right. That saves us a lot of effort."

They spent the next hour getting organized, grouping locations together, places Jack had gone more than once.

"All of these locations are in or between Glasgow and Edinburgh."

"Aye, he didnae go to Troon. He didnae go to any port towns."

"We've got nothing here that ties Jack to Grant or his shipping business." Elizabeth let out a frustrated breath. "I understand now why the police don't seem interested in Grant."

Then they got down to the hard work—matching each GPS coordinate with a destination. They started with the places he'd gone the most—home, the supermarket, the same handful of petrol stations, a bakery, Hannah's house, the pub, the hardware store, a nightclub, Holyrood.

He'd run errands for his family after work most nights, errands that would now be left to Ava to manage on her own with two wee ones.

Poor Ava.

Elizabeth typed in another location. "That looks like a soccer field."

Quinn had more experience with satellite images. "Those are goal posts. See? That's a rugby pitch—and over here, doll, it's no' soccer. It's football."

"Whatever." She smiled. "It's all just men playing with their balls."

He leaned over, pressed a kiss to her nose. "As I recall, you like men's balls."

After three tedious hours, they were left with a few unknowns—the place he went every Friday night, likely for Whitehall's social events, and a handful of spots downtown where several businesses shared space in a single building.

Elizabeth stretched. "We can work on the rest tomorrow."

Quinn stood, walked behind her, rubbed her shoulders. "I've got a few ideas about how we can spend the evenin'."

"Mmm." Elizabeth's eyes drifted shut. "So do I."

"IT'S RIGHT *in front of you, Shields. Why can't you see it?"*
Comstock glared at her.

She looked down at the page. There was nothing but scribbles and gibberish that seemed to be different every time she tried to make sense of them. "I can't read this."

"It's right in front of you! For God's sake, look!"

"I don't see anything." Now the page was blank.

How could that be?

"You're better than this. You're distracted. Focus!"

Elizabeth sat upright, felt a rush of relief to find that it was only a dream.

Quinn stirred, raised his head, rested a hand on her arm, his red hair tousled. "Are you okay, Lilibet?"

She lay back down, her pulse still tripping. "I dreamed I was still in training, and one of my instructors was yelling at me, telling me I needed to focus."

"Did somethin' happen wi' him? Is he one of—"

"No. Comstock was amazing. He taught me to get past my expectations and prejudgment to look at things critically, to see what was there and not what I wanted to see. I learned so much from him."

"Then it was just a dream and nothin' more."

Maybe. And then again...

"I can't shake the feeling that I'm missing something." She drew a deep breath, released it, her mind full of GPS locations and phone numbers. "The dream is right in one respect. I *am* distracted—because of us."

She turned to face him, pressed her cheek to his chest, felt the beating of his heart. "What are we doing—you and I? We both know this can't go anywhere. We knew that from the beginning. One or both of us would lose our jobs."

"I dinnae want to think about that, no' yet."

He kissed her then made love to her with his lips and tongue and cock, bringing her to a shattering climax once, twice, three times.

How could she give this up? How could she give *him* up?

As they lay together in the early morning darkness, she discovered she didn't want to think about their future, either.

ELIZABETH STOOD ON THE SIDEWALK, her feet freezing, Quinn beside her, rain pelting their umbrellas. "There's a nail salon. We can assume he didn't go there."

"He liked Indian food, so he might have stopped there for a wee bite."

"There's a sports bar, an Asian grocery, and a pet food shop. Maybe he went to get supplies for the puppy."

They had called the breeder this morning and discovered that Jack had, indeed, bought a little Labrador puppy for his daughters. The breeder had been trying to reach him because the little thing was weaned now. Quinn and Elizabeth had arranged to pick up the puppy—a female—later in the week. They would deliver it to Ava and her girls as the surprise Jack had intended her to be.

Elizabeth pointed. "There's also a post office branch. Maybe he bought stamps."

"When I still lived here, I bought mine at Tesco—the supermarket. It saved me the time and the trouble of findin' parking. I only went to the post office when I needed to post a package."

The ordinariness of it all was infuriating. They'd been all over Glasgow, trying to figure out where he might have gone in those cases in which more than one business occupied the space at a particular GPS location. Apart from identifying the store where he'd bought his new phone, it was a guessing game. Italian for lunch or ice cream? Coffee or a sandwich? Puppy food or curry?

She'd been expecting something sketchy or unusual.

It's right in front of you, Shields. Why can't you see it?

She brushed her dream aside. "This was the last known location of the old cell phone. After this, it vanishes off the face of the earth."

"Do you want to go from shop to shop, show clerks his photo, and ask if anyone remembers seein' him?"

"Why not?" They had nothing to lose. "You take the post office and pet food store and I'll—"

"We stay together, aye?"

Ten minutes later, they had no new information.

Quinn looked out at the parked cars. "Maybe he met someone here."

"Or maybe what we're looking for was on his work phone." This was starting to feel pointless. "I thought for sure his phone records would hold answers—threatening messages, repeated calls from some unidentifiable source. But my feet are soaked, and we've gotten nowhere."

Quinn glanced down at her wet shoes. "You need wellies."

He drove her to a store where a kind clerk helped her pick the right size and sold her a warm, dry pair of socks.

"Now that we've gotten that sorted, let's get some food, aye?"

Talk of curry had left them both craving Indian food, so they stopped at Quinn's favorite Indian spot for a late lunch, the food and chai tea warming Elizabeth.

"You're no' lookin' so scunnered."

"So ... what?" She couldn't help but smile.

"Grumpy, upset."

"Maybe because my toes are warm again."

"Aye, that'll do it." He reached across the table, held her hand, regret and worry in his gaze. "I'm grateful for your help, Lilibet. I'm sorry it's been so difficult."

She looked straight into his eyes. "It hasn't been all bad, you know. Some of it has been really good—incredible, mind-blowing, fantastic."

His lopsided grin told her he'd caught her meaning. He leaned closer. "I love to hear you screamin' my name."

Heat rushed into her cheeks. "I love to feel you, the big tough operator, breaking apart in my arms."

He insisted on paying for the meal, and they walked back to the car together, Quinn opening her door. "Where next?"

"All that's left is the location in Edinburgh."

"Let's leave that for tomorrow. You've spent enough time muckin' about in the wet. We can see Edinburgh Castle during the day and head over in the evening."

Elizabeth liked that idea. "Jack was always there on Friday evenings until late. Maybe that's what we should do."

"Och, well, that's it then. I'm takin' you out tonight. Do you have a nice dress?"

"Yes." She'd brought a little black dress just in case.

Not that she'd planned on sleeping with him or anything.

"I'll drop you off back at the Fortress and go and get somethin' for myself. We'll go after supper."

The Fortress was their nickname for their new abode.

"Go where?"

He grinned. "To the dancin', aye?"

He dropped her off in front of the building, watching

until she was safely indoors. Then he disappeared around the corner.

She took a hot bath and shaved, then did her best to make her stick-straight hair look stylish, tying it in a kind of messy bun. She'd just put on the dress and started on her makeup when she heard him enter.

He looked in on her. "Och, you're bonnie."

"What did you get?"

"No keekin'—no' yet." He disappeared across the hall.

She finished her make up and went to sit in the living room, imagining him in a suit like the one he'd worn in Afghanistan while escorting the senator—very GQ with that beard and his red hair.

It was almost twenty minutes later when he stepped out into the hall.

A bolt of lust shot through her, making her belly clench.

"Oh. My. *God*." Elizabeth stared.

He was wearing a kilt.

QUINN KNEW he was hitting the whisky hard, but, och, he was out dancing in Glasgow with Lilibet, and he felt like celebrating. "I'm goin' up next. I signed up when you went to the loo."

"You're singing karaoke?" She smiled but shook her head. "There's not enough alcohol in the world to make me do that."

If he lived to be a thousand years old, Quinn would never forget the look on her face when he stepped out of the room wearing the kilt. Her gaze had moved over him, desire naked on her sweet face. Then she'd asked what he was wearing beneath it, and he'd showed her.

He'd thought for a moment she was going to faint. Instead, she'd dropped to her knees and given him the best blow job of his life right then and there, climax all but making his knees buckle.

His Lilibet wasn't a cunning linguist for nothing.

She's no' yours.

He tossed back the rest of his whisky, tried to ignore that thought. They were together for tonight. She was here with him, not some other man.

They had already danced together until they were out of breath and sweating, Quinn unable to take his eyes off her, that little dress hiding all the delicious curves he'd come to know so well this past week. He couldn't wait to get her back to the flat.

The woman ahead of Quinn finished some tune he didn't recognize to the cheers of her friends then all but stumbled off the stage, clearly steamin'.

Quinn kissed Elizabeth hard. "This is for you."

"Oh, no, don't blame this on me!" she called after him, laughing.

Quinn took the stage. He knew the lyrics to The Proclaimers' "I'm Gonna Be (500 Miles)" like he'd written the song himself, and he felt every word as he belted it out, his gaze fixed on Elizabeth's. Och, he really would walk a thousand miles for her.

He'd give his life for her.

As he sang the last notes and the club exploded into applause, it hit him.

You're in love wi' her.

He stood on the stage, stunned, his heart pounding.

You're mad wi' it. It's just the whisky.

Naw, it was the truth. He was in love with a woman he had no business loving, a woman who didn't love him back, a woman he couldn't have.

Someone took the mic from him. Somehow, he found his way down the stairs to the dance floor, where Elizabeth rushed up to him and threw her arms around him.

"I didn't know you could sing like that."

He kissed her, long and hard. "I need a drink."

"Haven't you had enough?" She walked with him to the bar, looking worried.

Annoyance stabbed at him. "Dinnae worry yourself. I can hold my liquor."

He drank another shot and another and another, trying to still the emotional storm inside him. When that didn't work, he led her onto the dance floor again, the two of them dancing to a bloody awful rendition of some old disco tune —until a man slammed into Quinn, pushing him off balance so that he stepped on Lilibet's foot.

Quinn turned, confronted the bastard, fists clenched. "Bolt, ya fuckin' arse."

"Ya want to fight, ya daft bastard?

"Quinn, it's okay. It was an accident. Come on. You're both drunk." She took hold of his wrist, pulled him away. "Please, Quinn. I want to go home."

"Ye'd best listen tae yer American piece there."

Quinn didn't like to back down from a fight, but he didn't want Elizabeth getting caught in the middle of this. He followed her to collect their jackets and umbrellas and walked out toward the car.

She stopped him. "Oh, no, you're not driving. Give me the keys."

"Aye, you're right. Are you sure you know the way back?"

"As if." She dropped the keys into her handbag, pulled out her phone, and called someone. "Hi, it's Elizabeth Shields. I'm terribly sorry to bother you so late at night, but we're at the Temple. Quinn has had far too much to drink, and I've had wine. I'm not sure I can drive without wrecking this vehicle. Thanks so much. We'll be here."

"Who the bloody hell was that?" Quinn wasn't feeling so good.

"The security desk at the Fortress."

"You called fuckin' British Intelligence to give us a ride back?" The whole thing suddenly struck Quinn as hilarious. He laughed, a deep belly laugh. "I bet that's the first time they've been called out for that reason."

Elizabeth shook her head, her mouth a grim line. "Based on his reaction, I'm guessing not."

"Och, are you angry wi' me, Lilibet?" He didn't want that.

She glared up at him. "I was having a great time with you tonight until suddenly I wasn't. You drink too much, Quinn."

He opened his mouth to deny it—but closed it again, afraid he was about to get sick in front of her.

17

E lizabeth steered Quinn through the door to the flat, turning to face Nigel. "Thanks for coming out so late to pick us up. Thanks, too, for getting the car safely back here. We're both grateful."

Nigel grinned. "We've all been there. Work hard, play harder. Isn't that right, McManus?"

"Aye." Quinn had been quiet the entire way home.

He walked into his bedroom and disappeared into the bathroom for a good ten minutes, probably throwing up, leaving Elizabeth to wrestle with her emotions.

She kicked off her heels, peeled off her pantyhose, and went in search of every bottle of booze in the flat, starting with the new bottle of whisky he'd picked up today.

Tonight had been wonderful—at first. Seeing him in the kilt, watching him sing to her, knowing that he meant every word of it. Her heart had melted.

But when he'd come off that stage, he'd behaved as if emotional demons were chasing him. He'd slammed down shots, one after the other, seeming agitated on the dance floor, almost getting in a fight over nothing.

Anyone watching Quinn tonight would assume he was an alcoholic. Elizabeth might have believed that, too, if she hadn't known that he went for weeks and sometimes months without drinking a drop.

Cobra did not allow drinking on missions.

No man had ever made Elizabeth feel as cherished as Quinn. Most had been too busy competing with her, trying to prove that they were better at the job than she was.

But Quinn had never once put her down or tried to one-up her. His respect for her was evident every day on the job. It was one of the things that had drawn her to him. The fact that he was also big and ripped and handsome as hell hadn't hurt. Now she knew that he fucked like a god, too.

None of that would matter if he couldn't control his drinking. She couldn't build a life with a drunk.

The thought took her by surprise.

Was she thinking of this as a relationship now?

You're in deep trouble, girl.

Maybe so, but now it was her turn to show him how much she cared.

She carried the bottles to the kitchen, opened them, and dumped their contents down the drain. She was so wrapped up in watching the amber liquid disappear that she didn't hear Quinn walk up to her.

"What the bloody hell are you doin'?" Quinn's voice boomed through the flat, startling Elizabeth, making her jump. He yanked the bottle out of her hand, the blind fury on his face making her take a step backward, her pulse skipping. "You cannae just dump a man's Scotch down the drain! You're no' my fuckin' ma!"

Tears pricked Elizabeth's eyes, but she blinked them back. "Keep it—if that's what's important to you. But you and I don't stand a chance if you keep drinking like this. I won't get into a relationship with an alcoholic."

He jerked as if she'd struck him.

But she was done.

She turned and walked out of the kitchen toward her room.

"Elizabeth, I'm sorry. I didnae mean to shout at you. I... *Fuck.*"

She heard true remorse in his voice, stopped, faced him.

He leaned back against the kitchen wall, sliding down until he was sitting on the floor, still in his kilt, despair on his face. He held out the bottle he'd grabbed from her. "I'm sorry. Finish dumpin' it."

She walked back to him, took the bottle, poured the rest of it into the sink.

Quinn sat there, the anguish on his face putting a hitch in her chest.

She sat beside him, the tile cold on her bare thighs. "What is it, Quinn? You can tell me anything. You know that, don't you?"

For a moment, he said nothing, tension rolling off him.

When at last he spoke, his voice was quiet, almost devoid of emotion. "I grew up in social housin' just like Nicola—the damp seepin' through the walls, syringes in the halls, vomit and piss in the lift."

No wonder he'd been so tense when they'd gone to Thurston Tower.

"My da was a drunk. He never held a job for as long as I knew him. When he was drinkin', he beat me and my ma. Fists. Belt. A coat hanger." Quinn rubbed a small white scar on his forehead. "One time he struck me wi' a bottle."

Elizabeth took his hand. "I'm so sorry, Quinn. That must have been terrifying."

"When you're a child, you dinnae know that it disnae have to be that way. It's just the world you're livin' in, aye?"

"I suppose so." What a sad and terrible thought.

"As I got older, and after my sister was born, I tried to defend my ma, but she didnae want me comin' between her and my da's fists."

"It sounds to me like she was trying to protect you."

But Quinn was lost in memories and didn't seem to hear Elizabeth. "I grew angrier and angrier. I joined the South Bank Boys and took my rage out on the world. One night when my da was beatin' my mother, I threatened to kill him. I meant it, too."

"I can understand that."

"The next day, when my da went out to the pub, my ma packed up her things and Paige's and left. I wanted to go wi' her, but she wouldnae take me. 'You're too much like your da,' she said. She told me I frightened her. I stood there, watchin' as they walked out the door, the pain of it worse than any beatin'. That was the last time I cried."

Tears filled Elizabeth's eyes, her throat tight, her heart breaking for him. "How old were you?"

"Fourteen."

QUINN WAS glad he'd already emptied his belly. Talking about this turned his stomach. He hadn't planned on telling Elizabeth any of it, but he couldn't get past the look of fear on Elizabeth's face when he'd yanked the bottle away from her, a similar scene playing through his mind.

His mother had been right. He was too much like his father.

Get oot ma hoose, ye fuckin' bastard! Yer nae son o' mine.

Dinnae be comin' back or I'll beat the life oot o' ye, so I will. This is yer hame nae mair, ya worthless fuck!

Quinn held tighter to Elizabeth's hand, her touch an anchor. "One night when I was seventeen, I decided I'd had enough. I took every bottle of drink in the flat and poured it down the drain. He came up behind me, started shoutin'. I told him that he was mean when he was drunk, and that I wouldnae let him give me a doin' again."

"That was incredibly brave of you."

"I dropped one of the bottles in my surprise, and the next I knew, he was layin' his belt across my back. I stood and jerked the belt away from him. Then I punched him in the face. Och, it felt good, so I did it again and again. I beat the bastard bloody."

He willed himself to meet Elizabeth's gaze, prepared to see shock and disgust.

Instead, she was in tears. "It sounds to me like he deserved it."

Maybe she'd misunderstood.

Quinn tried again. "I beat my own da until he was bleedin', Elizabeth. That's the kind of man I am."

She shook her head. "No, Quinn, that's what you did to survive. It doesn't define you. It's what you've done with your life since then that tells me who you are."

He snorted. "You think I'm some kind of hero because I fought with the SAS? But that's no' true. My da threw me out that night. I had nowhere to stay, nothin' to eat, no way to get out of the rain. I saw a recruitment office, walked in, and signed up."

He told Elizabeth how he'd explained to the recruiter that he had no home and no food or money and how the man had taken pity on him, setting him up with a place to live and food and even spending money to get him through until recruit training.

"The army became my family. I went from beatin' my da to learnin' how to kill professionally. But I didnae do it for noble reasons. I did it to fill my belly—and to make sure my father never stopped fearin' me."

For a moment, neither of them spoke.

Elizabeth sniffed, let go of his hand, straddled him, sitting on his thighs, her hands cupping his face. "If you think tonight was a replay of what happened when you were seventeen, you're wrong. You didn't beat me with a belt. You didn't lay a hand on me. Yes, you startled me and raised your voice, but you didn't hurt me. Do you hear that?"

"You backed away from me. I saw fear on your face. *I* did that."

"Only because I was startled. I didn't know you were there. Yes, the shouting unnerved me a bit, but I'm fine. I wasn't afraid of you. And as for the army, you paid your country back by becoming an elite fighter. You gave them a decade of deployments, risking your life. I think that debt is paid in full."

But some part of Quinn couldn't accept this. "I'm no' a good man, Lilibet."

Tears spilled freely down her cheeks now, her smile quavering. "Do you remember when you pulled me away from Kazi's men in Kabul? I'd never been more afraid in my life. They were talking in Farsi about raping me, selling me, beheading me. And then you were there, angry as hell and armed to the teeth."

Quinn had wanted to rip them apart. "Aye, I remember. I saw fear in your eyes."

"They shouted at you to stand back. One held that rifle to my head. You told him you'd cut off his balls. You moved in on them as if you weren't afraid of them at all. You pulled me away from them and said, 'I've got you, Lilibet.' And I knew it was going to be okay. *That* is who you are. You will always be a hero to me, Quinn McManus."

He wiped the tears from her cheeks, her words a balm to the raw, broken place inside him. "Och, Lilibet, do you know what you mean to me?"

Because he couldn't bring himself to tell her, he kissed her, soft and slow, his heart aching for her.

She lifted herself up, pushed his kilt up his thighs, and stroked him to hardness. Then she moved the crotch of her panties aside and took him inside her, her gaze locked with his as she rode him. God, she was beautiful, the most beautiful thing in his world, the motions of her hips carrying him up and up until he was pounding into her from below and no longer knew where his body ended and hers began.

Scorching pleasure. Precious torment. A taste of heaven.

"*Quinn!*" Her head fell back when she came, bliss golden on her face.

He fell over that sweet edge with her, salvation washing through him as she carried him to paradise.

ELIZABETH LAY with her head on Quinn's chest, tenderness for him overwhelming her. He'd poured his heart out, bared his soul to her. "You're nothing like your father. You've always been protective of women. You're kind, thoughtful, caring."

"The day I met Jack, I called him a right wee prick. He kept goin' on about honor and servin' our country. He told me I was messed up. He was right. I learned so much from him—how to hold a fork properly, how to handle a disagreement wi'out beatin' someone's face in, how to be a man. I wouldnae be who I am today wi'out him."

She had to fight not to cry. Now, at last, she understood his absolute faith in Jack. "He really was a brother to you."

"Aye, he was." In a moment, Quinn was fast asleep.

But Elizabeth stayed awake into the early morning hours, unable to take her mind off the boy who'd had to beat his own father and join the army to survive.

I'll find the bastard who took Jack from you and Ava. I promise.

ELIZABETH WALKED with Quinn back to the car, feeling like she'd just spent the day in another world. "I think the Great Hall was my favorite part. When the crowd thinned out, I imagined James the Fourth and Margaret Tudor there, surrounded by courtiers."

"You've got a good imagination. All I saw was tourists."

Poor Quinn. He'd stuck to the plan of bringing her to see the castle even though he was emotionally drained from the night before—and more than a little hungover. He'd suffered through countless stairways, two museums, high tea at the tea garden, and every square foot of the castle open to the public with good humor.

"The view from the Argyle Tower was amazing. Oh! I loved the crown jewels, too. How about you?"

"Och, well, some of the weapons were interesting—the Lochubar axe." He spun her around, pretended to hold a sword to her throat, making her gasp. "I like the great swords, too. And you like being' overpowered, so you do."

Her cheeks burned. "Don't tell anyone."

"Your secret is safe wi' me, doll."

They ate dinner with the same view of the castle they'd had last time, lingering over their conversation and dessert. Then they used the car's GPS to find the last location from Jack's phone data.

"That's it. Wow. It's a mansion." Elizabeth looked out the window as they passed. "All the lights are on, and there are security guards at the front gate. Would they be Jack's former coworkers?"

"Aye, I suppose they would."

It was strange to think that Jack had been at this same villa every Friday night until exactly two weeks ago, when he'd gone to work but never come home.

"Ava said Jack came home upset on a Friday night exactly one month ago tonight. She remembered it vividly, which tells me that his behavior was unusual enough to stick in her mind."

"You're thinkin' that whatever upset him happened here."

"Possibly." She never wanted to assume anything.

"What does this have to do with that bastard Grant? I'm certain he's the one who planted drugs on us."

They had talked about this, and Elizabeth wasn't so sure. "I don't think his goons have the skill to hack door locks."

Quinn parked down the street from the mansion. "What if he's got someone else workin' for him—a cleaner, some fella who lurks in the background until he's needed."

Elizabeth laughed. "You've watched too many American TV shows."

They got out of the car, Quinn taking care to arm the alarm, and made their way down the street, the dull thud of bass audible from several houses down.

"It sounds like one hell of a party." She stopped before they reached the house. "Look. There are cars pulling up to a side entrance. There must be an alley or back driveway."

"Aye, I see it."

A teenage girl stepped out of a shiny dark BMW, followed by an older man, no doubt her father, the noise from the party growing louder for a moment when they walked through the side door, the older man's hand shifting to the girl's butt.

So, the man wasn't her father.

"I'm going to try to get in. Maybe we can talk with this MSP—Jack's boss." She'd dressed nicely for exactly this reason, passing over heels for less dressy but more comfortable flats.

"Aye, we can try."

"Just act like you belong here."

"You want me to impersonate a pompous arse?"

She bit back a laugh. "You're a patriotic Scotsman who served his country. Wear that tonight."

"What the fuck does that mean?"

They walked up to the front gate, where two men in suits stood guard, equipped with radios.

Elizabeth put on her game face. "Elizabeth Shields and Quinn McManus."

The men looked at them and then looked at each other.

"Have you got an invitation?" the older one asked.

Elizabeth shook her head. "I'm only in town for a short time, and I was hoping to speak with the MSP. We're friends of Jack Murray's."

Alarm.

Elizabeth saw it in their eyes.

"I served wi' him and Andrew Lewis in the SAS," Quinn said. "I think Lewis works for the MSP as well. He and I are good friends."

The older of the two guards stepped back, spoke into his handset, his accent English. "I've a couple here who say they're friends of Murray's—an American woman and a Scot who says he fought with Murray and Lewis in the SAS."

Elizabeth gave him their names again, watched as he relayed the information over the radio. He was jumpy, his gaze darting between her and Quinn.

He knew something.

He ended the radio call. "He's going to talk to Lewis and the MSP."

"Lewis is here?" Quinn grinned.

But Elizabeth wanted answers. "We're heartbroken about Jack's death. It must be hard for all of you, too."

"Oh. Yes. An awful business."

"Were you two friends of his, too?"

The looks on their faces answered that question.

"Yes, ma'am," the older man said. "Murray was a good man. Roberts here didn't know him well, did you?"

"No, I didn't know him well at all."

Then the older one took up his handset. "Yes, sir. Understood. I'll tell them, sir."

He met Elizabeth's gaze. "Mr. Lewis says that he and the MSP can't meet with you tonight. He suggests you schedule a meeting with his office in Holyrood."

Elizabeth hadn't expected this.

Quinn wasn't happy. "That's a load of pish. Give me the radio and put Lewis on."

The guard stepped back. "I'm sorry, sir. They're not available."

"What the f—"

"Thanks." Elizabeth cut across Quinn. "Tell the two of them to expect a call."

She and Quinn had just turned to walk back to the car,

Quinn cursing, when the front entrance opened. An older man leaned down and kissed a young teenage girl, the teen dressed in a revealing cocktail dress. Then the teen walked down the steps and out the front gate, the street light hitting the girl's face.

Elizabeth stared. "Nicola?"

18

Q uinn just had time to recognize her when Nicola
ran, dashing in a panic down the street. Elizabeth
ran after her, giving Quinn no choice but to follow.

Elizabeth called out for her again. "Nicola! Wait!"

Nicola was wearing high heels, so Elizabeth and Quinn
caught up to her quickly.

Nicola whirled on them, her gaze shifting to the villa.
"Leave me be! I cannae be seen talkin' wi' you, or they'll
kill me!"

"Who, Nicola? Who will kill you?"

Nicola turned and walked as quickly as she could.
"Please go!"

Elizabeth followed. "What were you doing there?"

"It's a party. I'm fourteen now, so my da says I can come
to the parties here, but he willnae let me stay late, not
anymore. I have to go."

Quinn could see the girl was afraid. He also saw the
white residue on her nose. "I'll no' let anyone hurt you. Who
wants to kill you for talkin' to us? Is it your da?"

"Och, you're an eejit. My da wouldnae touch me." Nicola

turned to face them again, her gaze once more on the villa, fear on her face. "Fuck off wi' you!"

This time when the girl ran, Elizabeth didn't follow.

"She's terrified. Someone has her scared to death." They turned and walked back toward the villa.

"Aye, I saw that—and the powder on her nose." Quinn looked up and down the street, watching for trouble. "That old bastard who was pawin' at her—he was old enough to be her da."

"Or her grandfather." Elizabeth looked up at the villa. "What the hell is going on in there?"

Quinn thought that was obvious but before he could say so, he spotted the young guard blatantly taking a photo of their license plate number with his phone. "What the fuck are you doin'?"

The man backed off. "You're disturbin' the peace. I'm goin' to call the police."

"The police?" Quinn laughed. "You do that, ya rocket."

He opened the door for Elizabeth then climbed in on the driver's side, watching his rearview mirror in case anyone tried to follow them. "Somethin' about this isnae right. Lewis and I fought side by side. He would never send me away or tell me to make an appointment. I cannae believe he wouldnae see me."

But Elizabeth was lost in her own thoughts. "What's the age of consent in Scotland?"

"I think it's sixteen." Quinn had never had to worry about that.

He was attracted to women, not children.

Elizabeth did a search on her phone. "You're right. It's sixteen. Nicola is fourteen. The other girl I saw couldn't be much older. The men looked like they were in their fifties and sixties. Sexual contact with those girls would be a criminal offense."

"Aye, so would plyin' them wi' drugs." Quinn checked his rearview mirror again, half expecting to see police lights flashing or someone following them.

"Yes, drugs, too." Elizabeth looked at her calendar app. "Ava said Jack was hired to be part of MSP Whitehall's personal security team a few months ago. He was here every Friday night. Four weeks ago, he came home upset and told Ava that the world was an ugly place."

"Maybe that's when he discovered what was really goin' on there. Maybe he threatened to report them, and they killed him for it."

"That's the first plausible theory we've had so far. Then again, why would he wait *three months* to report them? Maybe he played some role in it—like being their drug courier."

Quinn still couldn't believe Jack would do anything like that, but he'd said that so many times already that he didn't bother to say it again.

"Nicola said 'they' would kill her. Both times she said it, she looked back toward the villa. Someone there doesn't want her talking to us, and she was afraid they were watching."

"Or maybe that was the cocaine talkin'. Drugs can make a person paranoid."

"She also said her father lets her come to the parties but no longer lets her stay late. Wouldn't he care that she's there with those men?"

"No' necessarily. He might be for it if she brought home money—or drugs. I dinnae know much about women's clothes, but I doubt she bought that sparkly dress herself."

"Good point." Elizabeth rubbed her temple.

"Another headache?"

"Yes." Her brow furrowed in frustration. "It's right here in front of me. I'm just not looking at it in the right way."

Quinn took her hand, his gaze on his rearview mirror again. "Dinnae be hard on yourself. You've had a concussion, and you're tired. Let's get you home."

IT WAS TEN at night by the time they got back to Glasgow.

Elizabeth went straight to the office, dropped her jacket on the desk, and picked up a marker. "Let's go through this again but from the killer's point of view."

"Not until you've taken something for that headache." Quinn disappeared down the hall and returned with a glass of water and a paracetamol tablet. "Here."

"Thanks." She took the pill and swallowed it. "Okay. The killer is someone Jack knows fairly well, someone who knows that Jack is wearing body armor."

"One of the other guards would know that."

"True." Elizabeth wrote that on the board. "The older guard tonight—he lied about being friends with Jack."

"They werenae happy to be talkin' wi' us."

Elizabeth smiled at him. "You know, you're pretty good at reading people."

"I'm no' like you. You read people's minds."

"Hardly." She turned back to the board. "The killer lures him to an out-of-the-way location and inflicts a lethal knife wound, taking his phones, wallet, and watch. He doesn't use the credit card. He doesn't sell the phones. They vanish at approximately the same time he was killed, probably shoved into some kind of Faraday container. As far as we know, the watch hasn't shown up anywhere either. So, what was his motive?"

She studied what she'd written down.

"Maybe Jack's belongings have nothin' to do wi' this. Maybe the killer just wanted to silence him and make it look like a robbery."

"I agree. It wasn't a robbery." Elizabeth wrote that down, too. "Less than a week later, someone—probably the killer—breaks into Jack and Ava's house and rips the place to pieces. He was looking for something but was interrupted by a certain good-looking *eejit* and stole Jack's laptop. Why the laptop?"

She paused again, rubbed the ache in her temple.

"Maybe you should go to bed. It's been a long day."

She wasn't stopping now. She was close to putting the pieces together. She could *feel* it. "Then the same person breaks into our suites. He searches yours, so we can assume he searches mine, too. Then he plants drugs on us and tips off the police to get us out of the way. But why did he search our rooms? What is he trying to find?"

It's right in front of you, Shields. Why can't you see it?

She stared at the board. "What was he looking for?"

Adrenaline—it started in a slow trickle then hit her with a rush.

"Where are his phone records? Where did I leave them?" She hurried to the desk, tossed her coat to the floor, grabbed the pages, sorted through them.

And there it was.

Chills skittered down her spine.

"I don't know why I didn't notice this before. Look." She held the pages so Quinn could see, comparing the data from Jack's calls to his GPS location, barely able to contain her excitement. "He called you from here. That's the building with the puppy food store and the Indian restaurant—and the post office."

"Aye, I remember it."

"I'm betting he mailed the original phone to you to keep it safe. That's what these bastards are looking for—his original cell phone."

There was no other way to explain it.

"I'm callin' Denver." Quinn dialed Tower's number.

It was after three in the afternoon in Colorado, the middle of the business day.

"Hey, it's McManus." Quinn brought Tower up to date, telling him about the villa and what they'd seen. "Shields believes Jack Murray mailed his original mobile phone to me in Denver. Is there any way you can go check? Thanks."

Quinn gave him the passcode information for his apartment in LoDo then ended the call. "He's sendin' some guys off to check."

They made tea and waited for Tower to get back to them, Elizabeth's mind sorting through the scattered pieces.

"Jack came home upset early on a Saturday morning after being out most of the night. He bought the new phone the following Monday. He kept the old one on him at all times until he mailed it to you shortly before he was murdered." Elizabeth could think of only one reason for that. "There has to be something on it—a call or conversation he recorded or photos or a video. Maybe he had proof of what was happening there, just like you suggested."

"You're thinkin' the killer murdered him to retrieve it."

Elizabeth played with that idea. "He killed Jack, took his phones, concealed them somehow. When he discovered that what he was looking for wasn't on that phone, he put the pieces together—or hacked the phone records—and learned that the phone he had was a new one, not the one he wanted."

"And he's been tryin' to find it since."

Elizabeth took a sip of her tea. "That's why he broke into Jack and Ava's place—to find it. That's why he searched your room. He must have the same phone records we have. He would see that Jack called you before the phone disappeared."

Quinn's phone buzzed. "McManus here. Och, are you serious? The bastards! It disnae matter to me. Thank you. Right. It's there then?"

Elizabeth interrupted him. "If they found the package, tell them *not* to open it. They need to do that in an EM-proof environment."

Quinn conveyed the information then ended the call. "Someone broke into my condo and trashed the place. Tower has contacted the police."

"Oh, Quinn, I'm so sorry." Had the killer gone after the phone there?

"He says nothin' is missin' as far as he can tell. My TV, my firearms, my computer—they're all there. He had someone check the mailroom at Cobra HQ, and there was a package to me from Jack. Jack didnae mail it to my home. He was too smart for that. He mailed the phone to Cobra."

They had it. They had Jack's old phone.

At last, they were getting somewhere.

QUINN AND ELIZABETH woke up the next day to the news that Tower had found an EM-proof room at the Denver research lab of a US military contractor. He and some members of what everyone affectionately referred to as

Cobra's "geek team" had taken the phone to the lab to open the package and crack the phone's password, though Elizabeth insisted Jack had probably removed it.

"Whatever was on there—he'd want you to be able to see it. I'm betting he thought getting the phone into safe hands was life insurance for him."

Once they had access to the phone's contents, they would upload everything to Cobra's cloud server. The phone would remain in the lab until Jack's killer was arrested.

Because Denver was seven hours behind Glasgow, Quinn and Elizabeth found themselves with time to kill. Though Tower and the rest of the staff at Cobra would no doubt be fine working around the clock, the military contractor stuck to business hours.

"It's three a.m. there. We've probably got five hours until the lab opens." Elizabeth was clearly impatient to move forward.

"I'll take out my stitches, and then we can go visit another castle."

"Only if you really want to. I feel like I tortured you yesterday."

He kissed her. "I'm just teasin'. I love seein' your face light up when you see somethin' that excites you."

"We can get the doctor to remove your stitches."

"I can do it myself. I've done it afore many times."

When his stitches were out, they rode the lift down to the garage and set out for Dumbarton Castle, a drive of about thirty minutes from their hotel.

Quinn looked at his gas gauge. "I need to stop at a petrol station."

"Are there any that have convenience stores? I need to pick up a few things." She wrinkled her nose in dislike. "It's almost that time of the month."

Quinn drove north on A82, pulling off the highway when he saw a BP with a good-sized convenience store. "Stay in the car while I fill up, and then I'll go wi' you."

He didn't want her going anywhere by herself, not after that guard had photographed their license plate.

He refilled the tank and then walked into the convenience store with her.

"You're not embarrassed to be seen with a woman buying tampons?"

He chuckled, slid his fingers through hers. "A man would have to be a right wee prick to feel embarrassed about that."

He opened the door and followed her inside, his gaze searching the place. Apart from the cashier, who had his face buried in a comic book, they seemed to be alone.

While Elizabeth went off in search of tampons, he looked for Scottish Blend. The boys from British Intelligence had stocked the kitchen, but they'd left him with English Breakfast tea. Clearly, the bastards had no taste at all.

He found a box of Scottish Blend with eighty bags on the lower shelf and grabbed it. Then he looked over the top of the aisles to find Elizabeth. He didn't see the top of her head, but she was probably bent over. "Are you findin' what you need, love?"

No answer.

He strode the length of the store, looking down the aisles, spotted a box of tampons on the floor.

His pulse tripped. "Lilibet?"

Still no answer.

Quinn turned to the cashier—and his heart gave a hard knock, a thud of pure dread. The boy lay on the floor behind the counter, still breathing but unconscious.

"Elizabeth!" Quinn ran to the restrooms, threw open the door to the women's room. "Elizabeth?"

Empty.

He checked the men's room, too.

Then he saw it—the door that led to the back of the store.

He pushed through it, found the back door wide open, and saw a white van speeding away. He drew his Glock, ran after the van, but knew he couldn't fire without risking hitting Elizabeth—if he managed to hit anything at all.

"Fuck, no! Goddamn it!"

They'd taken Elizabeth. She was gone.

19

Quinn holstered his weapon, pulled out his phone, and ran through the store and out the front door toward his car, dialing the emergency number. "There's been an abduction and an assault at the BP off the M8 about five kilometers north of town. Elizabeth Shields, an American citizen, was taken by someone drivin' a white Ford van, and the clerk is alive but down."

He gave them the license plate number. "The van was headin' north on the M8. Get your asses up here—*now*. I'm goin' after the van."

He opened the driver's side door, threw himself into the seat, dialed Corbray's home number.

Corbray answered.

"They've got her. They took her right from under my nose."

How the *fuck* had he let that happen?

He gave Corbray the whole story as he tore out of the petrol station parking lot and drove as fast as he could toward the highway. "I'm headin' after them."

Corbray swore in Spanish—a string of words Quinn

didn't understand. "I'll get Tower's ass out of bed, and we'll have a team in the air within an hour. We'll track her phone, coordinate with the British government, and see if we can't get them involved. Keep me updated—and don't get yourself killed charging in on your own. Got it? Shields is tough. She'll make it through this."

"They killed Jack. They'll kill her, too, if we dinnae stop them." Quinn ended the call, speeding up the highway, looking for that white van.

His phone buzzed.

A message from Elizabeth.

He tapped it—and his mouth went dry.

She lay, unconscious, duct tape over her mouth, her wrists bound.

Beneath the image was text.

If you want to see her alive again, do exactly as I say. If you try to rescue here, I'll slit her throat.

Och, Jesus. Elizabeth.

Fear turned his blood to ice, scattered his thoughts.

He forwarded the message to Cobra, swerved to miss a car, and pushed on the gas, the van nowhere in sight.

Then his training kicked in.

Focus, man! You cannae help her like this.

He left the highway and pulled into a parking lot. Then he closed his eyes, leaned his head against the steering wheel, and drew three deep, slow breaths.

It would be at least eleven hours before the Cobra team landed in Glasgow, longer before they'd be ready to go into action, especially if the British government refused to let them get involved in the search.

A dark blue BMW pulled up beside Quinn, its tinted window sliding slowly down to reveal Leo Grant.

Quinn was out of the car, pistol drawn and pointed straight at him. "You fuckin' bastard! What have you done wi' her?"

Leo Grant got out of the car, hands raised. "I'd put that away afore someone sees it—or one of my men gets the wrong impression and shoots your damned head off."

The other windows lowered to reveal three men—two plus the driver—all armed.

Quinn lowered the pistol, slipped it into his holster. "Where have you taken her?"

"Do you think I'd go after a former CIA agent? I'm no' that stupid. But I know who is—and I know where they're takin' her. How about I sit in your vehicle, and we talk?"

Quinn didn't trust this man, but if Grant had wanted him dead, he'd wouldn't be standing here. If the fucker truly knew where Elizabeth was... "Aye."

Quinn unlocked the doors, watching as Grant got in beside him.

"Murray and I went our separate ways after he joined the army." Grant chuckled. "He didnae approve of my plans for makin' my fortune. Aye, I sell drugs up and down the coast, McManus, but I didnae kill Jack. I loved him. And I've nothin' to do with your piece bein' abducted, either."

"You know who killed Jack?"

"I figured it out the day after you came to see me. I've a source in the police station. Sometimes she says more than she realizes. I got enough information from her to know who it had to be. You and I both know Jack would never sell drugs."

"Aye." On that they could agree. "Why didn't you go to the police?"

"I believe in justice—an eye for an eye. Will the courts give us that?"

Quinn saw his point, but that's not how the law worked. "Are you certain?"

Grant nodded. "One of my men infiltrated their organization. He's been feedin' me information. You met him last night when he photographed your license plate."

"That bastard works for *you*?"

Grant grinned. "We set up a sort of picket, followed you back, saw where you were livin'. We followed you here. He knew they were going to take her, and I came to warn you. We were too late."

"Fuck."

"After dark, my men and I are movin' in. I meant it when I said I would kill the man who killed Jack. We'll do our best to keep your woman safe, but gettin' inside is no' goin' to be easy. I've got photographs, numbers of men, and the layout of the warehouse, but I dinnae have your tactical skill. If you get us inside, you can take your woman and go. My men and I will handle the rest."

Quinn thought through the hundred or so reasons why this was a bad idea. These men were criminals, not disciplined military men. He had no idea how they would behave in a fight. They clearly planned to kill the man who'd murdered Jack, and, as right as that felt to Quinn, it was still illegal. If he was a part of it, he might end up in prison, too—or get killed. And then there was the possibility that Grant would turn on them.

This wasn't what Corbray had meant when he'd ordered Quinn not to go after Elizabeth by himself.

Quinn glanced at the image of Elizabeth, tied up and unconscious, thought of all the things that could happen to her in the long hours until the police or Cobra went into action. Tower had ordered him to keep Elizabeth safe.

"How do I know you'll let the two of us go rather than killin' us?"

Grant looked him straight in the eyes. "I give you my word as a friend of Jack's. Neither I nor any of my men will harm her—or you. Not today, anyway."

The enemy of my enemy is my friend.

Quinn measured Grant's words, his mind telling him one thing, his heart another. He held out his hand, and they shook. "I'm in."

But there was one other thing. "Give me a name. Who killed Jack?"

ELIZABETH WAS cold and so thirsty, her head throbbing. She heard herself moan—a muffled sound. She tried to raise a hand to her head but couldn't.

A man's voice whispered to her. "Lie still, aye? You dinnae want them knowin' you're awake. I'll take the tape off your mouth when I know you understand me."

She opened her eyes to find herself on a cold concrete floor in an unheated warehouse, her hands and feet tied.

Her heart pounded, adrenaline washing away the cobwebs.

She'd been abducted.

Where was Quinn? Did they have him, too? Had they killed him?

She looked up at the face that hovered over her, nodded.

With a painful rip, the tape was gone.

"I'll tell them you were havin' trouble breathin'. I dinnae

think they mean for you to suffocate. That bastard has questions for you. Pretend to sleep. It will buy you time."

Then she recognized him.

He was the younger guard, the one who'd taken a photo of the car's license plate. Was he trying to help her? It certainly seemed so.

Bits and pieces came back to her then until she remembered all of it—the phone Jack had mailed to Cobra, the EM-proof lab, the drive to the gas station. She'd been looking for tampons and had felt a prick like a bee sting.

Then … nothing.

She opened her mouth to speak, but he shook his head and backed away.

A door opened, its hinges squeaking.

She closed her eyes and slowed her breathing, pretending to be unconscious.

"Why did you take the tape off her mouth?" An English accent.

"She was havin' trouble breathin' and was startin' to turn blue. I didnae think you meant for her to die till you've had a chance to talk wi' her."

So, whoever had her intended to kill her—but not yet.

Great.

"How much did those idiots give her?" Footsteps. "Call me when she wakes up."

"Aye, sir."

The door closed.

A moment later, the guard was there again. "Here's water."

She drank, slaked her thirst. "Thank you. Where's Quinn?"

"Shh!" The guard glared at her. "I cannae say where he

is, but he's no' here, if that's what you're thinkin'. They only took you. They want somethin' from him."

The phone.

There was no way they'd get their hands on that, but she didn't say so. Right now, that phone was likely the only reason she was still alive.

QUINN LOOKED out over the dark water as they made their way in a small cargo ship up the Clyde estuary. The sun had just set, the Cobra team still over the Atlantic somewhere.

Hang on, Lilibet. I'm comin'.

So far, Grant had been true to his word. He'd outfitted Quinn with body armor and given him an M4 rifle and ammo.

Quinn had turned the M4 over in his hands, racked the charging handle. "How the bloody hell did you get somethin' like this?"

"If I tell you, I'll have to kill you." Grant had laughed at his own joke.

It was like going on a mission with Cobra—except that everyone on board this ship, apart from him, was a hardened criminal or a terrorist or both.

Quinn's plan was to dock not far from the location where that fucking bastard had taken her and then move in under cover of darkness in the shadow of the riverbank. Grant's man on the inside would unlock the gate to let them in. Grant and his men would take the warehouse while Quinn went after Elizabeth.

Grant wanted only vengeance.

Quinn was happy to let him have it. It had gutted him to

hear who was behind all of this, left him feeling sick. But he didn't have time to dwell on that now.

"Gather your men." Quinn said to Grant. "I'd like to have a final word."

Grant pulled his men together behind the ship's wheel-house. "All right, you bastards. Listen to what our friend has to say."

Quinn outlined the plan one more time then focused on important details. "The rounds in your weapons can pene-trate walls. Be sure you know who's on the other side afore you start sprayin' bullets. Make your shots count. When a target is neutralized, leave him. Dinnae waste precious time takin' souvenirs."

This drew snickers.

"Listen!" Grant bellowed.

"The moment this bastard hears the first shot, he'll likely move to kill his prisoner, so dinnae be pullin' that trigger afore we're inside and there's a true need. If you can take a target down wi' a blade or the blow of a rifle butt, do it. Dinnae panic and start shootin' every bastard you see. You'll only kill each other that way."

When Elizabeth was in Quinn's hands, the two of them would get on another boat and sail up the Clyde, leaving the bastard and his men to Grant. Quinn would take Elizabeth back to the Fortress. The two of them would hopefully be ready to leave the country by the time Cobra's private jet touched down.

None of this was legal, of course, but Quinn would rather spend the next twenty years in prison than let anyone harm or kill Elizabeth.

The fucker had sent him two more text messages. He was using a burner now, not Elizabeth's phone. He'd given Quinn till tomorrow morning at oh-six-hundred to bring

Jack's mobile to a location in Glasgow. Then he'd promised to let Quinn and Elizabeth go. But Quinn knew better.

The son of a bitch planned to take the phone and kill them both.

Quinn had pretended not to know who was on the other end and had agreed to bring the phone with him, making a few threats of his own.

`If you touch her, I'll rip off your balls.`

Grant walked up to Quinn. "Five minutes."

STILL GROGGY, Elizabeth's heart began to race the moment the man with the dark hair stepped into the room. Whoever he was, she knew he had murdered Jack. The wound on his left cheek where Quinn had stabbed him told her that. She also knew for certain that he didn't intend to let her live—not now that she'd seen his face.

"You're awake. Good. Let's have a little chat."

He wanted to talk? Fine.

Interrogation was a game she knew how to play.

"What should we talk about—the weather in Scotland, whether rugby or soccer is the better sport, why you killed Jack Murray? Let's talk about that last one."

His pupils dilated.

So, she'd taken him by surprise.

"Excuse me, sir." The guard said. "I need to take a leak."

He nodded, then pulled a chair over and sat in front of Elizabeth. "You and McManus have something I want."

"Jack's original phone. Yes, that's true. You can't have it." She and Quinn had been right about that.

There was something on the phone, something tied to the parties in that villa.

Whoever this bastard was, he must work for Whitehall.

His brow furrowed, proof that she'd surprised him again. "I've told him that if he wants you back alive, he'll deliver it to me in Edinburgh. Then you can go."

"Liar." She willed herself to laugh. "You've got no intention of letting either of us go. You're just using me as bait. When you get your hands on the phone, you'll put a bullet through our heads. Otherwise, we'll tell the police that you killed Jack."

"I prefer to work with knives." He drew out a knife, flipped out its blade.

A frisson of fear shivered down her spine.

"The weapon of a brute." She tossed out something she knew about him, tried to get him to reveal himself. "Jack trusted you."

"That was his mistake, the noble idiot. He and Quinn are alike in that way—the two Wegians. Big hearts and small brains."

His response narrowed things down for Elizabeth.

She laughed again. "You call *them* idiots? If you think Quinn is just going to turn the phone over to you, you're dumber than you look."

Now, he was angry.

Good.

She was throwing him off-balance.

"If he double crosses me—"

"You'll do what exactly?" Then it clicked. "Everyone is going to know it was you, *Andrew*."

He flinched, proof she was right.

Andrew Lewis, who'd served in the SAS with Jack and

Quinn, the man who'd gotten Jack the job at Holyrood, was Jack's killer.

"The best thing you can do is make a run for it. Otherwise, they're going to catch you. After today, the truth will come out one way or another. If you kill me, you'll make it worse for yourself."

He was afraid now, but he tried to hide it. "Quinn will do what I tell him to do. He always has. He's a good little soldier."

"Do you want to know where the phone is right now? I'll tell you. It's in an EM-proof room at a secured facility in Colorado. Jack mailed it to Quinn in a Faraday bag. Right now, a Cobra team is getting ready to extract all of the data so they can share it with British Intelligence and Police Scotland."

Lewis glared at her. "That's not true. McManus brought it with him."

Her mind still muddled by the drug, Elizabeth tried to remember details. "Jack mailed it to Cobra's Denver facility on October twenty-eighth from that post office near the pet food store. Quinn was in Afghanistan until November fourth. You called him shortly after he'd gotten off the plane. He flew to Glasgow that night. The package arrived after he'd left for Scotland. Do the math. He doesn't have the phone."

The blow took her by surprise, pain leaving her stunned.

"You're lying, you fucking CIA whore."

Head spinning, she tried to seem unfazed. "Sorry, but they never paid me to do that sort of work."

Was that a gunshot?

Elizabeth's pulse skipped.

Lewis shot to his feet and turned toward the door just as the guard ran back in.

"There are men at the gate, sir," he told Lewis. "Three or four."

"It's McManus." Lewis glared at the guard. "What the fuck are you doing here? I'll get rid of her. You get out there and do what you're paid to do."

The guard disappeared, leaving Elizabeth alone with a murderer.

Lewis turned to stare down at her, knife in hand. "I'll make certain McManus knows this is *his* fault."

Elizabeth saw in Lewis' eyes that he intended to kill her now, her heart beating so hard it hurt. She needed to buy herself time. "What twisted you? What made you turn on men who loved you like a brother? You betrayed them."

More gunshots—closer this time.

A muscle in Lewis' jaw twitched. "Jack turned on *me*. He was going to tell the police about that stupid girl's death. All he had to do was keep his fucking mouth shut. And now McManus. He could have stayed out if it, but he had to charge in like a fucking white knight. I tried to get you both out of the way by planting drugs in your rooms, but somehow you knew and got rid of it."

Elizabeth didn't have time to wonder what dead girl Lewis was talking about, her gaze on the knife in his hand. "We set up security cameras."

"Ah. Clever." He nodded. "It would have been better for you to go to jail. After you showed up at the villa last night, I knew you had the phone. I knew you were onto us. It's your fault that you're here right now."

"No, it's entirely your fault."

Shouts.

"Don't worry. I'll make it quick. I've done it before. You'll be unconscious in a few seconds and dead in a minute at most. It's a shame, really. You're smart, pretty. I see why McManus wants you in his bed."

Mind racing, Elizabeth curled up in a fetal position as if afraid, drawing her knees to her chest, tucking in her chin to protect her throat. She knew he'd be fast, so she had to move first.

He bent down, brought the blade close. "Say goodnight."

She thrust her feet out together as hard as she could, catching him on the knee. "Fuck you!"

He cursed, fell backward, the knife clattering to the floor.

She rolled onto her side, wriggled toward it, trying to reach it first, but with her hands and feet tied she wasn't fast enough.

He grabbed it, his face red with rage. "You fucking bitch!"

She tried to roll away, but he pinned her with his body. Then he fisted a hand in her hair, forcing her head back, baring her throat for his blade.

And Elizabeth knew it was over.

Please don't blame yourself, Quinn. I love you.

20

Quinn fired two shots, dropping a bastard with an LiA1 and moving as quickly as he could down the corridor toward the back room where Grant's man said Lewis had taken Elizabeth. Grant's men were inexperienced, and that had cost them precious minutes as they'd tried to infiltrate the warehouse. He'd give his bollocks to have the Cobra crew with him right now.

I'm almost there, Lilibet.

He came to a closed door, kicked it open, and moved in, rifle raised.

And there was Lewis bent over Elizabeth, blade at her throat.

Quinn had no choice. He pulled the trigger—a single shot to the ankle.

Lewis cried out, fell back, the knife clattering to the concrete.

"Quinn!" Relief washed over Elizabeth's face.

But Quinn still had Lewis to deal with. "You fuckin' son of a bitch!"

Quinn moved in on him, stepped on his knife, put

himself between Lewis and Elizabeth, who was bound wrist and ankle and couldn't stand. "I trusted you like a brother. You betrayed me, and you betrayed Jack."

Lewis clutched his ankle, blood running between his fingers. "Jack betrayed *me*. I got him the job, and he fucking paid me back by trying to turn us in to the police. He got what he deserved."

"Move! Back away from her!" Quinn wanted Lewis as far from Elizabeth as possible so he could bend down and cut through the ties that held her fast.

"How am I supposed to move when you shot me in the fucking ankle?" Lewis scooted on his ass, leaving a trail of blood, his gaze on the knife beneath Quinn's foot.

"You want this?" Quinn took the knife, freed Elizabeth, and helped her to stand. "Are you okay?"

"A bit dizzy." There was a fresh bruise on her left cheek —proof that some bastard had struck her. "They drugged me."

Quinn put her behind him. He wanted more than anything to hold her, but now wasn't the time, not when the warehouse was full of armed criminals and Lewis sat only a few feet away from them. Even injured, he was dangerous.

"How do you think this ends, McManus? If you kill me, you're a murderer. You'll go to prison."

"He's no' goin' to kill you." Grant stepped into the room, HK416 slung over his shoulder. "I am."

Lewis' face went white, his eyes wide. "*You.*"

"Have we met?" Grant knelt down, looked Lewis in the face, pretended to study him. "I dinnae think so. I'd remember a stinkin' piece of shite like you."

"I know who you are." Lewis glared up at Quinn. "You hang out with drug dealers and terrorists now, McManus? And you think you're better than I am."

Grant stood. "You're accusin' me of bein' a criminal when you give drugs to teenage girls and rape them?"

"The girls are all willing."

Grant's expression turned to disgust. "They're no' old enough to be willin'."

"They want the money—and the drugs. I don't have anything to do with the girls, anyway. That's Whitehall. I just clean up his fucking messes."

"They're underage. That's a sexual offense." Elizabeth wobbled, clutched Quinn's arm to steady herself. "And then there's Katie Cameron. Yes, I figured it out. She overdosed on drugs *you* gave her. You dumped her body in a ditch."

This was news to Quinn. Who the hell was Katie Cameron?

Elizabeth explained. "Jack must have recorded something about her on his phone. That's why they murdered him."

Grant grinned, a feral, vicious smile. "I'm goin' to enjoy endin' you."

But Elizabeth had more questions. Of course, she did. "Did you force Jack to carry drugs for you?"

"What's it to you, bitch?"

Grant kicked Lewis' injured leg, making him shriek. "Dinnae be talkin' to McManus' woman like that."

Lewis groaned. "Jack was a righteous prick. He refused."

Quinn's face burned with fury. He took a step toward Lewis, itching to kill the bastard. But he'd made a deal with Grant. "You planted drugs on him, just like you planted them on us. You broke his wife's heart, and you stole him from his wee ones. Their lives will *never* be the same. Then you tried to sully his memory, too. You're no' the man I thought you were. You're no' a man at all."

Lewis opened his mouth as if to say something, then his eyes went wide.

The guard Quinn had seen last night stepped into the room.

Lewis shouted to him. "What the fuck are you doing? Shoot them!"

"The warehouse is secure, sir," the guard said, looking not at Lewis but Grant.

"Shoot them!" It took Lewis a moment to catch on.

"I dinnae work for you."

Grant chuckled. "I've had my eye on you for a while now. If we were just competin' for drug sales, I'd have let you be. Business is business. But you cut down a man I loved like a brother."

Grant met Quinn's gaze, thrust out a gloved hand. "It's been good workin' with you, but it's time for you to take your woman and go. You dinnae want her to see this. I'll wait until you're away. If you ever turn to the dark side, let me know. We could use a man wi' your skills."

Quinn shook his hand, gave him Lewis' blade. "Thank you for your help. I willnae forget it."

"I'm always happy to help out another brother of Jack's." Grant chuckled again. "But stay the hell away from Troon, aye?"

"Aye." Quinn handed the M4 to Grant's man, put his arm around Elizabeth's shoulders to steady her, and faced Lewis. "There was a time when I'd have followed you into hell, even given my life for you."

"You're going to leave and let this fucker butcher me? McManus!"

Quinn ignored his pleas, guiding Elizabeth from the building and onto the dock where a small boat waited for them. It would carry them up the estuary into the River Clyde and on toward Glasgow.

He helped her climb aboard and led her inside the heated wheelhouse, giving a nod to the captain—one of Grant's men. "Evenin'."

"We're off home, then, aye?"

"Aye." Quinn sat Elizabeth on a bench, wrapped his arms around her. "Och, you're shakin' like a leaf."

"I-I'm cold."

Quinn took off his jacket, wrapped it around her. "We'll get you warmed up."

She clung to him. "I thought I was dead. I thought..."

It had been close—much too close.

Quinn kissed her forehead, held her tight. "You're safe now."

STILL WOOZY, Elizabeth dozed off and on while the boat made its way upriver. The captain let them off just outside Glasgow, Quinn leaving his body armor on board.

Then Quinn called Nigel. "McManus here. I've got her. We're near Victoria Bridge. The bastards drugged her. She'll need to see your doctor. I think she's in shock. I'll explain when we get there and I know she's okay. Aye, thanks."

"It's cold. You should take your jacket back." Elizabeth started to remove it, but he stopped her.

"You keep it. I'm fine."

Still, the wind cut through her, chilled her to the bone. Maybe she was cold from lying on that damned warehouse floor. Or maybe Quinn was right, and she was in shock.

It took Nigel only ten minutes to reach them. He pulled up in a black Land Rover. "Good to see you, Ms. Shields,

McManus. We'll get you home and have our doctor check you out."

"Thank you."

The car was warm, city lights and Christmas displays passing by outside the window. Christmas? What day was it?

November 16.

She must have dozed again because the next thing she knew, Quinn was lifting her from the car, settling her onto a gurney. "You don't need to do this. I can walk."

"We'll let the doc decide that." Corbray stood there, wearing full combat fatigues, Tower, Dylan Cruz, Malik Jones, and Thor Isaksen beside him.

Her throat went tight. "You're here."

They'd come for her.

"Where else would we be?" Tower smiled.

"Nice of you boys to show up." McManus shook their hands.

"It looks like you took all the glory, McManus," Dylan teased.

"You couldn't save any of the action for us?" Malik chuckled

"That's what happens when you're late for the party," Thor said.

Tower narrowed his eyes. "McManus, we need to talk."

"Aye—but no' yet."

Quinn stayed with Elizabeth while the doctor examined her, standing beside the gurney, holding her hand, concern on his handsome face.

The doctor took her pulse, her temperature, her blood pressure, and checked her oxygen saturation. "You're slightly hypothermic, so we need to warm you up. They injected you with a high dose of a sedative—maybe Versed or Demerol. We're lucky you didn't stop breathing. You'll probably feel drowsy for the rest of the evening, so it's best if you just rest. I'll get you a heated blanket."

"Thanks."

The doctor walked away, leaving Elizabeth alone with Quinn.

She raised Quinn's hand to her lips, kissed it. "You came for me."

His gaze was soft. "Aye, I did. I'm sorry I let them get to you. I'm sorry I didnae get there sooner."

"You joined forces with a drug dealer and possible terrorist to save me."

He ran his thumb along the curve of her cheek. "I'd have made a deal wi' Satan himself if that's what it took to get you back. I love you, Elizabeth."

Her pulse skipped. "You ... *what?*"

"I love you. I know that's not what you want to hear. I know you—"

She pressed her fingers to his lips to quiet him. She needed to tell him. He needed to know. "When he held that knife to my throat, I knew it was over. My last thought before you stormed in was that I love you."

He searched her gaze, clearly surprised. "You cannae mean that. You could have any man you want—"

Tears filled her eyes. "I want *you*, Quinn McManus. I never expected to feel this way about anyone."

He kissed her, soft and slow, then wiped the tears from her cheeks. "We've really made a mess of it, haven't we?"

"I suppose we'll be fired."

He nodded. "I'll probably wind up in prison."

"Prison?" Her heart sank.

She'd been so out if it that she hadn't thought about that. He had risked everything—his life, his career, his freedom —to save her.

"Aye, prison. It's okay. It was worth it." He gave her that smile, the one that melted her insides. "A perfect time to fall in love, aye?"

The doctor returned with a heated thermal blanket. "This ought to warm you up."

Quinn helped him tuck it around her. "Is that better?"

Warmth enfolded her, seeping into her skin. "Oh, that feels good."

And despite every effort to stay awake, Elizabeth drifted off again.

QUINN WATCHED SLEEP OVERTAKE ELIZABETH. He kissed her and dragged himself from her side, leaving her in the infirmary and riding the lift with Smith upstairs.

It was time to pay his debts.

He sat down with Smith, Corbray, and Tower in Smith's office and told them everything—except for the private details about his relationship with Elizabeth. Then he answered their questions, one after the next, until it was just shy of midnight.

Smith took notes, preparing a report for the police, who would likely show up to arrest Quinn sometime tomorrow morning. Already, word of a shoot-out at a warehouse near Clydebank was on the news—reports of nine found dead and millions of pounds worth of cocaine and heroin recovered.

Quinn had been at that warehouse. He'd carried an illegal weapon. He'd watched men kill other men—criminals, the lot of them—and he'd done nothing to stop the carnage. He'd left Lewis with Grant, knowing Grant would make Lewis suffer.

Aye, Quinn deserved to go to prison.

At least Elizabeth is safe.

"Why didn't you wait?" Tower asked at last. "I believe that's what you were ordered to do."

"If I'd waited, she'd be dead." The memory of Lewis holding the blade to her throat made Quinn's gut twist.

"What concerns us is your refusing to follow instructions."

"You also ordered me to keep her safe." Quinn spelled it out for them. "I knew it would be at least eleven hours afore you got here, and every minute of that time, she'd be in that bastard's hands—a man who slit a friend's throat, who gives drugs to teenage girls so politicians can assault them. Then Grant pulled up, said he had a man inside Lewis' organization and knew where Elizabeth was. What would you have done?"

The three men looked at him, their expressions grave.

Smith tapped his notepad with his pencil. "I've been taking notes, and I'd like to run my summary by you before I turn this over to the police."

"Aye, go ahead." Quinn steeled himself for the words that would send him away.

"On the evening of sixteen November, two rival crime syndicates got into a lethal conflict at a warehouse near Clydebank, leaving nine dead. One of those syndicates has associations with MSP Whitehall, who has an appetite for underage girls and drugs, some of which he imports through ties to British veterans who served in Afghanistan."

That was news to Quinn.

Smith went on. "Among the dead is Andrew Lewis, who was found beheaded."

So that's what Grant had done to him.

Smith kept reading. "Lewis helped import and distribute illegal drugs. He was responsible both for concealing the overdose death of Katie Cameron, aged fourteen, and killing Jack Murray. Footage taken from Murray's phone and delivered to British Intelligence by Cobra this evening shows Lewis and other men in MSP Whitehall's employ loading Miss Cameron's body into a vehicle. Her body was subsequently dumped in a ditch. Is that everything, Mr. McManus?"

Quinn blinked, stared at Smith, momentarily speechless. The man had said nothing about Elizabeth's abduction or Quinn's involvement.

They're letting you off the hook, man.

Quinn nodded. "Aye, that's it exactly."

Smith stood. "You're wondering why you're not being led away in handcuffs. I'll explain. The intel you and Ms. Shields provided has proven to be most interesting. You two exposed two drug dealers, revealed a possible IRA cell, solved a murder, and uncovered a sexual exploitation scheme, resolving the death of a teenage girl and leading us to a leak in the police station."

"The leak—you found it?"

Smith nodded. "PC Patel has been feeding information to Grant for years. She also had a relationship with MSP Whitehall, who was manipulating her, using her to feed information to the media. It was Whitehall, through Lewis, who told her that you and Shields were distributing drugs. DS Wilson suspected her after the drug raid at the hotel. We knew we had her when he discovered that she had illegally prepared the warrant to search your suites *before* the tip from Lewis came in."

Smith stood, Corbray and Tower, too. "Thanks for your help."

Quinn stood as well, shook his hand, unable to believe he was going free. "Thank you, sir. I'm grateful."

"You help us. We help you. We're the good guys, right?"

Still reeling, Quinn stepped out into the hallway, followed by Corbray and Tower, who shook Smith's hand and thanked him.

What the hell had just happened?

He walked with Corbray and Tower to the lift. "If you're goin' to fire anyone, it should be me."

"McManus..."

"None of this was Elizabeth's doin'." Quinn had to make certain they understood. "She only came here to help me and—"

"McManus!" Tower shook his head. "No one is being fired."

Corbray clapped Quinn on the shoulder. "Get some sleep, man. You've had a busy day. And, hey, remind me never to go on vacation with you."

"Aye, sir."

Corbray and Tower stepped into the elevator.

"Aren't you coming up?"

Quinn shook his head. "I'm goin' down to the infirmary to check on Lili... Elizabeth."

The two men looked at each other as the doors slid shut, both grinning.

Jesus.

Quinn needed a drink.

No, no more drinking. He needed Lilibet.

21

Elizabeth woke the next morning to find herself in Quinn's arms, his warmth surrounding her. She snuggled into him, her face pressed against his heartbeat.

"Oh, man! He blew your fuckin' head off."

Men's laughter.

She sat bolt upright.

Dylan was out there in the living room. Malik, too.

But what...?

Memories from yesterday crashed in on her, adrenaline making her pulse spike. Setting out for the castle. The bee-sting prick in her arm. The warehouse.

And Quinn...

He'd risked everything to save her from Lewis.

"Hey, it's all right, love." Quinn sat up, rubbed a big hand over her bare arm, kissed her shoulder. "It's over."

"And you're not being charged with anything?" She vaguely remembered him saying something along those lines last night when he'd brought her upstairs.

"Naw. Smith thanked us. You've got a debriefing wi' him at eleven."

"Oh, yes." Then she remembered something else, something that made joy blossom behind her breastbone. "Quinn McManus, you told me you love me."

"Aye, I did." His blue eyes looked into hers, not a hint of teasing. "I've loved you since the day we met. It just took me a while to own it. I didnae think a woman like you would even look at a man like me."

"A man like you?" She rested a hand on his chest. "You mean a courageous man who would risk anything for me? A man who's sexy and ripped and strong and fucks like an angel?"

He chuckled. "I've no' spent much time in church, I admit, but I dinnae recall hearin' much about the sex lives of angels."

She laughed, imitated his accent. "Ya daft bampot."

"I'm no' educated like you. I've no talents aside from combat—and carryin' heavy things."

"That's not true." She wished he could see himself the way she did. "You're funny. You're brave, intuitive, and smart. Yes, I said smart. You dance really well, and you sing. You've got the biggest heart of any man I know. You must have broken a half dozen laws to save my life."

"I'd do it again."

"I know." She stroked his beard. "I think I've loved you since you barged into the airport and threatened to feed that bastard's nuts to your dogs. Do you know how romantic that was?"

He chuckled. "I do like to sweet-talk you."

She was serious now, her throat going tight. "That's the most afraid I've been—until yesterday."

He drew her against him. "When I discovered they'd taken you, I was scared, truly fuckin' scared. If I'd lost you, Lilibet—"

He held her tighter, Elizabeth yielding to his embrace.

Shouts and laughter came from the living room.

Elizabeth drew back, looked up into Quinn's eyes. "If I didn't love you before, I would have fallen in love with you on this trip. You never lost faith in Jack—not for a minute, not when the evidence seemed to pile up, not when I was certain he was dealing. *You* are the reason he'll get justice now. You're the best friend a person could have."

Grief slid across Quinn's face, his jaw going tight. "He was my brother."

Elizabeth's stomach growled. "Sorry."

"You're hungry."

"Famished." She hadn't had anything to eat since breakfast yesterday.

"Are you ready to face those bastards out there? They're on the wrong side of the clock. Jet lag. They've been playin' video games for a few hours now, yellin' at each other to be quiet so you can sleep."

"I guess our secret's out."

He pressed his forehead to hers. "Dinnae let it worry you. We'll work it out."

She nodded. "You're right."

They got up and dressed, Elizabeth wearing jeans and her warmest sweater over a T-shirt, Quinn wearing jeans and a dark green Henley.

They opened the door and stepped out together, holding hands.

Three men turned, grinned.

"The red-headed lovebirds are awake." Cruz paused the game and got to his feet. "How are you feeling, Shields?"

"I'm okay."

"You want to tell us what the hell happened?" Malik stood too, tossing his game controller onto the sofa. "One minute you're here for a funeral, and Shields is on vacation. The next, you're chasing killers, and she's been abducted. What the fuck?"

"It's been on the news all morning." Thor took the remote, switched from the game to the BBC. "They arrested the fucker behind all of it."

There, on the screen, was Alastair Whitehall in handcuffs.

"Doin' the perp walk." Dylan glared at Whitehall's image. "*Cabrón.*"

"Guys!" Elizabeth needed food. "I haven't eaten since yesterday morning, and I need some coffee—on the double."

That got their attention.

"Time to move. Shields needs her coffee, man." Dylan headed down the hallway, the other two following. "Good thing I brought some Puerto Rican beans and salsa. Huevos, anyone?"

Quinn smiled down at her. "They almost lost you, too."

"AND YOU JUST LEFT LEWIS WITH that Grant dude?" Cruz stared at Quinn. "Brother, that is stone cold. I like it."

Malik poured himself another cup of coffee. "You did what you had to do to get Shields back in one piece. That took balls."

Thor sat there, staring at Quinn. "I can't believe you're not in a jail cell right now."

Quinn chuckled. "It's a surprise to me, too."

He told them what Smith had said last night and how his name and Elizabeth's had been left out of the report completely.

"I'm just as amazed that we haven't been fired—yet." Elizabeth seemed more herself now. She had devoured her huevos rancheros and was on her third cup of coffee. "I don't suppose the three of you could forget to mention the fact that Quinn and I are sleeping together."

The three idiots sitting across from Quinn grinned.

Cruz chuckled. "Will everyone who's surprised to find out that McManus and Shields are lovers please raise their hands?"

No hands went up.

"We've known that you two were hot for each other for years." Jones rolled his eyes. "We're just glad *you* finally figured it out."

"I guess they haven't checked their work email," Isaksen said.

"What?" Quinn looked from one man to the next, but none of them spoke. "Come on, ya bastards. What are you goin' on about?"

"Are we fired?" Elizabeth asked.

The three men burst out laughing, keeping Quinn and Elizabeth in suspense until Quinn wanted to punch them all in the face. "Okay, you've had your fun. Out wi' it."

It was Cruz who finally told them. "They've removed the 'no hookups' policy."

"What?" Elizabeth stared at Cruz in wide-eyed amazement, then smiled, her fingers tightening around Quinn's. "Oh, my God!"

Relief washed through Quinn.

Thank you, Corbray and Tower.

Malik grinned. "It's hard to enforce a rule that your boss breaks."

Then it was time for Elizabeth to get ready for her debriefing with Smith.

They showered together then dressed and rode the lift to the ground floor where Smith met them and took them upstairs to his office.

He sat across from them. "I'm so glad to see you alive and well, Ms. Shields."

"Thank you—and thanks for your help."

Elizabeth gave him the story again, this time from her perspective, explaining how they'd put the pieces together.

Quinn couldn't have done this without her.

"If you're looking for teens who were victims of this, I'd talk with Nicola MacDonald—Clive MacDonald's daughter. I'm pretty sure Whitehall either paid her or bullied her into having an abortion. That's why her father went to Holyrood and threatened Whitehall's life."

"Interesting." Smith looked up from his notes. "When they raided Whitehall's office this morning, they found drugs and child pornography. They've charged him for that, as well as for ordering Lewis to kill Jack Murray. I imagine they'll file more charges when they get a good overview of what was happening at that house."

"There was a video on Jack's phone, right?" Elizabeth asked.

Smith opened his laptop. "Videos, images, recorded conversations, license plate numbers, notes. Whitehall won't be the only man in prison when this investigation is over. Jack gathered evidence the entire time he worked there—until Lewis found out."

Smith turned his computer to face them, pulled up a video, clicked play.

From an upstairs window, Jack filmed four men loading a girl's body into the boot of a car. The camera moved in, got the license plate number, then the men's faces, and the girl's, her vacant eyes staring at nothing.

"Katie Cameron," Elizabeth said.

"Yes. A damned tragedy."

"Lewis." It turned Quinn's stomach to see what the bastard had become. "He's the one tellin' them what to do."

Then Lewis looked up at the window, seemed to notice Jack.

The hair on Quinn's nape rose. "That's why they killed him. Lewis caught him and wanted to silence him."

That was the end of the video.

"Lewis wanted to silence him—and get that phone," Elizabeth said. "But why would Jack meet Lewis in the middle of the night when he knew Lewis had seen him?"

Now that Quinn knew what had happened, he understood. "Jack thought of Lewis as a friend. He couldnae imagine that Lewis would kill him in cold blood."

Smith closed his laptop. "Jack Murray died a hero."

THAT AFTERNOON, they picked up a squirming Labrador retriever puppy and drove with her and a car full of puppy things to Paisley to see Ava and Hannah.

"It looks like you've brought trouble," Hannah said, eyeing the puppy.

"Who's this?" Ava took the puppy into her arms. "Aren't you sweet?"

Quinn explained. "Jack bought her from a breeder as a surprise for you and the girls. He was killed afore she was weaned. We found out about this from his phone records and went to get her for you."

Hannah covered her mouth with her hand. "Oh, God."

Ava gaped at Quinn, her eyes filling with tears. "She's from Jack?"

"Aye, she is."

"A last gift. Thank you, Jack." Ava held the puppy close, tears spilling down her cheeks, its tail wagging. Her voice quavered as she called her daughters. "Olivia, Isla, come and see what Daddy got you. It's a puppy."

The girls were delighted. The puppy was happy, too, the three of them instantly the best of friends, the girls squealing as the puppy slathered them with kisses.

"Thank you." Ava wiped the tears from her face. "I would never have known."

Hannah made them tea, and they sat together in the kitchen, Quinn and Elizabeth telling them a sanitized version of the story, leaving out some of the violence but sharing with them every good and brave thing Jack had done.

"I didn't hear that on the news," Hannah said about Elizabeth being abducted and Quinn rescuing her.

"It's a secret," Elizabeth explained. "Quinn might go to prison if they knew he was there."

Both women's eyes went wide.

"We certainly won't tell anyone," Hannah said. "No' a word."

"Do you remember the day I said that Jack had died for nothing?" Ava asked Quinn. "You told me he'd never done anything without a reason and that we would find out in the end that he'd tried to help someone. You were right. Even when I doubted, you still believed in him. My husband died trying to protect teenage girls from those *monsters*. It breaks my heart, but I can make peace with that."

Elizabeth took Ava's hand. "Your daughters will grow up hearing how their father was a hero."

Then Hannah spoke. "You saved my brother's reputation. Our family will never be able to repay you—either of you."

"Jack..." Quinn's voice cracked, his throat tight. "He was my best friend. He saved me. He showed me the way. I finally had the chance to return the favor."

Hannah blew her nose, stood. "I hope you'll be stayin' for supper. We plan to head into the city to watch the Christmas lights switch-on at George Square. We're trying to keep things normal for the children. They're too young to understand, and it *is* Christmastime. There will be fireworks and music. We'd love for you to join us."

Quinn looked at Elizabeth, who nodded. "Aye, thank you for invitin' us."

THE NEXT FEW days felt chaotic to Elizabeth. The Cobra team went back to Denver, while Quinn and Elizabeth moved out of the Fortress and into a hotel closer to Ava. Because Lewis was dead and Whitehall wasn't being charged with the crime of committing Jack's murder, the Procurator Fiscal released Jack's body, enabling Ava, at last, to hold his funeral.

Quinn helped complete the funeral arrangements. He also installed a new alarm system on Jack and Ava's house so that Ava could feel safer.

"Life will never be the same for them." Quinn held Elizabeth close, watching Jack's girls play with the puppy.

It broke Elizabeth's heart that Jack never got to see how happy his gift had made his wife and children. "No, it won't be the same. But you've made it better."

~

JACK WILLIAM MURRAY was laid to rest on a sunny Saturday morning with full military honors. Elizabeth sat behind Ava and Hannah, who were surrounded by friends and family, the two little girls, who clearly didn't understand what was happening, sitting beside their mother.

But Elizabeth's attention was on Quinn.

Ava had asked him to say a few words at the church service, and he was nervous. He wasn't used to the limelight, and this was so close to his heart.

He was grieving, too.

Elizabeth had helped him put his thoughts into words, helped him practice. "You'll do fine. I'll be right there."

He looked so handsome in his dress uniform, standing at attention near Jack's casket, which was draped with a Union Jack, Jack's beret resting on top of it.

"Greater love hath no man than this, that a man lay down his life for his friends," said the rector. "Those are the words of our Savior, Jesus Christ, who, like Jack, was betrayed by a friend. How much greater the love in a man's heart when he gives his life for strangers. Jack didn't know the girls who were being abused in that house. He didn't know their families. But he did know right from wrong— and for that, he was killed."

Elizabeth dabbed her eyes with a tissue, saw tears running down Quinn's face.

The rector finished his homily and stepped aside.

Another man in uniform came to take Quinn's place in the honor guard, the two of them trading crisp salutes before Quinn went up to the lectern.

He wiped his tears away with a handkerchief, which disappeared into his pocket, then cleared his throat, note-cards in his hand. "Jack Murray was the finest man I've ever known. As a veteran of the SAS, I've known a lot of good men.

"He and I met in recruit trainin' and served in the army together afore we signed up for the SAS selection process. Both of us were Glaswegians who'd grown up on the breadline, livin' in social housin'. I asked him why he'd joined the army, and he told me he wanted to serve his country and make somethin' of himself. I thought he was a right numpty, so I did. I had joined because I had no home, no food, no shelter, and wanted to get out of the rain."

Quiet laughter.

Quinn smiled, a heartbreaking smile. "No matter how rude I was to him, Jack was kind to me. It wisnae long afore I saw that he'd meant what he'd said. He wanted to serve his country."

More laughter.

"If I told you everything I learned from Jack about being a good and decent human being, we'd be here until midnight. So, I'll just say this: He and I joked that if we'd no' joined up and met in the army, we'd have met in prison. But the truth is he'd no' have landed in prison. I would have."

Tears spilled down Elizabeth's face.

Then Quinn looked directly at Ava. "Ava, Jack loved you wi' all of his heart and soul. I've never seen any man happier than Jack was on your weddin' day. He loved Olivia and Isla, too. He'd have gone to hell and back for you. I make a pledge now. Those of us who served wi' him will stand by you and help you through this. We'll be there for your girls as they're growin', helpin' to keep Jack's memory alive.

"Jack, my friend, my brother, I never got to thank you for all you did for me, but I have to believe that wherever you are now, you're lookin' down on this—and wonderin' why the hell we're all cryin'." Quinn's voice cracked. "Rest in the peace of heroes."

Quinn was Elizabeth's hero. Wiping her tears away, she couldn't have loved him more.

QUINN STOOD at Jack's graveside. "I still cannae believe he's dead."

Ava and the others had gone, leaving Quinn, Elizabeth, and a few other stragglers.

"You did a great job today." Elizabeth tucked her arm through his. "You made everyone laugh and cry. Jack would have been proud. I know I am."

"The three-volley salute scared the wee ones."

"Yes, I think it did." Then Elizabeth stiffened. "Wilson."

Wilson walked up to them. "I wanted to apologize on behalf of the station for what Patel did and for no' seein' through her. I'm grateful for your help. I'm no' sure we'd have gotten to the bottom of this wi'out you."

He held out a hand to Quinn and then Elizabeth.

They both shook his hand, and thanked him, and then watched him walk away.

Elizabeth motioned with her head. "Leo Grant is here."

"What?" Quinn followed the direction of Elizabeth's gaze and saw him.

Grant stood at a distance in the shade of a tree, wearing a hat, sunglasses, and a trench coat. After Wilson got in his car, Grant walked toward them, glancing around as if to see whether he was being watched. When he drew near, he pulled off the sunglasses, and Quinn could see that his eyes were red from crying.

"That was a good eulogy. You captured Jack's spirit, so

you did. He was a good man—better than this fuckin' world deserves."

"I'm no' good at public speakin', but I had some help."

Grant smiled at Elizabeth. "You two make a formidable duo. You should go into the superhero business. I can play the villain."

He chuckled at his own joke.

Elizabeth took his hand. "Thanks for helping to save my life."

He raised her hand to his lips. "My pleasure."

"Did it make it better—killin' Lewis?" Quinn had wondered.

Would his grief be lessened if he'd killed the bastard himself?

"It was satisfyin' for a moment, but nothin' can bring Jack back." Grant glanced around and slipped on the sunglasses again. "Things have gotten too hot for me here, thanks to the two of you. Och, dinnae worry yourselves. We're no' comin' after you. You didnae mean to expose me. You wanted what I wanted—justice for Jack. But I'm leavin' Scotland for a time. You two watch your backs, aye?"

"You too, Grant."

They watched him touch the coffin and walk away.

Then Quinn, too, walked to the grave and touched Jack's coffin as the workers began to lower it into the ground.

"Goodbye, friend."

"Quinn, look!" Elizabeth pointed to the sky.

Quinn glanced up to see a sea eagle soaring over the cemetery, its white tail leaving no doubt as to what kind of bird it was. The workers, too, stopped and stared.

Quinn watched it soar. "They never come here."

"This one did. Maybe Jack's saying goodbye."

Quinn's heart lifted at that absurd suggestion, a suggestion he was willing with all his soul to believe. "Fly free, my friend."

They turned and walked back to the car.

Quinn took her hand. "I couldnae have done this wi'out you—not just findin' Jack's killer, but gettin' through today, speakin' in front of all those people."

"You would have been fine, but I was happy to help." Elizabeth smiled. "And so, our first vacation together comes to an end. Maybe Tahiti next time? Bali?"

"If that's what you want, that's what we'll do."

They were scheduled for a mission to Ukraine next and were meeting the Cobra team in Frankfurt tomorrow. But Corbray and Tower had assured them they'd be home in time for Christmas.

Elizabeth looked up at him, her sweet face shining. "I've got the feeling that life with you is going to be one big adventure."

Quinn smiled, his heart light for the first time in weeks. "Always."

EPILOGUE

Six months later

Quinn walked with Elizabeth toward the restaurant, the Inverness sunshine not quite warm enough to melt away his nerves, butterflies fluttering in his stomach.

"Would you relax? Everything's going to be fine."

"I hope so." Quinn had never expected this day to come.

He was about to be reunited with the sister he hadn't seen in twenty-two years.

The whole thing had been Elizabeth's idea. She had located Paige and then asked whether Quinn wanted to contact her. At first, he'd been reluctant. Then Elizabeth had reminded him that it hadn't been Paige's decision to walk out and leave him.

With his approval, Elizabeth had gotten in touch with Paige, and she and Quinn had begun writing emails back and forth, catching up on two decades of life.

Paige was twenty-seven now and newly married. She and her husband raised sheep on a croft outside Inverness.

He'd been as surprised by that as Paige had been to learn that her brother was an SAS veteran who lived in America and worked in private security. She'd had lots of questions for him, and he'd told her about Jack.

"I saw that on the news," she'd written. "I'm so sorry your friend was killed, but it's really cool that you helped solve his murder."

He'd told her about Elizabeth and how the two of them were getting married in July, and Elizabeth had sent them an invitation.

She'd told him she and David couldn't afford the trip. The farm, it seemed, survived at least partly on EU subsidies, and those were uncertain now.

"Tell her we'll buy their tickets, and she and her husband can be the wedding gift we buy for ourselves," Elizabeth had said.

She always knew what to do. Quinn loved her more now than he had in November—if that was even possible.

"Here we are." Quinn opened the door to the pub, held it for Elizabeth, then followed her inside.

"Oh, I see her!"

"Aye." Quinn found himself grinning like an idiot, his butterflies gone.

Paige wore a pair of overalls, her red hair in braids. She waved, jumped up, and hurried over to him, throwing her arms around him. "Quinn! I recognized you the moment you stepped inside. Och, you're so tall!"

Still grinning, Quinn looked into her face, saw the little girl he remembered. "I recognize you, too."

"And you're Elizabeth." Paige hugged her.

Elizabeth smiled. "I'm so happy to meet you at last."

"My husband, David, is sittin' at the table."

They were blocking the front entrance and needed to move.

"Let's no' keep him waitin'." Quinn followed Paige, shook hands with his brother-in-law, some part of him unable to believe this was real.

He'd gotten his sister back—thanks to Lilibet.

Quinn had a family.

"WHAT DO you remember from the night your ma took you away?" David asked Paige, taking her hand. A slender man with dark hair and a handsome face, he seemed to Elizabeth to cherish his wife.

The fact that Paige bubbled with life and energy clearly didn't hurt.

"I remember Ma covered in bruises, cryin' and packin' our things. I remember looking back and seeing Quinn standin' there. You looked so sad. I held out my hand for you, but she pulled me through the door."

"Aye, I remember. She didnae want me. She was afraid of me—afraid I was just like Da. The bastard took his belt to me when he got home. He didnae believe me when I said I had no idea where you'd gone."

"Oh, Quinn. I'm so sorry." Tears shimmered in Paige's blue eyes, so much like her brother's. "I thought of you often. I kept you in my prayers at night. We moved first to Aberdeen and then here to Inverness. Ma changed our names so Da couldnae find us. How did you find me?"

Elizabeth smiled. "I used to work for the CIA."

Paige and David's eyes went wide.

"I thought of you, too." Then Quinn told Paige about the

night he'd left and joined the army. "I beat Da bloody, so I did."

"He was a beast when he drank. He deserved it for all the pain he put us through. I'm glad you got away."

Quinn took a sip of his beer. He'd stopped drinking whisky. "He threw me out, so I joined the army just to have a meal and a place to sleep."

Paige and David had so many questions. How was SAS selection? Where had he gone? Had he ever been injured in combat? What was it like to work in private security? Did he like Colorado? Had he learned to ski?

Elizabeth listened, relieved that this was going so well, her fingers threaded through Quinn's. It had been such a long journey for him to this moment. Since the terrible days of last November, she'd watched Quinn learn to trust himself more as a man, not just a fighter. He was so much more at peace with himself, and she hoped that this reunion would help to fill that tender, broken place inside him—the one created by his father's fists and his mother's rejection.

As for Paige, she was a delight, a living ray of sunshine.

"No, that scar isnae from combat." He showed them his arm. "I got that when Jack's killer—that bastard Lewis—chibbed me last November."

Whitehall had been sentenced to thirty-five years in prison and would probably never walk free again. Nicola and her father had helped to put him there, giving depositions against him that were used to get a confession with regards to trafficking girls, pornography, and giving drugs to minors. Nicola had also been able to give a deposition about Katie Cameron's overdose. A jury hadn't believed Whitehall when he'd claimed not to know about Katie or that Lewis had murdered Jack, especially not after seeing evidence of communications between him and Lewis that discussed both.

The long prison sentence—by Scottish standards, anyway—couldn't bring Jack back, but it was hard-earned justice.

"Have you ever jumped out of a plane?" Paige asked Quinn.

It was then Elizabeth spotted her—an older woman with a care-worn expression who stood inside the entrance staring straight at Quinn.

Quinn followed her gaze. "Paige, is that Ma over there?"

Paige glanced over her shoulder, her eyes going wide. "I'm so sorry. I dinnae know what she's doin' here. I didnae bring her or invite her to come. I'm no' even sure how she knew where to find us."

David looked sheepish. "That might be my fault. I told her where we'd be today. I didnae think that she'd decide on her own to show up."

Elizabeth leaned closer, spoke for Quinn's ears alone. "You don't have to see her if you don't want to."

But Quinn stood, motioned to her to join them, then sat again. "I know what it feels like to be rejected and left out."

God, Elizabeth loved him.

SOME PART of Quinn wanted to get in his mother's face and tell her exactly what she'd done to him by cutting him out of her life and leaving him with an alcoholic abuser. But the moment he got a good look at her, he felt nothing but pity.

The woman he remembered was gone.

At fifty-three, she looked seventy—and not a healthy seventy, but worn down, weary, broken. She had no teeth, her skin lackluster and sallow, her red hair thinning and streaked with gray.

Paige stood. "You sit here, Ma."

Quinn didn't stand but took Elizabeth's hand, her presence steadying him. "Mother."

She looked at him, a bit breathless, tears filling her eyes.

Och, he didn't want her tears.

She ducked her head in a mousy gesture that he recognized as fear. "Yer all grown, a big man now."

That's what happens to a boy in twenty-two fuckin' years.

He thought it but didn't say it. "This is my fiancée, Elizabeth Shields. Elizabeth, this is my mother, Margaret."

God, it felt strange to say his mother's name after all this time.

Elizabeth had sworn she'd cuss his mother out if she ever met her. Instead, she gave her the smile Quinn loved. "Hello, Margaret."

"Fiancée? So, yer gettin' wed, are ye? And to an American by her speech."

"I told you she was American, Ma," Paige said.

"Och, well, aye, I remember you sayin' somethin' aboot it."

"She used to work for the CIA," Paige said.

Quinn's mother gaped at Elizabeth. "Is that no' too dangerous for a woman?"

Elizabeth laughed, gave Quinn's hand a squeeze. "No more dangerous than it is for a man, and I enjoy risk."

His ma looked like she didn't know what to say to that.

"Quinn was answerin' all of my questions about his time with the SAS. My big brother is a hero." Paige filled her mother in on some of the stories Quinn had shared.

But it was clear to Quinn that his mother wasn't really

listening. She seemed agitated, uneasy, her gaze moving over Quinn.

She cut Paige off mid-sentence. "It broke my heart to leave you."

Sweet sufferin' shite!

"Ma, I dinnae want to hear it. You—"

"I loved you, but you scared me. You'd come hame and talk aboot the boys in the gang and the fights you'd been in and whose heid you'd busted and who you wanted tae stab. I wanted peace, and you were all fists."

Her words opened the door to a dark, wounded place inside him. A surge of rage flowed through him—but ebbed as he saw things from her point of view for the first time.

"Ma, please go now." Paige stood. "You werenae supposed to be here."

His mother started to stand, her chin quivering, tears in her eyes. "I'll go. I only wanted tae see you."

"It's okay, Paige. Ma, sit." He waited until she was settled again. "I did talk tough. You're right. But it was all shite. Mostly, we got drunk. But I talked like that at home because I wanted Da to quit hittin' us. I wanted *him* to be afraid for once. I never meant to scare you. I tried to protect you from him, so I did."

She ducked her head again, nodded. "Aye, I remember that. I tried tae stop you because I knew he'd only take it oot on you. You didnae listen."

"After you left, I was the only person he could hit. That's when it really got bad."

Her face crumpled. "I'm so sorry. I'm sorry."

He heard the apology, some part of him rejecting it. He'd been the child, and she'd been the adult. She ought to have protected him, not left him crying and alone. His tears hadn't moved her. Why should he feel any sympathy for her now?

"It disnae matter. I got my licks in afore the bastard died. I beat the shite out of him the night I left home. I left him bleedin', and then I joined the army. I built a new life for myself."

"Can you forgive me, son?"

Quinn closed his eyes, saw his mother in the doorway, telling him she was leaving him behind. He felt his four-teen-year-old heart break. But that was so long ago.

He opened his eyes. "Aye, Ma. I forgive you."

His mother closed her eyes, clutched his free hand, relief washing over her face, tears spilling down her cheeks.

When she opened her eyes again, he saw new light shining there, and a weight he hadn't realized he was carrying lifted from his shoulders.

"YOU AMAZE ME, QUINN McMANUS." Elizabeth lay beside him, the two of them sweaty and spent, the bliss of orgasm fading into a glow.

"Och, well." He grinned. "It's my tongue game, aye?"

She laughed, levered herself up so she could see his face. "I'm not talking about your talent for oral sex—though it's incredible. I'm talking about what you did today. I'm not sure I'd have had the strength to forgive Margaret if she'd been my mother. Then you invited her to our wedding."

He frowned. "It wisnae easy."

He told her how angry he'd gotten when Margaret had described how she'd been afraid of him. "A part of me wanted to shout at her, to tell her to get the fuck out, to remind her that I'd been the child and she'd been the adult. But what she said was true."

"What do you mean?"

"I came home every night after hangin' with the other South Bank Boys, my pride held together by pure rage. If I could hammer some bastard or threaten him or even pretend that I had, I wisnae the weak one, the boy who got beaten up at home. I would never have hit her or Paige, but how could she have known that for certain?"

Elizabeth's throat went tight. "The look on her face when you said you'd forgiven her—she came alive, Quinn. I think leaving you haunted her. What you gave her today was nothing less than redemption."

"That's what you've given me." Quinn gave her a sleepy smile. "I'm no' the man I was, and that's your doin'. You changed me, Lilibet."

"You did that yourself. It's that big heart of yours." She pressed a kiss to his breastbone, tasted the salt of his skin. "As long as I've known you, you've let it guide you, even when it got you into trouble. You've become the man you were always meant to be. I love you, Quinn. You're everything to me."

His eyes were closed now, afterglow cooling into sleep. He had, after all, outdone himself. "I love you, Lilibet, and I always will."

THANK YOU

Thanks for reading *Hard Justice*. I hope you enjoyed this Cobra Elite story. Follow me on Facebook or on Twitter @Pamela_Clare. Join my romantic suspense reader's group on Facebook to be a part of a never-ending conversation with other Cobra fans and get inside information on the series and on life in Colorado's mountains. You can also sign up to my mailing list at my website to keep current with all my releases and to be a part of special newsletter giveaways.

ALSO BY PAMELA CLARE

Barely Breathing (Book 1)

Slow Burn (Book 2)

Falling Hard (Book 3)

Tempting Fate (Book 4)

Close to Heaven (Book 5)

Holding On (Book 6)

Chasing Fire (Book 7)

Historical Romance:

Kenleigh-Blakewell Family Saga

Sweet Release (Book 1)

Carnal Gift (Book 2)

Ride the Fire (Book 3)

MacKinnon's Rangers series

Surrender (Book I)

Untamed (Book 2)

Defiant (Book 3)

Upon A Winter's Night: A MacKinnon's Rangers Christmas (Book 3.5)

ABOUT THE AUTHOR

USA Today best-selling author Pamela Clare began her writing career as a columnist and investigative reporter and eventually became the first woman editor-in-chief of two different newspapers. Along the way, she and her team won numerous state and national honors, including the National Journalism Award for Public Service. In 2011, Clare was awarded the Keeper of the Flame Lifetime Achievement Award for her body of work. A single mother with two sons, she writes historical romance and contemporary romantic suspense at the foot of the beautiful Rocky Mountains. Visit her website and join her mailing list to never miss a new release!

www.pamelaclare.com

www.ingramcontent.com/pod-product-compliance
Lightning Source LLC
Chambersburg PA
CBHW030157200626
46812CB00017B/2265